BOUND BY DUST

KEELA JONES

*For those that daydream of fantasy worlds they likely wouldn't
survive in,
but experience them deeply from the safety of their couch.*

Emerain
The Arid

SAHIR
GROTH
OASIS
AUDUN
OUTPOST
MOIRA
TASHIA
MEGARA

CHAPTER I

I will not hope for change. I will not hope for ease. I will not hope for happiness. I will not hope. At least I will try not to.

I watch Jo hope. Somehow the world has not beaten her down into the very sand we can never escape. If I didn't have Josephine, I would have no reason to continue. She keeps me out of my own head, which is a tempting place to reside and decompose while living in these dunes. For eight years we have battled the sandy Arid together and I watch every year as the water in our oasis diminishes. The birds do not fly over us as they did a year ago. When the water dries up, the camel will die, the goats will die, the crops will die, and we will wither away leaving nothing, not even our footprints will remain but a few moments, and the sand will bury our bones.

We have to keep mapping the Arid.

In truth, I've mapped miles out from our oasis. In every direction, besides the abandoned city of Audun. Just thinking of it sends a shiver down my spine. I'm also certain there are things outside of the Arid. The problem is that we can't pack enough supplies to make the journey. We've tried.

We've nearly died while maintaining the "keep going" mindset.

Eight years have gone by and we continue to have no choice but to return to our oasis, regroup, and try again.

Jo hopes for bird sightings. It has been 196 days since I last saw a desert sparrow. I will not hope for a sighting that I know I will not find. Besides, I have Jo, who has enough optimism in her to keep both our feet moving. Jo is days away from her fourteenth year. Somehow, she has not hardened into the shell of a human I was at fourteen. I like to take credit for her happiness because it also sparks happiness in myself. I have raised her since she was six. We both lost everyone after the Blight hit. I found her because of the birds doing circles in the sky, impatiently awaiting the moment her body finally gave out. In all honesty, I thought the birds were starting to circle what I could potentially fill my shriveled stomach with, and push off starvation for another week. But as I got closer, I discovered a child. Her hair was astonishingly curly, even encrusted with sand I could see the rich color so dark brown it could be black. Her lips were cracked and her eyes were closed with sand caking her long eyelashes. I poured my water into her mouth and her labored breathing seemed to get a little stronger. I still dream of her wheezing sobs when I try to sleep.

The sky was turning orange as the sun went down in the west. "We'll stop here today," I tell Jo as I hand her my walking stick, which was technically just a whittled branch I finished last week. She takes it and her own and starts setting up shelter with our two tarps. I begin working on the fire. Lately, I've been giving in to building fires. The warmth at night is just too appealing. That, and I no longer fear being discovered as I once did. Sometimes I think an unsuspected attack might be an easier way to go than the slow death we face when we inevitably run out of water. I look over at Jo in her sleep sack. Her face is so at peace, I can only assume her dreams consist of birds and water, and whatever family she's lost. I only hear about them when she mumbles their names at night. Maybe I do have a tiny particle of hope because if Jo's family is out there, I will get her home to them. I think better of the fire and put it out.

My mother reaches for my face. I can see her mouth moving but I can't hear her. Her eyes don't look right. They are starting to match her red hair. I move toward her, only to realize that she's not reaching for me, she is shooing me away. I don't want to go. "Mom!" I yell for her, yearn for her. I can help, my arms stretching out for her. She starts crying but her tears are not clear. The liquid falling from her eyes is red. Blood leaks from her eyes and nose.

She tries again to speak to me but more blood runs out of her mouth. For the first time ever, she screams, "Go, Jemma!"

I sit up in a panic, "Jemma, we have to go!" Jo yells at me. The effect of my nightmare quickly wears off as I jump up. Jo is throwing our bags over her back as I look around to find the source of our alarm. My eyes adjust; it's still night time and the moon provides our only light. I can make out Jo's face and turn toward what must be the cause of her distress. I can barely make out a cloaked figure. My mind is already sending me into flight mode; I grab the top of Jo's pack, pulling her with me as we settle into a run. We leave the tent, leave the tarps, leaving the walking sticks.

The figure is at least seven feet tall; I do not allow myself to turn around to double-check until I know we have put more distance between us. Jo is barely over five feet, her head only coming up to my chin, and I have to slow my strides allowing her to keep up with me. I look behind us and the cloak is moving our way. Our pace is too much for the cloak to gain on us.

We continue in silence. Jo has always been an incredibly fast learner. Breathing in through our noses and out through our mouths, moving with adrenaline-created haste. We've already put two miles between us and where we were camped for the night. I guide Jo North West of our oasis, if the figure continues to follow us it will not know the direction of our home. I have mapped this part of the Arid enough times to know where the abandoned bunker lies. I check over our shoulders one last time to make sure we are in the clear before shoving Jo down the nearly invisible opening into the bunker. She lands with a thud and turns around ready to pummel me. I quickly throw my hand over her mouth before she can start in on threats. I silently warn her to keep her mouth shut and we move to a squat to look out of the narrow opening of the bunker. My eyes scan the dunes as I focus on catching my breath.

I'm confident that we've lost the cloaked figure when ten minutes pass and there's no sign of company. "What was that thing?" Jo whispers.

"I'm not sure," I turn to look at her. Jo's eyes are so rounded that I have no choice but to pull her into my arms. It is painful to see her adorable face full of worry. Jo's small frame would make anyone believe her to be delicate. Paired with her doe eyes she has constantly been viewed as innocent and weak. She enjoys using this to her advantage. I know from experience that she is far from fragile. It has been over a year since we've found ourselves in trouble since company across the dunes is becoming scarce. We've found other Blight survivors but with the land going to ruins, any people we stumbled upon only wanted us for our nutritional value.

Stealth was Jo's starting strategy on all our adventures; she is quick and can fit into any hiding spot. However, on the rare occasion that we fall into the grasp of the less desirable, her childlike appearance grants us an escape window. Underestimated is my favorite thing to be.

I look over the bunker opening again. And there, just barely within my vision, I can see the top of a cloak coming over one of the dunes. This time it is accompanied by two more figures behind it. Shit.

Shit.

I point out the three of them to Jo. She drinks from her waterskin and then offers it to me. I shake my head. "You're going to need this before we start running again," she presses.

"We aren't going to run." The opening to the bunker is nearly invisible, especially at night. I only discovered it last year accidentally when one of my boots slid into the entrance. I had to limp all the way back to the oasis after the incident resulted in a sprained ankle. I whisper to Jo, "The wind is on our side, so we haven't left any prints. We are going to let them pass over us." As much as I curse the sand, in this moment I am thankful for its ever-changing waves.

I whisper, "Keep on, keep on, keep on," willing them to continue in the direction we had been running and not discover the bunker accidentally. We watch them grow closer and I have to use my eyes to remind Jo to be quiet. Sitting still and being patient has never been her strong suit. I realize I have misjudged their size the closer they get to our hiding spot. These cloaked individuals are at least eight feet tall. I start to make out details as they come into view. Everything is dark and I can't get a look at any facial features but I can see their long fingers hanging out of the cloak sleeves. From palm to fingertip, their hands must be the length of my arm. I swallow back the vomit threatening to come up. I look at Jo and immediately regret it when I see that her eyes are the size of two large saucers.

I grip her hand and feign confidence that we will not be discovered. By now I can hear their footsteps. They are close enough that when I peek out of the bunker their heads are too high to be seen. Sand falls around us. One must be standing on top of the bunker. They communicate in hisses I can not understand. Jo's hand is sweaty in mine. Or maybe it's my hand that's sweating. We hold our breath and with another step, more sand falls around us.

I listen and hear them making their way across the dunes putting distance between us. Jo finally exhales and I can see sweat beading across her forehead as I'm sure mine mirrors her. We wait another hour and they never return. As relieved as I am that we were not uncovered, nausea washes over me because our dwindling oasis is only three miles from here and our lands are no longer empty.

CHAPTER 2

We have to go. I take in our oasis. We settled here seven years ago. It took time but time was all we had. Our patch of land is small and hard to find and as everything dried up around us, birds and other animals stopped passing through. The first thing we lost was meat since hunting became almost impossible. But we adapted and expanded our crop growth. Our collection of dates, figs, corn, and a few other fruits and vegetables thrived at first. Looking at our supply now is difficult as the water level falls lower every day. In return, our produce is diminishing as well.

I look at Jo who is also reeling in what once was.

"We'll eat one of the goats and bring the other. Start collecting what you can. We load up and leave tonight." Jo is quiet. We've been avoiding this conversation. I try to ignore her sniffling while I fill the four waterskins. Wherever we go, we have limited water and food. Rationing is nothing new for us, but being unsure if we will find another refuge before the end of our supply is going to make this journey the mental battle of our lives.

"I don't understand why we can't stay and keep mapping. We still have some time left, the water won't dry up today," Jo whines.

"We are not alone here anymore. It will be no time before the cloaks find this. Better to take what we have and stay ahead. I won't die a sitting duck." I won't let you die a sitting duck, is what I want to say. Jo has to make it.

"But if—"

"Wash your clothes, and let them dry while you bathe. This is the last time you'll have that privilege for a while."

My daggers are concealed under my tunic and my sword is secured at my hip. Jo doesn't carry as many weapons but she operates her daggers with undeniable skill. She is lethal and grace all wrapped up into one lovely, little terror. I get our camel loaded, he's mostly packing water. Dehydration will kill us faster than starvation. The Arid is many things, but forgiving is not one. We have to make sure every move is calculated. Most of my mapping has expanded miles from the Oasis with no real refuge to be found, especially not water. The direction that has the least amount of collected data is southeast of here. The only knowledge I have of that region is that we will have to pass through my homelands. I have avoided the city of Audun for a reason. Having to navigate past my deceased mother and father is one of them.

The look of dread on Jo's face, when she finishes her supper, is nearly enough for me to call it off. But the thought of the cloaked figure's long fingers wrapped around her neck propels me forward. We have enough resources to get us through ten days of travel. And when all else fails we have our goat and camel. I take a final look at the dying trees that sway over our underground hut. Jo grew from a seven year old to a thirteen year old in those mud walls. I wish I could somehow know what her fourteenth year will look like. I look at Jo's big brown eyes, full of tears. But she doesn't let a single one fall. My resilient little optimist. We both tuck our hair into our shemagh. I can only see limited inches of her face, from the bridge of her nose to the middle of her forehead, but I can already tell that her face has shifted from grief to determination.

Audun is between ten and fifteen miles from the oasis. It's been seven years since I traveled this path. The closer we get to the city the more unsettled my stomach becomes. Along with my queasy gut, the goat is not a great travel companion and I can already tell his stubbornness is slowing us down.

"Is it too early to turn him into jerky?" Jo asks.

"No, I actually think that's a great idea." I know the city is getting close. It's starting to smell like my childhood. I wasn't prepared for that to smack me in the face. I thought the Arid smelled like the Arid. But if I close my eyes, I can hear my mom telling me to stop giving Ray date candies.

Ray.

No.

My throat is suddenly smaller than it was a minute ago. I cave and help myself to our limited water to rid myself of the lump I can't swallow. But the water won't help. I was thirteen.

I was thirteen.

I was *thirteen.*

I couldn't care for a three-year-old. I was such a child myself.

I gave her away. I gave her away. *I gave away my sister.*

My hands are shaking. I can't see twenty feet in front of me. Jo grabs my hand and it's too much. I throw up everything in my stomach. What a waste. What is the point of rationing if I won't be keeping anything down? Jo rubs my back but she shouldn't be here. I should have Ray. I can hardly picture her. Her little red curls would turn such a bright orange in the sunlight. She was only three and already had clusters of freckles dusting across the tops of her chubby cheeks. I can imagine her but I can't really see her. For years I never looked at my reflection in the water at the oasis because those same freckles are scattered across my cheeks. Our freckles were the only thing we had in common. I was an anomaly in my family. My mother, father, and sister all shared the same pale skin but even from birth my skin was bronze. My mother and Ray both had curly red hair while my father's was wavy and brown. His hair wasn't as dark as mine but we did share the same silky waves. Though I could find similarities to my parents, overall I stuck out while Ray was a perfect mixture of their best features. Ray's real name is Darian. In the sun, her hair glowed orange; a beacon of dazzling light. Dad called her his "Ray of Sunshine," and I guess Ray just stuck.

And I gave her away.

I put her on that wagon with the other small children. She cried and I looked away. I didn't even watch the wagon roll out of the city.

I love Jo. I will take care of Jo as long as my body allows. But my heart knows that I would have left her for dead when the vultures circled her if the guilt of giving up Ray wasn't eating me alive. Jo was a second chance for me. And for her, I will be the sister I was supposed to be.

We are upon the city by the time I can talk my mind off the ledge. For years I have managed to keep the thoughts at bay but walking through this city may be the beginning of my end. We pass an adobe I don't recognize. This is good. The less I remember, the more intact my mind will remain. I watch Jo take it all in. I still don't know where she is from. She's never told me, and I wouldn't be surprised if she doesn't know herself. She was six when I found her and sometimes trauma has a way of hiding things from you. I wish I could forget the way it seems like she has. I wish I didn't remember, wish I had been young enough to block out everything that happened before the Blight. The bliss of knowing that something terrible occurred without witnessing it.

But I remember.

We're a couple of miles into the city when Jo asks, "Is your home somewhere around here?"

"No. We won't be passing it. We don't have the resources to explore. We need to head straight through town."

"I can't imagine that a few minutes detour would be the difference between life and death."

"When you become the backbone of operation 'keep us alive' you can make decisions." I'm getting agitated. And it isn't Jo's fault. But we need to keep moving. There might be water on the other side of the city. Probably not, since I have yet to see any wildlife. But today I will be the image of optimism since Jo seems to be lacking her usual buoyancy.

We have almost passed through the city when I see an adobe that has collapsed. A tarp is blowing in the wind, still attached to a large open window. I recognize the faded green of the fabric. Mom used to purchase bread from this stand. Which means two blocks to my left is my home. I will look straight. I will not veer off course. Jo drops a canister of olives and startles the goat. "Shit! Jo! Why are you sneaking olives?"

"I'm sorry! I'm stressed!" She tries to grab the goat's rope but he skips out of her reach. I only wish I could run with such joy in my steps. I let Jo run ahead to gather the goat. Our camel is only a little shaken but is willing to follow our lead. We follow the goat and of course, he's moving left of the street we're on. I know it's close. I know if I allow it I'll be steps away from the doorway.

And then I see it. The arched doorway is still the same as the last time I ran out of it. The window frames that Mom begged Dad to stain blue are only a little sun-bleached. I can't help it. I step inside. Almost all of our belongings are missing. During the Blight panic, some fled; some stayed and collected the belongings of the dead and deserters. The living area is empty and I'm grateful. I don't think my heart could take seeing all of my mother's favorite knick-knacks on display. I walk into my old bedroom. The ceiling has fallen in, in the corner. There is no furniture, only ruble. Connected to my room is Ray's. The tears are flowing freely when I see her toddler bed still perfectly intact. The bed can't be more than three feet long. She used to fit so snugly in her bed. She turned eleven a few weeks ago. I wonder how tall she is now. I won't dwell on the likelihood that she probably never outgrew this bed.

My parent's room is the last one down the hall. The old curtain still hangs, acting as the door. The curtain was such a rich purple when she brought it home. At this point, it hardly has enough pigment left in the fabric to be considered lavender. Much of it has unraveled and almost the entire bottom of the curtain is left frayed. I push it out of the way. I can still hear my father telling me to go. Mom was sick. She didn't look like Mom anymore when I went to see her. I couldn't look directly at her. I caught a glimpse of the blood that wouldn't stop. It poured slowly out of her eyes, nose, and mouth. She tried to wipe it away and put on a brave face but when she smiled her teeth were stained with blood. The last words my mother said to me I couldn't look her in the face while she said them. When I walked out the door, I passed my dad, whose nose had started to bleed. "It's time to go, Jemma."

Their bed is here. And so are their bones. My mother's remains lie there still tucked into my father's.

If love were a cure for the Blight, my parents would still be alive.

Jo is standing with the goat and camel when I finally come out. I know my sobs could have been heard from outside the city. My throat is raw and the possibility of speaking is stuck, trapped in the walls of my childhood home. I keep my head down and walk to our camel. Before we leave, I tie a ribbon I ripped from my mother's purple curtain onto the strap of my waterskin. Jo doesn't ask and we continue South of the city.

I've seen death before. I've seen death more in the last eight years than most people see in a lifetime. The first time I saw death, I wasn't old enough to grasp what I had walked in on. I was six. His name was Wahab. He was my friend. Wahab's father indulged heavily in the consumption of Audun's bourbon. He drank until killing his wife seemed like a good idea. He drank until Wahab joined his mother in death. He drank until he spilled his own blood to accompany them to the afterlife. There was so much blood, I couldn't tell where Wahab's started and his mother and father's stopped. A piece of myself is still trapped in the room where I found them all.

Nightfall is approaching. We stop in an adobe on the city's outskirts.

I tie up the animals while Jo gets our sleep sacks laid out just within the adobe. "Do you remember anything from this side of Audun?" Jo asks.

"No. When I fled, I headed North. Supposedly, the Arid ends that way. And I was hoping to find Audun's sister city. It was said that Audun was forced south by something and that the land to the North was rich and magical. It was all stories, but the tales were all I had." Even after my exploring, I never found anything more than infinite dunes. Sometimes I imagine something amazing is out there, I just didn't travel far enough.

"Why would Audun's people move South if their lands were so abundant?"

"Supposedly we were forced out. At least that's what we were told in Fundamentals," I tell her. Almost everything I was taught in Fundamentals, I've passed along to Jo. Starting at age five, every child was sent for training and education. Intelligence and survival skills were desperately forced down our throats. Instructors had us all convinced there would be a war tomorrow. At the time, I thought that was just an angle they would use to motivate us to do our best. But then the Blight came. Since then, my training has saved my life more times than I can count.

"Maybe you were wrong. What if the land South of Audun is as plentiful?"

But I know I isn't. Everything South of Audun was said to turn to jagged rock. Tashia, *The Land of Sacrifice;* I don't tell her what might await us. We are out of other options. We are out of other directions. If we go another way, we will run out of supplies before we reach any land I haven't already mapped. We must continue or risk drying up with the rest of the land. It's a gamble to head toward a place we were taught to have nothing. But a gamble is all we have left.

CHAPTER 3

A piercing sound jolts me awake. Jo is still fast asleep next to me. I focus on being silent so I can decipher what startled me awake. There's a faint chirping. A desert sparrow bird singing. I'm sure it must be a dream. But the sound continues, moving, like the bird is flying above us. I nudge Jo. "Listen," I whisper.

Her sleepy eyes start to sparkle, and she smiles. I haven't seen this smile in days, and it warms me to see the hope blossoming within her. Something swells within my ribs, and I squander the untrustworthy feeling. There's a better chance that we've both gone crazy and are hearing things than the possibility of a real bird.

I hear another sound but it's not singing.

A howl.

A howl so full it rattles the walls of our shelter.

A grunt and labored curdling sound comes from just outside the adobe. My heart rate swoops into overdrive as I slowly, slowly, *slowly*, peek out of the window above our heads. A tall, cloaked being has its hand stuck through the side of our camel. The goat is already ripped apart. Blood covers the ground and the creature's long, gray fingers with nails that better resemble claws. I slide back down beside Jo and motion for her to be silent. Not that I would be able to hear her anyway. Adrenaline pumps through my veins and strangles my eardrums.

We need a plan.

I make sure my knives are still safe under my tunic and grab the hilt of my sword. Jo already has both her daggers ready in each of her palms. I try not to notice, as there isn't time to comfort her, but her chest rises and falls at a rate only created by adrenaline and fear.

We can't run or hide this time. Jo and I startle as deep gurgling and weak bellows are released from our camel as its last breath is stolen. God, it's loud. The ripping of flesh, a noise forever ingrained in my brain. Quickly, I move to the other side of the doorway. We aren't yet spotted but I know the creature will soon investigate the inside of this adobe. Quiet falls over the static swirling in my brain and my heart calms. I'm ready.

There's a crunch by the door. The smell of blood, metallic and coppery, invades my senses. I ready my sword in anticipation of the beast coming through the door. Instead, its hand reaches down through the window grasping Jo by the back of her neck, and drags her out of the window.

Her yelp propels me.

I burst out of the doorway and fear washes over me. The figure is every bit of the predicted eight feet tall and Jo is dangling high above me as its hand brings her neck closer to its face. I lunge and swipe my sword across where I'm hoping the back of the being's knees are located. The resistance in my swings ripples along my arm, telling me the sword did find purchase. Part of the fabric is sliced revealing a silver leg that, thank God, is bleeding. The legs extend down to what I thought would be feet, but these resemble the skeletal structure of a wild animal's hind paws, all accompanied by claws big enough to rip me clean in half.

The cloaked being turns toward me, exposing its vile face. Foggy, yellow eyes connect with mine; I'm taken back by its gray skin. Its long nose is scrunched and wrinkled like that of a wolf. Its mouth is big enough to take up the bottom half of its face and lined with jagged, razor-sharp fangs. Each tooth is off-white and dripping with blood that reaches the fabric clasped at its neck.

Panic pools in my stomach.

I can handle blood. Camel blood. Goat blood. Not Jo's blood.

Jo's dagger sinks into the creature's forearm and she is released. She drops and I can tell by the impact that she's hurt her ankle. We circle the creature, while it continues to face me. Forgetting Jo, it lunges toward me and its hands go over my head as I duck and slice across its midsection. The creature is so tall I will have to aim high if I'm to land a lethal blow. It reaches for me again, reaching lower this time. Its movements are slow but the sharp nails cut my back as I run to the right. As it bends down I catch Jo leaping onto the back of the cloak. She's hurt so her jump doesn't put her very high on its back. She sinks a dagger into its spine and starts climbing, forcing another dagger in higher as if she were scaling a frozen mountain with a pickax. The creature screeches in agony.

The distraction is enough for me to slip close to the being's front and I slice again, deeper through the midsection. Blood pours profusely from its abdomen. It falls to its knees as Jo plunges her dagger into the back of its neck, severing its spinal cord. The cloak lands in a heap face down in its blood and Jo crawls off its back as I take in our new state.

Our camel and goat are gone. The creature slashed through

all of our waterskins except the one I kept with us while we slept. It still has the lavender ribbon tied snugly and kept close to my chest. I collect what few things we have left and pack them onto my back.

We have to move. The other cloaked figures traveled in three. More company could fall upon us at any second.

"This is bad." Unlike Jo, I prefer not to dwell. Dwelling never changed anyone's circumstances before. Jo limps around the fallen beast, "How far can we get with this?" She gestures toward our sad collection. Far enough. It has to get us far enough to make it. She has to make it, there's no other option.

"A few days if we ration responsibly. But distance will be cut down when you factor in your ankle."

"It doesn't hurt that bad. I just need to walk it off." She winces as she tries to take a couple of steps. *Walk it off*, my ass.

"Sit down, I'll wrap it." I was eight when my dad showed me how to use compression wraps. It's kind of an art. Behind the heel. Over the foot. Under the foot. Something about the action is soothing to me. "Alright, arm over my shoulder, only put as much weight on it as you can tolerate. We need to go. Last time there were three creatures together and we can't be here when the other two show up."

We head out. I catch a glimpse of the bright sheen in her lovely eyes. She won't let the tears fall but it doesn't mean they aren't there. There's never been anything more devastating than feeling the empty air around us; Jo's hope has finally depleted.

CHAPTER 4

Three days pass. Our pace is not as it was before Jo injured her ankle. I don't have any ointment for the cut across my back that the Cloak left and it's warm to the touch. It's infected but there's nothing to do besides clean it with water and cover it back up. We move day and night, only resting when our bodies give us no other choice. Water is low and our food supply is gone. I should have salvaged more after the attack but I knew I could only carry so much when Jo would be leaning on me for the journey.

We've made long treks before, even nursing injuries or illness. But the certainty that we would be back at the oasis soon always provided us the ability to keep placing one foot in front of the other. Here, we have no destination, only dreams, and even those are dwindling.

We take a break.

The sun is directly above us. I remove my shemagh hoping that a deep breath of air will replace my need for water. Our thirst is getting the best of us. I know better than to exhaust us by moving during the day, but fear of another Cloak pushes my feet forward, regardless of where the sun is in the sky.

"We know something is out there. We heard the sparrow," Jo encourages. I hate when she can see my lack of faith. I look at her cracked lips when she takes off her shemagh. Mine must look the same. I take a sip from my waterskin; there are only drops of moisture still remaining. I pour the rest into Jo's mouth. We lean back against a hollow log and she pulls her foot from her boot.

"Don't do that. It will swell and you won't get that boot back on," I warn. She ignores me and unwraps her ankle. It's purple and I swear I can see it protruding before our eyes. Her relief is short-lived when I stand and tell her it's time. She goes to put her foot back in and cries out but her body doesn't have enough water left to muster real tears.

We decide against the boot and I store it in my pack. At this point, Jo's foot barely touches the ground. I have become her crutch, carrying most of her weight as she hobbles with one foot for another several miles. It might be easier if she wasn't so much shorter. It's killing my back to accommodate the eight-inch difference between us. I don't know how far we've gone and my sense of direction is wavering. "Do you hear it?" she asks. "The water?" No. *No.*

"You're losing it, Jo. There isn't any water."

The land has flattened around us. The dunes and soft sand harden. We don't leave footprints here. The cracked surface of the ground doesn't cushion our footfalls. Jo needs to stop and rest again. The sun is about to set on our second full day without any water, not that we were drinking much of it before we completely ran out. I give her a minute then urge her to get up. "No. We rest here." She's decided not to move again today and I no longer have the energy to argue with her. We lay our heads on my pack and give in to exhaustion.

"Jemma, you have to protect her," she says. "Listen. This is important. Your decisions from here on out are yours alone. I know you have the strength to make the right ones. Protect yourself, protect your sister." And then she starts screaming. I try to cover her mouth. I can't think of anything better to do. I think it's the shock. Mom has never screamed and now her cries rattle my bones.

I try to conceal it.

I try.

"Mom!" My eyes snap open.

Jo is screaming and gripping her calf. I spot the sand viper, grab it by the head, and toss it away. I turn to Jo and roll up her pants. There on her calf is the bite. Two small puncture holes in the cushion of her calf. And it's already swelling.

In other circumstances, we could handle this. A sand viper bite doesn't have to be lethal. But being stranded in the Arid, with no water, and no chance of finding the help we need means death. Jo understands this; the resignation on her face is splitting me in half. She hunkers back down on the rotten tree trunk.

This is unacceptable.

I stand, clench and unclench my fists. Squint my eyes. Maybe there's something in the distance that I missed earlier. Check every direction. Check every square foot of dark blue sand connecting with the black sky. She just needs to hold on. In a few hours, the sun will illuminate what we need.

I look at her long eyelashes resting on her cheeks. She doesn't have a few hours. I sling my pack over my shoulder. I'll go and get help.

"Stop." Her voice is distorted, sand already rusting her vocal cords. "Stay with me," it's hushed, nearly whipped away by the wind between her mouth and my ears. There are so many places I need to be. I need to find water, find food, find a place for us.

I take a seat, prop her up beside me, and hold her. This is where she needs me most. A couple of quotation marks, winding around the other, our backs to everything else. The only spaces in this world that matter are the ones we occupy together.

I contemplate going and grabbing the snake so it can bite me too. Maybe we can meet our maker together.

I play with her hair, the spirals wound tightly. Her breaths are even. I can almost convince myself she's just going to sleep. I'm not going to look at the bite. I'm just going to rock her to sleep like I did every night during the first years we spent scavenging.

I lightly run my fingertips from her forehead, down her nose, over her lips, to her chin. Again. Forehead, eyelids, cheeks, and chin. Again.

And again.

And again.

I run my fingertips over her hands, from her palms to the ends of her fingers and back down again. Jo whispers, "Thank you for being my sister."

"Of course." I kiss her forehead. I can't speak anymore. My throat won't allow it.

"Do you know where I lived before I met you?" she asks. I shake my head. "I don't remember much of it. I know I had a family there. Not the kind of family you had. Most of what I remember might not even be real. I can only really see it in my dreams now," she whispers and it feels like she is comforting me when it should be the other way around. "I was in a kid's home. I never met my parents, but neither did a lot of the other kids. The fire got almost everyone in the building. My Niki got me out but he couldn't get out himself. Niki has the same birthday as me. He was born exactly ten years before me." Jo sighs. "I'm not even sure he's real anymore. My mind probably made him up. But in my dreams he protected me. And then one day I woke up and didn't need him anymore because I had you." Somehow tears well in my eyes. There isn't enough for any to escape and fall down my face. But I know if she'd told me this a few days ago, I'd be a blubbering mess by now. She recites her favorite poem,

"What is broken,
Sure will mend.
If not, sometimes,
We must pretend.
For if our hope do ever perish,
There's not a thing for us to cherish."

It's gut-wrenching having to listen to the life in her voice fade away.

I hum the happy birthday melody. The corners of her mouth lift slightly despite the morbid ache in my chest. Her lashes rest, still, on her cheeks.

I hum her an old lullaby until she falls asleep. I hum until the sun starts to come up again. I hum until time means nothing and until the hums are only breaths. I think she's breathing. Or is that just me?

"Jo," I say but no sound leaves my lips. I try again. Nothing.

I reach for her but I can't find her. How could I not have noticed if she moved off of my shoulder? Did I fall asleep? My eyes are crusty. Sand and tears have mended my eyelids closed. I reach up to rub my eyes. Or I think I do. My arms don't feel like they're attached to my body. Their movements are delayed. I can tell my shemagh is still covering most of my face.

I get my eyes to open so I can focus on the face in front of me but it's covered by a black turban. The eyes are enough to sober me up without having to see the rest of the face. This is a man. His eyes are surrounded in darkness, whether it be by his dark, heavy eyebrows, or the thickest lashes I've ever seen. But the most striking part of this small fraction of his exposed face is the light green eyes. I've seen green eyes before but this green is so pale, it can't be right. This is a hallucination and I don't know where else to look. Or even how to look somewhere else. I don't trust my consciousness now. This isn't real. Water is poured on my face and down my throat. I cough but don't have the strength to turn to the side. Someone shoves me over so I can catch my breath. "Jo," I gasp.

A bag is pulled over my head.

CHAPTER 5

The back of my skull knocks into something sturdy behind me. I must have been moved because I am no longer on sand. My hands are tied behind me but there's a scrape of wood against my fingertip. From the constant jostling, I assume I'm in some kind of wagon. I scoot back until I'm flush with the wall.

"Jo!" I wheeze but get no response. I know she's dead. It feels like someone has pushed on my chest so hard that it actually cracked in half. I can't breathe. "Jo!"

I'm heaving and choking on the limited air under the bag. I can't reason around this heartbreak and panic. There are no coping mechanisms built strong enough to get me through losing her.

"Shhh, you have to breathe," an unfamiliar voice comes close to my ear. "She's okay, just unconscious. If you stay calm and quiet, they'll take care of you both. But if you make this difficult, they'll toss you both out and leave you for dead." The voice is soft but strong. Deep but gentle. "Here." There's pressure sliding at my shoulder, wedging in the space behind me, running down the length of my back. The rope around my wrists is cut off and my hands are guided in front of me. Small fingers are placed in my palm. It's Jo. I squeeze her hand but it remains limp, I run two fingers to her wrist. Her pulse is weak but it is there. The weight on my chest dissipates as I take deep breaths.

"Be still. I have to tie your hands behind your back again." I obey. I'm so relieved that Jo is alive, that I haven't fully faced our predicament.

Captured is better than dead.

Captured is better than dead.

Captured is better than dead. I think.

Time passes in eons and seconds. Time means nothing. I must have fallen asleep, giving in to the exhaustion from the past few days. Water is thrown on my head. I'm so thirsty that I bring pieces of the bag into my mouth and suck the moisture out of the damp fabric. The wagon comes to a stop and there's conversation too far away to understand. I remain still enough to make out some of the shapes in front of me through the bag. Just as I can finally make out the wagon side we start moving and any glimpses I could catch go dark. We must be moving lower than the Arid. It's getting colder with every rotation of the wagon wheel. I start shivering and all the light that I had minutes ago is gone. My limited vision is swallowed up by darkness.

Strong hands guide me to stand. I'm lifted over the side of the wagon and dropped to the ground. It's a struggle to get up while my hands are still tied and it's too dark to see anything. I'm pulled up by the back of my tunic and shoved forward.

"Jo," I say, "Jo stays with me!" Not that I've laid eyes on her in hours, but if I can get any say in what happens next, it's that she and I stay together. My outburst goes ignored and a new voice tells me to move.

There's a loud creak somewhere in front of me and lights pours into the sack over my head as, what I would assume is a door, slides open. I'm momentarily overwhelmed by light streaming in between the thread of the sack. Again, someone shoves me forward and I'm sent sprawling into the lighted space before me. The bag is ripped off of my head.

As my eyes adjust to the brightness, I scramble to locate Jo. I turn around and see her limp body being carried through the wooden door on a stretcher. She is still unconscious but her coloring looks okay. "Please, she's been bitten," I tell the man closest to me holding one end of the stretcher. I look around to find the green eyes that helped me before but he's gone. I focus on Jo. Her pant leg has unrolled concealing the bite. "Untie me, I'll show you. It's inflamed. She needs treatment." My voice is stronger than I expected and I'm grateful.

"We'll take care of her," a voice behind me announces. "Alert the med wing that we have visitors in need of assistance." I turn to find a man dressed head to toe in navy blue. His indigo attire compliments the striking blue of his eyes. Every bit of his appearance is alarmingly intense. His skin is pale, along with his hair and beard, so white. The contrast of his richly pigmented tunic on his milky skin makes it seem that he is glowing. Or does he glow because, when you take away the clash of colors, the man is still absolutely stunning? If Jo was well right now we'd be taking bets on his age. I'd have to go with 45, but he could say he's 30 and get away with it. The wisdom in his eyes gives away more years despite his lack of wrinkles.

"I need to stay with Jo. Where she goes, I go."

"Oh, there's no need for that. She'll be well taken care of." He smiles. "Simon, cut those dreadful ropes. These are our guests, not prisoners." The rope around my wrist is cut and my arms are released. "Wonderful! Go ahead and help, Jo? Is it?" I nod. "Yes, please escort Jo's stretcher to the med wing." I move to follow but the blond man grabs my arm. "Just a moment my dear."

He has a hold of my right arm. My sword is missing, it must have been removed when we were collected. I run the fingers of my free hand along the outline of a dagger still sheathed in my pant leg. With a slide of my palm, I ease the dagger hilt into my hand. "Play nice, sweet girl. We have a lot to discuss. And I would hate it if Jo never made it to the medical wing." The man tilts his chin and his eyes roam down my body before landing on my slightly exposed dagger. His voice is light, a perfect disguise for the edge of his threat. I sheath my dagger completely and remove my hand from the hilt.

I turn to take in the rest of the room. The tall walls are made of stone and mud. The colors here are similar to the Arid, minus the blue sky. Sconces are mounted every few feet holding a lit torch. Jo is being taken down one of the hallways by three soldiers dressed in shades of brown and cream with swords at their sides. It's difficult to tell the difference in any of the soldiers since they all still wear their turbans. My heart yearns to go with her. The door slams behind me and I'm left with two soldiers and my peculiar captor.

"This is not how I wanted to finally meet you, Jemma." The blond man lets go of my arm. "After I heard about your parents, I knew I needed to find you but you disappeared. The years stretched, I nearly gave up hope that you were still alive." My face must have been the perfect picture of disgust because he takes a step back and says, "Forgive me. My name is Amos. King Cerastes of Megara." He smiles wide, giving me a view of every one of his white teeth. I want him to be ugly. To say his appearance is anything less than perfect would be lying. And I hate it. I can't shake the alarm and discomfort that his presence is causing me. All of this beauty spent on a person that

I'm certain has a rotten soul. "Please, let's get you cleaned up. We can give you the royal tour while Jo recovers."

"How do you know my parents?" I press.

"What an excellent question, my dear. Perhaps after you get settled we can have a more in-depth discussion." Turning to the soldier behind me he says, "Take her to Sondra, then she can come to supper."

I'm motioned to move forward and the soldier walks me down another hallway lit with the same torches as the hall Jo was taken through. I know I should be keeping track of steps and turns and landmarks. But my mind is spent and my survival instincts are shot. I'm led into a large, well-lit space. Cream curtains hang as barriers between a handful of beds on the right wall. To the left are tables and foreign instruments. I've never seen a room so *clean*. I'm suddenly aware of the sweat and sand caked to every square inch of me.

"Ah! Hello! I'm Sondra." A blonde woman wearing multiple shades of cream steps around a table and offers her hand. When I shake it she pulls me forwards and inspects my arm, then the other. She grabs my face and proceeds to inspect my head and neck. "Any injury I should know about?"

"Um, I have a cut on my back." From the claw of a massive cloaked beast, I don't say.

She spins me around and pushes the tunic up over my shoulders. "Jesus," she breathes. "Gentlemen, I can take it from here." The soldiers leave the room and she helps me take the tunic off. "Lie here on your stomach." She pats the cushioned table. "I'll be right back with antibiotics." I lay on my bare stomach and watch her spin the pristine, pale layers of her outfit into a door in the corner. When I release the breath I've surely held since the bag was placed on my head, I can't help but shiver. I shiver from the distance spanning between me and Jo, the sterile smell of this table, and the cool air giving my unaccustomed lungs a shock. Without my tunic, along with the lower temperature here, I can't contain the goosebumps that spread all over me. Sondra cuts back into the space by the table. "Alright, this will heal you up by tomorrow." It stings when she cleans my wound and the ointment is cold as she layers it over my festering cut. A bandage covers the gash, a plastic wrap-like rectangle that blankets the entire injury. "This is just so it doesn't get wet during your bath."

I sit up and she waves for me to follow her around the corner where there's a huge white tub. I can see the steam coming off the water and my excitement is palpable. I'm helped out of the rest of my garments and soon fully submerged in the hot water. Sondra takes my clothes and boots elsewhere. She either told me she was going to clean them or burn them. I don't care. I could stay in this tub forever. I pray Jo is receiving treatment as incredible. My fingers and toes resemble raisins by the time Sondra returns. She holds open a towel and I step into it. "King Cerastes is requesting you for dinner. Let's get you ready. He's not the most patient man in the world."

CHAPTER 6

I t's been years since I looked in a real mirror. Sondra's closet is not only vast and bursting with the brightest, white fabrics, but it's also home to a massive floor-to-ceiling mirror, reflecting the ghastly expression of a stranger back at me. My face is thinner than I remember; higher cheekbones protrude in an unfamiliar form, and my eyes have taken on a shape I would almost consider feline. I'm years older now and my sharper facial structure encapsulates the passed time.

I try to ignore the constellations across my bronzed cheeks and nose; thinking about the freckles will only make me think about Ray. I wipe my sweaty palms on my thighs. My legs are also different. I knew I had grown into a taller woman, but to see the whole picture in front of me is foreign. My legs appear to go on forever compared to the rest of me. Sondra offers me a navy blue dress covered in gold embellishments. She slips it over my head and zips up the back. The sleeves cling to my slender arms and the neckline falls just below my defined collarbone. The rest of the dress has some stretch and it hugs every one of my subtle curves. There is a slight slit exposing my right leg, stopping just above my knee. I feel beautiful. Until I remember this is all for King Cerastes.

Sondra pulls my hair back into a low bun. I haven't had a haircut since I was thirteen. It must be magic that she can fit fifty pounds of hair into an elegant bun. She pairs the hairstyle with gold, teardrop earrings. A navy veil is placed over my head. Fabric is fastened above my ears and drapes over my face just under my eyes. I look in the mirror, the dress is exquisite, and I'm thankful for the fabric over my nose and mouth. My eyes look terrified enough without exposing the rest of my face. Sondra steps back to take in her finished product. "Perfect," she beams. "Garrith! We're ready!"

Another soldier steps into the room. This soldier wears all black, unlike the others. He has to be at least a foot taller than the rest of the soldiers. He's well over six feet tall and I can't help but feel small. I've never been intimidated by someone's presence alone.

His broad shoulders aren't far from taking up the doorway. Every inch of him is covered except his eyes. When he looks at me, I see his unnaturally pale, green eyes. The recognition smacks me in the face, this is the man who captured us. Captured us, saved us, I haven't sorted out the details yet. "Jemma, this is Commander Garrith, he'll see that you get to King Cerastes."

King Cerates. Dread courses through my veins. "Can I have my daggers?" I'm not sure where they ended up during my bath but facing the king has a choke hold on my nerves. Nerves that can only be calmed by being well armed.

"Absolutely not. There's no reason to have them. You're under the protection of the king's guard." She shoves me lightly toward the door. "Time to go." I would thank her for the kindness and hospitality, but I can't shake the feeling that she's only fattening me up like a pig for slaughter.

Commander Garrith walks me down the winding tunnel. I wonder how big this structure is. How many exits does it have? How many guards does the king have? It's amazing how much a bath can reawaken my instincts. With every step, I begin mapping. Garrith turns around and checks the space behind me, but quickly faces forward after his eyes fall to mine. Odd.

His steps fall slower, shorter, and each of my footsteps echoes in question. Apprehension rises in my chest and I'm about to ask when he whips around again to check behind us in the hall. This time, I snap my head to see what he could be looking at when he shoves me into an alcove in the wall.

"What the fuck!" I shout as I turn to face him. His giant profile takes up the opening to the alcove. Panic grabs hold of my throat. The feeling of being completely defenseless has grown old.

The realization of his intentions pours into my senses. I open my mouth to scream but there's a flash of movement and his hand is pressed against my mouth while the other pulls me in from the back of my neck. There's no time. I won't be granted the opportunity to scream. I've already missed it.

I am at his mercy. His grip is an iron fist clamped around me. I tug at his arms but a way out of this is nowhere to be found. A silent tear escapes my eye and I hate myself for showing such weakness. The years in the desert, clawing my way through every near-death experience, to protect myself, to protect Jo. Only to come down to this moment with no weapon and no advantage over this terror of a man.

This is why we killed them all. Every despicable man that stumbled upon our oasis became the grains of sand we traveled over.

All my efforts, reduced to *this*.

I wish we had died in the Arid.

I wish I were dead and Jo too. No matter how terrible the

next moments of my life have aligned to be for me, don't let her endure it.

Don't let her.

Don't let her.

Don't let her.

I'll put the dagger in her heart myself. Jo should never know such pain.

Let us die.

Right now. This second.

I pray my tears seal my requests.

Just let us die.

My tears seep between his fingers, the salt reaching my lips.

As if he's finally reading my alarm, his eyebrows fly to the fabric of his shemagh and he releases me. He's tripping backward as he says, "No. No! I'm not—" His eyes glowing wide and bright green.

Such green eyes.

Gleaming windows of sea glass, designed to disguise his evil intentions.

He is the epitome of wicked.

And I'm certain I will fall under the hands of a monster that has done such terrible things.

He sighs. "These are yours." He tosses me a sack. It's a trap but I've no other choice but to look inside.

In it, I find my daggers. I look up in confusion, with a million questions on the tip of my tongue, but I'm left speechless. "I'll be right outside." He steps away, leaving me in the alcove.

There's no time to reflect on a tragedy I thought was to happen.

My misjudgment. I will never convince my heart to recover. It beats at an unnatural pace.

But I can worry about my heart later. I have to act.

I quickly put the holster high around my right thigh and sheath three daggers. If anything happens at this dinner I can get to them quickly, thanks to the slit in this dress. I walk out of the alcove. Garrith remains a few steps ahead of me and doesn't utter a word about my horrific misunderstanding. "Thank you," I say. Emotion doesn't reach my voice, and I worry that my ability to properly express myself has been stunted by the encounter.

He doesn't slow his pace or turn around. "I wouldn't thank me yet," he huffs. "From the looks of it, a million daggers couldn't save you. Especially if your first reaction is to cry. They're going to eat you alive," he scoffs. Shame washes over my shoulders causing them to sink, all feigned confidence whisked away by one comment. I want to lash out and argue, but I don't. I know he's right. I keep my head down while I follow him through the tunnels.

He leads me into a massive room. Suddenly there are a ton of eyes on me. Commander Garrith presents me with a long table of many individuals that are clearly of importance. They stand. All are regal in appearance and bear the same variations of navy blue. I am dressed to fit the part. Garrith leaves me at the table, excusing himself. King Cerates is seated at the end of the long table with an empty chair to his right and he waves for me to be seated beside him. A servant dressed in brown pulls out my chair. All soldiers and servants have kept their shemagh on, sure not to expose anything more than their eyes. King Cerastes stands. "Gentlemen, I'm sure you are all curious about our new visitor, she is as beautiful as she is intriguing. This is Jemma Shayde, a survivor of the Blight and a fellow, former citizen of Audun." The table filled with at least two dozen people breaks out in applause.

Once the roar dies down, the king motions for everyone to

take their seats, and colorful platters are walked into the room, and placed on the table before us. The men do not hesitate and dig in as soon as the servants remove their hands from the plates.

Nothing seems real. I look up to find multiple chandeliers, packed with hundreds of skinny candles. In the spaces between the lighting and the walls, navy banners sway, adorned with golden threads that shimmer from the candle-light. So many parts of this room are decorated in gold, framing portraits of people I expect are dead. Anger and hatefulness are feelings I'm becoming very familiar with. The appetizers in front of me are out of place. Everyone is starving in the Arid. Or so I thought. I unfasten the cloth covering my face, take a bite of the vegetables in front of me, and peek to my right to find a handful of men looking at me. I put down my fork and slide my hand down my thigh to feel that my daggers are still with me.

One of the men at the table waves two of his fingers in the air and a woman standing at the edge of the room moves to him. Her face is covered but not by thick fabric like the servants or a sheer veil like mine. She wears a collection of golden tassels across her face. I can only see her eyes, lined thickly in black. The navy of her gown is rich and the cloth moves as if it were fluid. She is stunning.

She bends to listen to what the man says, then she is waved away to take her place on the wall next to another woman I hadn't noticed before. I look around in the few shadows of the room where these beautiful women are perched.

"Who are the women?" I can't help it. I don't want to talk to the King but curiosity gets the better of me. Surely servants would not be as decorated as these women.

Amos finishes chewing before he says, "Councilman's wives. Lovely aren't they?"

"Will they not eat with us? A council member's wife should be permitted to dine among their husbands, should they not?"

Amos chuckles without steering his gaze from his plate. "They have very fine dining quarters. Here, their job is to support their husbands." The men are murmuring among themselves when Amos finally looks at me. "So, where have you been hiding all this time?" His eyes roam over me and the vegetables I just swallowed threaten to come back up.

"The dunes of the Arid. Where else is there?" I answer. I try keeping my voice steady but it comes out as brittle as the biscuits stacked before me. I take another bite.

"But with the river dried up, how did you make it?" he presses. Our plates are collected and a piece of meat I can't identify is placed in front of me. I haven't used silverware in so long. Watching the others at the table, I mimic their actions and slice through it with the steak knife, and using a fork I bring a bite to my mouth. It's delicious, and I don't mean I've been starving for days so it's delicious. This taste is unlike anything I've ever had. The wheels turn in my head and I know before any escape can be executed I must also abduct the chef responsible for this meal. "Jemma?"

"Where is Jo?" I change the subject, not ready to share the location of our oasis.

The man across the table from me scoffs, "She wastes no time getting down to business, Amos."

"That's okay," he says to the man, without breaking eye contact with me, "I like a woman that means business." I have to actively keep from shuddering. Play nice, you don't have Jo, I tell myself. He leans back and sighs. "Jo should be in your room by now."

"And where would that be?"

"You'll get there soon enough." The lump in my throat tells me he's toying with me. If I get to my room and Jo is in anything but perfect condition I will light this place on fire. He can either read my mind or my thoughts are displayed vividly on my face because he assures me, "She has healed quite nicely, just resting. But we have some things to attend to before we release you, my dear."

The entire table has turned to face their king. He stands and holds out his hand for me. I take it and stand. What other choice is there anymore?

Torches are being lit by servants around the walls of the room. The corners grow from their darkened state, exposing hallways I hadn't noticed.

"This way, sweet girl." Amos leads me down a lit tunnel. I turn around and see that the rest of the room is following us. We turn left into a dim room. He holds my hand tightly as we descend a flight of stairs and through a doorway. With every step down, the darker my surroundings grow. My eyes won't adjust. "This is the part where we see what you're made of," he says close to my ear. He strikes a match and tosses it to the side. A tremendous fire erupts in front of me. Amos takes a step back and a cage door falls between us. I try to reach through one of the metal squares but he's too far away to choke. Anger is fueling my adrenaline. Whatever is about to happen, I will not cry.

I step back and look around. There's only one cage wall. Behind the cage, I can see the men from dinner all taking a seat to watch. The room resembles an amphitheater and they're all here to see the show. I turn away from them. The fire before me lights up a cave. I can't see anything in the cave while the fire is between us. My eyes won't dilate to adjust to the dark as long as I stay here. I walk around the fire and face the cave.

Thump.

It's hard to focus on any sounds before me with the crackling fire behind me.

Thump.

The sound is closer this time. Not only can I hear it, but I can feel it. The floor rattles.

Thump.

The hairs on my arm stand at attention.

The first thing I see is a mouth, and sharp teeth lit up by the light of the fire. The shape comes further into the light.

A wolf. But this wolf doesn't have any fur and its eyes are level with mine. Its eyes are the same milky, yellow as the cloaked creature, and skin the same gray. It stands on four alarmingly long legs, mocking me with dramatic steps as it sizes me up.

There has to be a way out. I run to the cage, feeling for any gaps that can help me escape. I hear several chuckles from my audience. I turn around and inspect the cave. There's nowhere to run. The wolf starts to walk around the fire. I counter his steps, keeping the fire between us until I have the cave at my back. And I'm off. I run deeper into the cave and make the mistake of looking back where I see the wolf leap over the fire. It's gaining on me and I won't make it far enough to think of a new idea. I'll have to fight. Turning to face the charging wolf, I pull up the dress and fetch my daggers, one for each palm.

I will not die today.

The wolf lunges for me and I fling a dagger directly into its left eye.

I will not die today.

It howls in pain and then tracks me with its good eye. Blood trickles from its wound, seeping into the corner of its mouth. Nothing but anger is left as a growl from deep in its lungs fills the chamber. I am short one dagger but the two I have left are enough.

I have enough. I will not die today.

The wolf runs toward me, I get ready to plunge a dagger

but the beast veers to the right and comes back to sink teeth into the back of my calf. I scream in pain and I'm slung into the cave wall. The wolf releases its jaw for a moment, only to clamp down on my thigh. The pain is blinding as I'm slammed up against the wall. This can't be happening. I'm quicker than this. I am smarter than a wolf. But my thoughts are muddled by the pain as the wolf's jaws lock into place.

I can't. The pain is too much. My back is smacked into the wall again and I scream. I need to build walls in my mind. Block the pain; put it in a box so I can think.

For a moment I see the wolf's other eye and act on instinct as I send another dagger into the eye socket. I'm released by the beast. It whines and backs up, running into the cave wall opposite me. It's moving sporadically. I'm afraid to approach it. Not that I even could, my leg is expired. I slowly come to stand, using the cave wall as support. My movements will need to be silent and effective, running is no longer a possibility.

I see the wolf's nose twitch. It's adapting to blindness quickly. Using the wall behind me, I slowly come to stand.

I will not die today.

The wolf turns to me and lunges, running into the wall inches to my left. I use what small amount of strength I have left to push off the cave and force my last dagger through its underside, right into the heart. It lets out a moan-like howl and struggles to take another step before collapsing on top of me.

My triumph is short-lived. I shove the wolf off me, the pain in my leg coming alive as the adrenaline wears off and the extent of my injuries swirls in my brain. My walls are crumbling and misery is pouring out into all corners of my mind. "Get her out!" A voice calls out, an almost familiar sounding voice. Think! I keep taking deep breaths through my nose. I can handle my wounds, I've done it before. Blood is flowing and my vision is getting spotty. Seeing my blood on the outside of my body is not something I've ever gotten used to. The bites are huge, the one on my calf left a gash that cut through the muscle. I need cloth or gauze, I need to keep pressure on it. Someone wraps my leg tightly and reaches behind my knees. A strong arm stretches across my back and I'm lifted off the ground. My head is spinning, surely an effect of the blood loss. But there's a tether here that I use to keep consciousness. It's a scent. It's intoxicating. I lean into it and inhale, thankful for the distraction. It's all freshness and citrus, my own personal anesthesia.

I'm jostled; we must be running. I'm not sure how long we've been moving or how far we've gone until the scent of sterile instruments replaces the citrusy heaven. I'm in the same room I was in earlier today.

"Sondra," the voice says.

"She's still alive?," I recognize Sondra's voice, and her tone doesn't hide her surprise. "This is the second one we've ever had."

"She was bit twice." Pain erupts as Sondra starts working on my leg and I can't help it, a cry escapes my lips.

"It hurts!!" I scream.

"No shame in giving in to the dark, Jemma. I won't let you stay there. It's okay," Sondra soothes. I know I could give in and let go.

"Jo!" I call.

Sondra puts her hand on my forehead and strokes. "She's on her way."

"Jo." My voice is weaker now.

"Jemma!" It's Jo. I can hear the panic in her tone and she takes my hand. Tears flow from my eyes and collect in my ears. I gasp as Sondra pours something on my wounds. It feels like fire and I can't hear Jo's words of comfort over my own screaming. I can't keep my body still. "Put her out! She can't take it."

"Jemma, deep breath, you're fine. Breathe in." Something smells off. It makes my head swirl. My brain feels detached but the pain is going away. I take in another deep breath and the room goes black.

CHAPTER 7

I am parched. I blink my eyes and it feels slow. I instinctively reach across my waist for my waterskin. Of course it isn't there. Memories flood my brain and anxiety racks every inch of me. I hear soft breathing beside me but my distress is replaced with relief. Jo is asleep snuggled into my side. There's never been a more comforting sound than her even breathing. The only light in this room comes from the hallway. There's a glass of water on the table next to me that I gulp but do it too quickly, sending me into a coughing fit. Jo sits up quickly, and takes in my state. "Wrong pipe?"

"Mmhmm," I try to say but it's in irregular spurts, trying to get the water out of my airway. After a moment I can finally breathe in. "How are you?"

"Great!" she exclaims. "I'm not sure what kinds of healing devices they have here but it's effective. My ankle doesn't feel like it was ever injured and the snake bite didn't leave a scar. And look at your leg." I really do not want to. Jo pulls the blanket down exposing my bandaged leg. She starts to remove the bandages.

"That's okay. I'm not ready to see it."

"No, look! I mean you've been out a few days so it didn't just heal overnight. Regardless, this still doesn't seem possible." I look at my thigh where there are only two large pink spots and several small ones that are almost invisible. My calf looks the same. All of that blood loss and I only have these pink dots to show for it.

"I'm really glad you're okay, Jo," I tell her. She is adorable in the cream colored nightgown. I'm wearing the same one. "So what have I missed?"

"Not much," she shrugs, "I just wait for you to wake up all day. And I eat. A lot. The food here is unlike anything we've ever had. Sondra takes me to the kitchen to eat, they haven't decided what to do with us yet so they don't want me seen in the dining hall until a decision is made. I like Sondra, she's been great company. Actually she should be along anytime to wake me up for breakfast. Are you hungry?" Now that she asks, I can feel that my stomach is empty, if it hasn't shriveled up and turned to dust already.

My face gives me away because Jo hops out of bed. "I'll go tell Sondra you're up and get some food for your belly." Jo smiles and it breaks my heart. She's too sweet, too cheerful for the less than ideal situations we have always found our way into.

Jo returns with Sondra and scrambled eggs and bacon. Jo and I have no self control and eat like wild animals. Sondra rolls her eyes and inspects my leg. She tells me that I should be fine to return to normal activity today. There's a bathroom to the right of the hallway door, and inside is a shower. I spend too long under the hot water. Sondra dresses Jo in a cream colored gown. It has sleeves that reach her wrists and the neckline mimics that of our tunics. Mine is the same, but in navy. I ask if I can wear something else, something with pants, knowing I can't conceal any daggers in this. "I think that's the point," Sondra retorts. When she goes to collect hair products for Jo's springy hair, I slip a sheathed dagger into my boot.

Sondra leaves my hair down and it falls in big waves ending just at my waist. I watch Sondra get Jo ready, taming all of her spunky curls. I see why Jo likes her. Sondra is less serious with Jo. They giggle and tease one another; Sondra is charmed. Jo has this effect on people; she can put cracks in anyone's hard facade. She is sunshine and innocence. And though I know she is strong and capable, the need to protect her at all costs has saved my own life just as many times as hers.

We are escorted by a soldier to meet the King and his council. Now that I'm conscious, we will find out what they are going to do with us. I assume that we are headed back to the dining room. It was such a formal setting, I expect this meeting to be just as formal. But we pass the large arch that leads to the dining hall, following our soldier down a tunnel I've not been through before. The tunnel turns sharply to the right and in front of me are ceilings so high and bright, my guess is it's mirrors. No, that is the sky! I can't stop myself. A smile spreads over my face. I glance at Jo and she is soaking in the moment too.We walk between two rows of massive stone columns. The detailing in the stone must have taken years. We pass under more stunning arches. I'm so busy admiring the architecture, I crash into the back of our guiding soldier. There's giggling and I step around him.

The most ornate, and unnecessarily massive throne is positioned at the top of the stairs. King Cerastes is seated, looking amused. The council members are in chairs to my left and right, leaving a wide aisle from us to the throne. King Cerastes' eyes are level with mine despite his seated position. There's two more seats placed on either side of him. The chair on the left holds another man who is much older than the king. He's frail, like a strong gust of wind can take him away. The seat on the right is empty. "Jemma!" King Cerastes claps his hands together. "I'm so happy to see you up and about again. You had us worried for a moment." You are scum. I don't say that. You are scum and you put me in there to watch me die for your own enjoyment, and now act relieved that I survived. I don't say that either. "I've called you here today to offer you something." His smile spreads and whatever it is, I've already decided to decline. "But before we get to that part, I feel I should explain how things are done here. This particular establishment relies heavily on those inhabiting it to be strong. To be resilient. We pride ourselves on the capability of our community. You, my dear, showed us that you belong here. You are strong, resilient, and incredibly capable."

I feel sick. Jo takes my left hand. King Cerastes' words are disguised as compliments but Jo can also feel they must be rotten on the inside. "You have proven yourself, Jemma. And I want you to stay here. I want you to take pride in us as we will take pride in you. I want you to fight for this community the way you fought the wolf. War is coming. And I want you to be on our side."

"I appreciate the offer," my voice comes out stronger than I was expecting, "but I must decline. I'm only interested in keeping Jo and myself safe, I do not want to be responsible for anyone but the two of us."

"So what are your plans? Leave here in hopes that a Howler doesn't find you. Even if you evade the Howlers you aren't going to find refuge out there. Or must I remind you how we first met?" *Howlers?*

My silence only proves my lack of plans. "I've talked this over with the council and we all agree to allow you to reside here. You won't have to fight in the war. You can stay in Megara. Better yet, you can stay here in our underground training quarters, Moria, safe and sound. Between you and me," nothing is between the two of us in this room of council members, "I think they want to keep you around if only for the happiness it brings them to... look at you." His eyes rake over me slowly.

Disgusting. I look down at Jo. I have no ideas. Outside is surely a death sentence. I can't take her out of here so I can save my dignity, not when she is so well taken care of and fed in these tunnels. I meet King Cerastes' gaze. He smiles back knowing that I have no choice but to stay here.

"We are ecstatic to have you, you have earned a place among us. But we still have yet to decide if Jo has what it takes."

"What do you mean?" I say, sensing a catch.

"You've faced a wolf. You are one of only two people to face a wolf and make it out alive and we applaud you for that. But Jo has proven nothing. She's only slept in our home and eaten our food. We can't keep tending to a guest that isn't worthy of —" Rage grabs hold of my mind and the space between us slips away as I launch myself up the steps. His face is only inches away when I'm thrown back. One of my arms is twisted behind my back as I kick forward, desperate to feel his airway cut off under the force of my hand.

I'm shoved to the ground but find my footing, ready to pounce again. Hands grab my arms, pulling my back against one of the soldiers and a sword presses into my throat.

"You will not send her into that cave!" I spit at the king. Rope is tied tight around my wrists and the sword is lowered from my neck.

"Always so invigorating to see you in action." He rubs his hands together. "I mean gentleman," he motions to me, "is this not the most exciting thing we've seen in a while? Yes, well. Jemma, it's really not up to you and your tantrums what we do with Jo. What do you say? Fight alongside Megara and allow Jo to be exempt from this tradition, or let her earn her place here with a visit to our wolf chamber?"

"You slimy, crooked—"

"Yes, yes," he waves me off, "I'm delighted to have you fighting by my side, dear." He has won. Everyone in this room is aware I would never send Jo to one of the wolves, especially knowing they would never let her get away with smuggling daggers the way I did.

"Am I late?" A voice asks from behind me. I snap my vision to a man coming up the same path Jo and I took into this room. He passes me without a glance and continues up the steps to the seat right of the king. Before sitting down, he takes the kings hand and bends to kiss his knuckles. His pale blond hair and skin is fascinating and familiar, it stops just shy of the detailed collar of his cream-colored tunic. Everything about him is dazzling and brilliant. He turns to sit and finally scans the room; my heart stops as his bright blue eyes connect with mine.

Reid. Correction, Reid Cerastes. I knew Cerastes sounded familiar. I never imagined that this is what would have become of him, son to a despicable king.

His eyes do not linger and he continues to take in the scene. He doesn't remember me. This isn't a surprise as he never noticed me before the Blight, but I couldn't calm my heart. I could feel my face heat and hear the blood rushing to my ears and neck. Suddenly I was thirteen years old again, aspiring only to be like Reid Cerastes.

"We were just welcoming our new warriors. If you had been here sooner you could have witnessed this beauty in action." Reid looks at me and smiles, carrying the same confidence I remember. Before the Blight, everyone under eighteen was sent to Fundamentals where we were trained in combat and survival against the elements. Reid was the sought after teammate, even at fifteen he was chosen by the seventeen and eighteen year olds to command the units. The way he carried himself and never faltered under pressure gave him an edge. Everyone near him knew he represented safety and a logical solution to anything. His confidence, even as a child, was evident in the set of his shoulders. It has been eight years since I last saw him. He's added at least a foot to his height, looking to have reached six feet, and though his shoulders are far broader and more muscular now, his stance still commands the same leadership. He's grown well into his body and is not the same lanky fifteen year old I remember.

He is beautiful. As much as I try to keep my brain from acknowledging this, my face still heats. Even blind, I think I would be able to sense the perfection that is him.

"This is Jemma and Jo. Jemma is requesting a tour of our training quarters." The king beams. "She's agreed to help us fight the Howlers of Groth. Perhaps you could make time to show her around, Reid? And Jo can help Sondra for today."

I look at Jo and Sondra has appeared behind her, likely in the excitement of my attempted king assassination. Jo is ushered away. She turns to look at me when Sondra assures her, "You'll see her this evening."

Reid comes down the stairs and offers me his hand. I take it and he winks. "We will see you at dinner, father," he says over his shoulder to the king. His father.

His father.

Once we are swept back around the tunnel, Reid lets go of my hand. "Sorry about that, he likes to talk in circles. It sounded like you were handling yourself, though." Reid smirks, definitely referring to my outburst. "How are you, Jemma? It's been a while." So he does remember me. He could have fooled me a few minutes ago.

"I'm fine." In all honesty, too much has happened. I don't know how I feel. It's just been one terrifying moment after the next. I can tell I'm full of anger, but I don't know where to put it. Jo is okay. She is well fed and alive here, which is more than I could say a few days ago when she was only with me. I'm angry because even if we leave, I can't make certain of our safety. I'm angry because Jo relies on me, yet none of my recent decisions have been my own. Yet, she's in better shape than she's been in months. Truthfully, I'm angry that I have failed. But Reid is untrustworthy, and he does not deserve to hear me vent. I wish Jo was here. She was always a saint when it came to listening; all of my problems got smaller when I would voice them to her.

"I'm sure you are fine. You're strong," Reid says, "My father comes off as the villain, but he really just knows how to survive, much like you."

"Do not ever compare me to that snake."

Reid lifts his hands in surrender. "Noted." He laughs. "So what have you been up to?" This casual conversation is making me uncomfortable. The only peaceful talks I have are with Jo, all others end in death. Anger pours over me and I turn and grab his arm.

"You don't get to know me. We are not friends. My purpose in life is to protect Jo. We are not here because we want to be. We are here because we've come up with zero other options. So do whatever your little prince duties are, and then show me back to Jo."

"Listen, sweetheart," he grabs my wrist and pulls my hand from his arm, "you are mistaken if you think I give a shit about my *little prince duties.* I have bigger things going on than worrying about your opinions and assumptions. Pardon me for keeping things light in this gone-to-hell world. You may have slayed the wolf, but you are insignificant. I'm just giving you a tour, so let me show you where you'll be reporting every morning until we go to war." His irritation is palpable. I suddenly feel small as the weight of knowing that we are all only pawns settles in my chest.

My steps become shorter and my lungs seem to shrink. I want to yell and scream, but I don't, and I feel stronger for fighting those feelings. Maybe not everyone here is out to end me. Or maybe Reid is just the perfect actor. He certainly made me rearrange my thoughts.

"Are you coming?" Reid asks. I nod and follow him to the training quarters.

CHAPTER 8

Training quarters reminds me of the physicals in Fundamentals. The ceiling isn't as high here but the width of the room is intimidating; I can't see where the wide cave ends. We maneuver through rows of mats where instructors are breaking down fighting techniques. Some of the mats have individuals learning basics and form. The farther we walk into the cave, the more aggressive the sparring gets. Blood is staining some of the mats and I'm torn between letting the nausea take over or the craving to partake in the violence.

Eyes keep connecting with mine, most with curiosity, some with malice. Everyone here is of pale skin, like Reid. And I stick out with my brown skin tone. When the Blight came through, only those of pale skin were affected. Audun turned on many of the bronzed, assuming we were the cause of destruction. There was always talk of another kingdom. Rumors claimed that the kingdom could wield magic. But those were only rumors. I guess in the confusion of the Blight, an unbelievable loss, people would start believing such unbelievable rumors. Blame was placed on anyone not sharing the majority of Audun's people with commonly light skin. I've never understood my own appearance. I remember wishing to have the same stunning complexion as Reid. I was my family's anomaly; they knew it too. Warning me to leave was the last interaction I ever had with my father.

"So this is where most training takes place, at least the underground portion of it does," Reid snaps me back to the present. "Through here," Reid motions me into a well lit room off the right side of the cave, "is where all of our strategy meetings take place. There are several boards, maps, tables, and chairs."

"What training doesn't take place underground? How do I sign up for that?"

Reid chuckles. "We do have above ground training exercises at the end of every week. It's how we come up with effective quadrants, find suitable leaders, and get a group of soldiers acquainted and working together. War is coming and it's a goal everyday to be more prepared than we were the day before." He turns to leave the room and heads back to the sparring mats. "So are you interested in a taste of training?"

"No. I just want to get back to Jo."

"Jo's fine, she's got Sondra wrapped around her finger. Come on," he taunts. He walks backward onto a mat and I follow.

"I'm not dressed for sparring," I say, looking down at the navy gown.

"You'll manage. Weapons on the bench," he instructs as he removes his sword and multiple daggers I never even noticed he had sheathed in plain sight.

"Sondra told me not to carry any weapons today, having to

meet the council and all." He doesn't say anything, just looks at me. He crosses his arms and continues to look at me. So I reach in my boot and take out the dagger. I place it on the bench. He smirks and walks back to the center of the mat.

"Alright, we're going to start easy. I'm only going to defend."

"Sounds like an easy way to have your ass kicked," I state.

He snorts. "Okay Jemma, give me your best." And I let loose. I start with a quick spin to bring his feet out from under him. It's kind of effective, he loses balance for a moment but he's agile enough to correct himself quickly. He's a few inches taller than me and his reach definitely gives him an advantage. I rise swiftly and send my fist toward his chin and he blocks it. It sends a jolt from my fist to my elbow. His arms must be made completely of steel. I try again with a combination that he blocks again. I try again. Blocked. He has started to lean forward, closing in on me.

"Finish her, Reid!" Someone chants from the next mat over. Reid sneaks a quick glance. I step and send my foot colliding with his chin, snapping his head back. Thank you God for long legs. His head shakes back into place and his eyes connect with mine. He's smiling. I try with my left leg to make contact with the side of his knee. He catches my ankle.

Shit.

I'm flat on my stomach on the mat before I can even blink, aware of the crowd that is gathering to watch. I get to my feet.

"Well Jemma, I think I have some ideas for what we can work on this week."

"I'm not finished!" Anger and irritation is taking over.

"You are finished. Grab your things, let's go." Pissed off, I slip my dagger back into my boot and storm towards the exit.

I round the corner and Reid grabs my elbow. "Hey," he

whisper shouts. I shake him off. "Jemma, listen to me. As much as I'd enjoy a real sparring match with you, we were drawing attention. And not everyone down here is happy about your presence." That gets my attention. "We will train in the morning, before training quarters is so occupied. That was foolish of me today. I'm sorry. There are things going on here that you aren't familiar with yet. You will be soon. But until then, I need you to trust me. Not everyone here is your enemy, but they're also not all your ally."

"And you are? Are you my ally? Or am I King Cerastes pet project that falls under your little prince duties?"

He mulls over this then asks, "Are you hungry?"

What the fuck? "I'm fine."

"You look hungry. And if I wasn't your ally, would I be willing to smuggle you something decadent from the kitchen?" We walk back to the wing that my room is in, along with the kitchen. I'm not sure how I secured such a conveniently located room. The torches on the walls light up the hall and I can see the door to my room. "Wait in there, I'll be right back." I'm about tired of his orders. No matter how much logic is instilled in his instructions, it still pains me to obey someone. I've grown so used to calling all the shots myself.

Jo is sitting on the bed while Sondra has assorted herbs laid out on the floor. Sondra is quizzing her. "You're back!" Jo exclaims. "What are *training quarters* like?" Jo mimics King Cerastes' accent.

"A little overwhelming," I admit.

A knock at the door startles us. I crack it open. Reid. That was fast. "Here." He hands me a couple sticks with meat on them. Shish Kebabs! "I hope these hold you over until dinner." He looks over my head. "Sondra! Put the girls in something really nice." He winks at Sondra and Jo and leaves.

I walk over to Jo and give her a kebab. I immediately begin eating mine, but when I look up Jo is giving me a knowing smile.

"What?" I say with a mouthful of food.

"What do you mean *what*? Am I the only one that just witnessed that handsome hunk of man deliver you food?" she teases.

"That's Reid," I shrug, "and you're not wrong, he is easy on the eyes. But he's son to King Cerastes, who we definitely can't trust." I laugh at Jo's disappointed face. "We are too smart to be charmed so easily, Jo." I tap the end of her nose.

"Let's finish up this lesson." Sondra tries to grab Jo's attention again. She quizzes Jo on the herbs and what they're used for as I walk into the bathroom to splash water on my face. I end up craving a shower once I feel the warm water on my hands. I'm awfully sweaty, despite how brief the sparring session was.We must be near a large water source if they have figured out how to get running water. Hot water at that. I try not to waste time in the shower but it's just too inviting.

"Sondra is ready to do your hair!" Jo shouts into the bathroom. I turn off the water and wrap myself into a plush towel. When I walk into the bedroom there are already dresses laid out on my bed. Mine is an off white color with gold detailing all around the neckline and down the sleeves. The sleeves! The bell of the sleeve's material cascades down to the length of the dress. I don't realize until I put it on that it's actually an off the shoulder design. It's beautiful. When I lift my arms up the material hangs from my arms and I look like an angel with spread wings. And I can't help but feel like a fraud.

My hair is pinned up in big rollers. I've never been more terrified of my appearance. Curls are the goal, but this seems rather extreme when I inspect my reflection.

Jo is stunning. Her navy blue dress shimmers when she

moves. She is grace and elegance. Her dress covers her almost completely, coming up to the top of her neck. The only places you see her tanned skin is her face and hands. The dress flows so beautifully, it makes her look like she is moving in slow motion.

Jo stands in the doorway of the bathroom while Sondra finally lets down my hair. The waves I usually wear have turned into huge voluminous curls spilling down my back and over my shoulders. Sondra adds light makeup to "enhance my beauty" or so she says. I look different. My eyelashes were already prominent, but with this makeup, they look impossibly long. The eye shadow is a little darker than my skin tone and it makes my eyes appear more feline. "No veil this time," Sondra tells me, "word travels quickly here and they all know you are a sight to behold." She brushes the backs of her fingers down my cheek. "Lovely," she whispers. I pull up the dress and sheath the only dagger I've managed to keep in my possession into the holster on my thigh. Sondra rolls her eyes.

I slip gold sandals onto my feet and grab Jo's hand. "Those kebabs were nice but I'm going to stuff my face when we get to the dining room." I laugh and Jo starts toward the door.

"Enjoy this meal, ladies," Sondra tells us, "when it ends they will take you to your permanent rooms. After tonight you are no longer guests, but a part of Moria inhabitants."

"Permanent rooms?" Jo asks.

"Yes, permanent rooms, or I guess dorm is a better word for them. You'll dine in the mess hall with hundreds of others, and you will have to wear the Moria uniforms and have schedules like everyone else here. How do you think we have accomplished this way of life? There are rules and duties that everyone has to abide by." It makes sense. I guess I've been expecting that we would have to carry our weight eventually.

"Will our rooms be separate?" Jo holds my hand tightly.

"That's up to the King." Sondra sighs. "I won't be seeing you as often, you'll get your schedules in the morning. Be safe ladies, and do not place your trust easily." She embraces Jo then turns to me. I'm pulled into her arms and she whispers in my ear, "Killing is inevitable to survive here, keep that dagger close, always."

CHAPTER 9

Commander Garrith is waiting outside the door when we step out of our room. Or I suppose it was never ours. Garrith's eyes meet mine. Even if he wasn't distinguishable by being the only soldier here in all black, his green eyes give him away immediately. I wish he would remove his shemagh. If his eyes alone are this beautiful, I wonder what the rest of— no. What am I thinking?

He's such an easy target for my curiosity. He saved my life when he smuggled me my daggers before facing the wolf and I have yet to know why. I know nothing about him. Garrith's eyes widen slightly and only for a moment when he takes in my appearance. I can almost convince myself it was just my imagination but his eyebrows are higher than normal. "You have freckles." It's a statement but I nod like he's asked me a question. Whatever raw expression he was wearing quickly disappears as the mask of a perfect soldier slides back into place. We clearly took him by surprise when we swung open the door to the hall. This interaction is bizarre and Garrith seems just as eager to put it behind us. He turns and walks down the tunnel; Jo and I follow.

The dining room is as beautiful as the last time. I forgot Jo's never seen it and her gasp when we enter is appropriate. Garrith leaves the room and we're left surrounded by mingling councilmen. Half the men are sitting around the table and half of them are up, gathered in clusters to talk and sneak occasional glances in our direction. That is until King Cerastes walks into the room and everyone stands. He is wearing a thin crown that rests at the top of his forehead. He wears a long, navy coat with white fur lapels. Navy, cream, and brown are the uniform here. Reid strolls in behind the king in all white. His suit is detailed with gold, similar to my dress. He glows. The intricately sewn gold embellishments shimmer as he glides to his seat. The king gestures for me to sit to his right again, and Jo sits next to me. Reid is right across the table.

I look everywhere. Anywhere that isn't Reid's eyes. It must be obvious because the king asks, "So Jemma, what do you think of my boy? I hope he didn't make training quarters seem too intimidating."

"No actually, I'm looking forward to training."

"Eager to choke out some of my soldiers?" he teases.

"Nope. Just you." I look down at the food placed in front of me. I have to actively work not to inhale the whole plate.

The king props his elbow on the table, brings his fist up to his chin, and rubs his fingers over his beard. "So feisty. You are the most dangerous little thing, wrapped in such a pretty package."

I look to Reid, but he's directed his attention to conversation further down the table. "Your parents were always so protective of you. Perhaps it's because you were quite the spectacle. You know, your great-grandfather played a large part in Audun's migration. When the kingdom moved from the north and settled in the desert, stories spread that he carried civilians, and acted as protector, his burgundy hair was a beacon of hope." King Cerastes chuckled, "Everyone knew he would continue an impressive bloodline. Bravery and strength were to be expected. Pure genetics, a given. But here you are lacking red hair and pure skin, yet somehow carrying all the grit of his legacy. I am in awe, my dear." He leans forward to start eating. "We were right to look for you."

I glance at Reid, who is also starting in on his food, but I notice the corners of his mouth are slightly upturned. Half of Jo's plate is already cleaned off so I dig into my own. Steak and a combination of vegetables I've never seen before but could definitely get used to eating disappear quickly. Servants come around the table to collect finished meals and pour a sparkling liquid into fluted glasses.

The king rises, holding his glass. "To Jemma and Jo, may their new citizenship bring as much light and excitement as their arrival has." A few council members snicker. "We truly are elated to have a capable duo joining our community. Tomorrow starts a new journey for the two of you. You will be challenged in ways you've never imagined and often pushed to your breaking point. But it's the price we all must pay to earn our peace. I'd share more but I wouldn't want to spoil anything for you." He winks at me. "Tomorrow we train. But tonight we will celebrate." A cheer erupts along the table as the king raises his glass, and everyone follows. I grab my own. "To our newest Moria soldiers, Jemma and Jo!" He brings his glass to mine and it's music around the table as other glasses clink together and we drink.

The liquid is delicious and warms every corner of my insides. Jo eyes it suspiciously and I slightly shake my head at her. She puts the glass back on the table. Servants circle the table again, delivering cake and refilling glasses. Jo selects an adorably decorated slice of cake, a pale pink color with truffles of white icing. My glass is refilled and several men around the table start getting up to mingle. "Reid, why don't you take Jemma around and introduce her to some of the other soldiers in her wing of dorms?"

"Jo stays with me," I tell them.

The king ponders my request and finally says, "I suppose we can arrange that. Take them to the dorms at the end of corridor two. Some of those rooms are large enough for two beds."

Reid gives his father a skeptical look. "You want her in two?"

"Yes. She's proven herself capable. She'll fit right in. And have someone stock their wardrobes." He turns toward me and reaches behind me to grab my glass off the table. "Enjoy yourself this evening, Jemma. Nights like these are difficult to come by." He places the glass in my hand and walks away to entertain a group of councilmen.

"Ready to go?" Yes, please. Reid guides us through the door we came in and down the hall. We turn down one of the tunnels I haven't been down yet and it opens up into a huge room filled with at least forty tables with chairs. "This is the mess hall. Breakfast is at 7:00 a.m. for those in corridor two through four and at 7:30 a.m. for corridors five through seven. Same with lunch and dinner. One is a shorter hall, where generals and councilmen reside; they have their own agenda, soldiers aren't permitted in their quarters." He sighs before continuing, "Lunches are 12:00 and 12:30; dinners are 5:00 and 5:30. Schedules are important to how things operate down here so stick to yours and don't be late."

The dump of information and schedules open up a million new questions. But the most pressing one I can think of is, "Why has your dad been looking for me?"

Reid smirks and guides me across the large mess hall. "Curious are we?" His strides don't falter and I increase my pace to keep up. "Dad can be a little cryptic. He thrives on secrets and using people's curiosity as motivation. Whether that be to encourage cooperation or make individuals squirm, I'm not sure." He chuckles but stops when he takes in my irate expression. "I don't know why he's been looking for you. That's something you'll have to work out with him."

My feelings toward the king are coated in distrust; breathing his air makes me nauseous. If he's wanting me to offer him cooperation in exchange for settling my curiosity, he is sorely mistaken. I will sort it out on my own. Determination flickers in my chest. My new challenge: mapping the king's secret agenda.

We're nearly across the mess hall. There are a few people that look around my age sitting at some of the tables. They don't hide their stares. In their defense, we are new faces. And dressed like royalty. There are three large hall openings on the far wall of the room and we are walking to the one with a large '2' above it. Hall is the wrong word. We enter and it opens into a massive cave with stairs and balconies scattering either wall. We pass people as we make our way further into the cave. It's lit with torches and the fire light reflects off the intricate carvings of the cave. It's beautiful. I'm torn between marveling at the beauty of my new surroundings and escaping at the first presented opportunity. The hall is coming to an end.

Reid motions for us to go up one of the staircases to the right. At the top of the stairs, we open a door up to a small room with two twin beds with nightstands and two wardrobes. That is all. The three of us standing in the room is a little crowded. "Right, well, one of the servants will be in, in a moment to give you your uniforms and toiletries. And the showers are the next door over. I got you as close to them as I could."

"Thank you," I say as I place my empty glass on the night-stand and start removing my earrings. Even though this room is not my home, tiredness has settled in my joints and my new bed is looking unnecessarily comfortable. I look up at Reid who looks torn. This is new, I've only ever seen him with unwavering confidence. Jo sits on her bed across from mine and kicks off her sandals.

"I get the feeling you are both ready to turn in for the night." He laughs lightly. "Maybe we can introduce you to some of your neighbors in this corridor another time."

"Where's your room?" I ask.

His shoulders stiffen. "I'm just across the cave from you. At the top of the stairs. My room mirrors yours."

"Excellent. I'll know where to find you if I need someone to smuggle us kebabs." The gleam in his eyes is extraordinary when he laughs, paired with his beautiful smile, so much of him seems magical.

"These rooms only lock from the inside. No keys. Be sure to lock this after the servants bring your new belongings." He gestures to a sliding metal piece on the back of the door. "It's important that you lock this. You are new here and sometimes violence will accompany our people's curiosity. I'll be by at 6:50 a.m. to walk you to breakfast." Jo and I nod as I start slipping off my sandals. Reid backs out of the room and while closing the door he meets my eyes and says, "Goodnight."

"Goodnight."

A few moments later there's a knock at the door and two ladies dressed in brown tunics come in with our new uniforms. They're all shades of brown with a few cream tunics. The boots are a rich chocolate color and they lace up to our knees. The servants fill our wardrobes and leave a bag of toiletries.

"So Reid has a crush on you," Jo states after the servants shut the door behind them.

"We've had a long day. Let's go to sleep." I try to redirect her to the sleeping gowns I pull out of a drawer.

"But you know I'm right." And relentless. But she's not wrong in noticing that Reid has taken his job of welcoming me to Moria very seriously.

I roll my eyes thinking about the king and his cryptic motives. What if Reid has his own games? "We're going to keep our heads down and be sponges. We have to absorb everything about this place if we plan on getting out. There is water nearby and that's where we're headed. Whatever tomorrow and our schedules bring, we blend. I know we will start as a spectacle but we need to become invisible. Got it?"

Jo nods and changes into her nightgown and climbs into bed. I go to lock the door and put on my nightgown. It's stiff but at least the material isn't thin. I lift my arms and the fabric falls more comfortably around my shoulders.

I try to distract my mind from homesickness. I miss the whistling sounds of wind outside our hut at the oasis. The air here is different, there's moisture in it. Funny, lack of water is one of the things that drove us out of the oasis.

I make my way to Jo and kiss her forehead before I nestle down in my bed.

She breaks the silence. "King Cerastes gives me the heebie-jeebies."

"He does for me as well." I laugh.

She laughs with me until she whispers, "I don't know about him, what if he tries to take you away from me?"

The seriousness in her voice is rare and it breaks my heart to hear it. "If he wants to keep his limbs, he won't even think about separating us."

"You promise? Me and you stick together."

"I promise."

CHAPTER 10

The cooler temperature underground is difficult to get used to. At any given moment there are goosebumps covering my arms. I go to snuggle down in my bed but the sheets are too thin to assist in sealing in my body head. Jo asks, "Can I sleep in your bed? I can't warm up over here." I wave her over and she crawls under my covers. Some nights would get chilly above ground, but our sleep sacks were the perfect repellent for cold air. I took that warmth for granted.

It's nicer with Jo curled up beside me, but she still shivers in her sleep. I wonder if Reid would have any extra blankets in his room. And his room isn't far. I'm already crawling out of the bed before logic catches up with me. Reid stressed that not all company outside this door is welcoming, but Jo needs another blanket. And curiosity gets the better of me. I put my boots on and unlock the door.

When I poke my head out I don't see anyone in the cave. I creep down our stairs to the floor. Only the torches throw light over some parts of the cave. I cross to the other side of the cave and climb the steps to Reid's door. I knock and the sound echoes down the cave walls. I wince. Reid doesn't answer. Maybe he's asleep so I knock again, louder this time.

I'm getting anxious when he doesn't answer.

There's sound echoing back down the cave, coming from the mess hall. I go back down the steps and hide in a shadowed indention in the cave wall. I don't see anyone and move to the next dark corner of the cave. My footfalls are silent as I slink back up to the entrance of our wing. The opening of the cave comes into view and I can make out some of the tables in the mess hall. Voices are coming in clearer now and I can hear at least three different people. One familiar voice pushes me forward. I can't see Reid yet, but I can hear him.

"It's not going to be that easy," he says.

I lean around the corner enough to make out the back of one of the councilmen from dinner. He's facing away from me and I can't decipher what he's saying. I go to take another step forward when I'm pulled back by the neck of my nightgown. A hand clamps over my mouth and pulls me back into the cave shadows. I'm thrown against the wall and a blade is pressed into my neck. I look up and directly into bright green eyes. Even in the dark, Garrith's eyes are undeniable. He removes the blade and grabs my arm, hauling me deeper down the corridor. He's dressed in his usual, head-to-toe black ensemble. I go to speak but he squeezes my arm and shakes his head no.

One of Garrith's strides is two of mine. To match his walking pace I have to start jogging. Once my room is within view, I stop and wrench my arm from his grasp. "What are you doing?" I whisper but it has more venom than I anticipated.

He turns to face me and closes the distance between us in an instant, my vision and nose suddenly full of him. I am not a short woman, but his height and frame make me feel tiny in comparison. His eyebrows set low over his eyes, making him seem impossibly dark. He towers over me and smells of soap and musk. "What am I doing? What are you doing? Do you wake up determined to die every morning?" He's pissed. His voice is low but terrifying. He's the type of person that could command armies or torture terrorists without ever raising his voice. "What are you even doing out of your room? Did Reid not tell you to lock your door?"

I'm still reeling and taking in the current situation when I notice that he is waiting for a response. "Jo. Well, I guess me too. Jo and I, both, were freezing. We aren't used to the cold down here. And I thought if I found Reid he'd give us some extra blankets." Garrith blinks then sighs.

He turns away and starts walking back to my room. "Come on," he waves me on to follow. But we don't go up the stairs to my room. He stops at the door directly below my room and pulls a key from his pocket. He unlocks it then holds the door open for me to enter. His room is the same size as mine but instead of having two beds, he has one and a desk.

"I thought the rooms here didn't have keys, they just lock from the inside," I note.

"I guess I'm just special." He opens a closet door and hands me several large, wool blankets. It's such a kind gesture. I search his face for any sign of emotion but still I can only see his eyes and they don't give away much.

"Thank you. Jo will be proud of me for making a friend," I joke.

"I am definitely not your friend."

"Really?" I lean back onto the wall. "Because twice you've granted me with things that have helped my stay here more," I ponder my words, "bearable."

"Bearable? You would have been dead without those daggers. And honestly, I'm not sure giving you those daggers was worth the trouble. You're clearly so keen on dying, I'm afraid my efforts will be in vain."

"King Cerastes thinks I'm a great addition to the force."

"This isn't the first time the king and I have disagreed. You slayed a wolf, congratulations." He rolls his eyes, "When I look at you, I see a weak girl who made it her highest priority to protect Jo, and she couldn't even do that." That got my blood boiling. Every piece of who I am and what I've done circles around keeping Jo safe.

"Who do you think you are? Every decision I've made was always with Jo's best interest at heart. I've been keeping her alive for years. How do you get off deciding that I didn't protect her?"

"You're here, aren't you?" He throws his hands up in front of him and takes a step toward me. I don't know how to answer that question. "You're here. In a prison disguised as a kingdom. Because you couldn't keep her safe out there. You are weak and unworthy of saving." Another step toward me.

"Then why keep saving me!" I throw the blankets on the floor. "Why don't you just butt out next time you feel the urge to interfere?"

"Fine! Take the blankets and get out!" I frantically gather the blankets, stepping on them and tripping over my own feet. My hands shake and I can't figure out if it's from rage or shame. I pull open the door to escape his room. He calls out behind me, "And lock your damn door!" So I slam his.

CHAPTER 11

Just like Reid promised, he's knocking on our door at 6:50 a.m. the next morning. Jo and I get dressed in similar uniforms. I put on a long-sleeved shirt and a pair of pants that are the same dark shade of brown as my boots, which I lace almost all the way up to my knees. The clothes look tight but I feel more supported than uncomfortable. I'm shocked at how well these clothes suit me; I've always struggled to find clothes that reach the distance from my waist to my ankles. I finish pulling my loose-fitting, cream tunic over my head before I open the door to greet Reid.

"Ladies," he takes in our appearance, "you look well rested. Glad to see it." Jo's complexion does look brighter today. She slept like a baby after I wrapped her in one of Garrith's wool blankets.

"When do we get to know our schedules?" Jo asks.

Reid walks us down the cave and I can't help but be aware of the lingering gazes that seem to follow us. "You'll be with Sondra in the mornings while Jemma has combat training. There aren't many children here but Sondra handles educating the ones we have. In the evening you'll have some sparring time but to keep our younger company uninjured, we limit their time on the mats." Reid continues toward the corridor entrance and the sound of a crowd grows near. We enter the mess hall and there are several tables full of people and a line forming where I'm sure food is about to be served. It was loud when we first stepped out of our hall but within a few steps, the room goes silent. Everyone has eyes on us.

If Reid notices the sudden tension in the room, he doesn't show it. I recognize a few faces from Fundamentals at Audun. It's been so long that I come up blank with names. We follow Reid across the room to a table that Sondra is seated at alone. She's quick to smile at Jo. "Are you ready?" Jo is so charming; she'll have no problem gaining friends here. All she needs is a few minutes to work her magic and everyone will be naming their babies Jo.

I don't rely on Jo, she relies on me. Or at least that's what I thought before today. I hadn't anticipated this feeling. All the hostility in the room is directed toward me and I am completely alone now. Even though I always act as Jo's protector. I had taken for granted the happy distraction her company brings from all the things I can't control.

Reid ushers me to follow the crowd when everyone starts to leave the mess hall. We are starting today on the sparring mats. I caught a glimpse of how it works yesterday, but today they will be assigning us, and matching us against one another. Though my skills in the Arid proved that I am capable of survival, I don't know of the talent these soldiers possess. Here, they train every day. Their tunic keeps their physiques covered, but it isn't difficult to recognize the muscles appearing in necks and arms. Some soldiers wear trousers tighter than others. I try not to think about the definition of their legs and the sheer strength they must hold.

I'm brought to a mat with nine other individuals. Reid had to report to a different corner of training quarters. A list is posted on the wall next to the mat. After everyone has looked it over I go to check for my name. I'm up last against someone named Tatum. I'm not sure of the gender. I pray it's a girl, and if it's a boy, please let him be small.

Two by two, the soldiers work their way through the lineup. We're scattered around the mat. Everyone has a person to stand by, talk to, and observe with. This is new. I remember Fundamentals, but the social aspect was not a problem; I always had friends. I haven't had to think about acceptance in a group of people since then. It's always been just me and Jo.

I don't see anyone of authority. I suppose the soldiers are just trusted not to kill one another. Panic is forming in my stomach. These soldiers won't kill each other on the mat. They are colleagues and friends, they eat together every day. But I am the outsider. There is no one here to make sure my neck isn't snapped today.

I look around but I can't find Reid anywhere.

I'm among three other people that have yet to spar. There's only one boy left and he's huge. I know it will come down to us. Luck has never been something I've found on my side and I know better than to start hoping for it today. Everyone watches the mat and the individuals throwing one another this way and that. But I study the man on the sidelines waiting his turn. This must be Tatum. He looks relaxed and it's doing nothing but add to my stress. My breakfast threatens to make a reappearance.

When one of the soldiers on the mat gets pinned to the floor there's cheering and shouting then, "Harrison and Delaney, you're up." Relief floods my body. I don't have to fight the boy, whose name must be Harrison.

My relief is short-lived. The only person left around the

mat who hasn't sparred yet is standing directly across from me. Her eyes are on me before I've even identified her. Tatum. Her hair is short and blonde. Her tunic is removed and she wears a tight, brown tank top that tucks into her pants. Her arms are bare and defined. I focus on Harrison and Delaney, eager to break from her gaze. She won't allow me to study her the way Harrison did. Even without eye contact, I can feel her watching me, sizing me up.

This girl is cunning. And girl isn't the right word for her. She is a woman and a strong one at that.

There's a gasp. Delaney clutches her now bloody nose. The blood gushes and drips, staining her light hair. The amount of pale-haired individuals in this room must be well over half. Harrison is one of the few with brown hair, but even his is a light, sandy brown. He stands at attention, concern written on his face. He steps to Delaney to assess her possibly broken nose. As soon as he reaches out a hand, Delaney takes it and spins. She is quick and has Harrison on his stomach in an instant with his arm bent behind his back in an unnatural position. Impressive.

Tatum steps onto the mat with a confidence I envy. She walks halfway around the mat, circling, and I mirror her. Her stance is ready and trained. I already know her strategies will be different from those that I've seen. But I also know she spars with soldiers who have been taught the same technique as hers. I have a different background and I need to use it to my advantage. I have rarely found myself in an attack without my daggers, but she practices that way every day.

She lunges but I'm quick and move to the left, evading her fist. At least I know my speed isn't lacking. I'll use that to stay away from her.

Training quarters have grown quiet.

Her face is calculating, taking in every move I make. She

lunges again but when I move to avoid her, her foot juts out the other way, sweeping my legs out from under me. She's on top of me before I've even hit the floor behind me. I screw my eyes shut, ready for the pummeling, ready for my bloody demise.

It never comes.

Tatum moves off of me. I open my eyes and she's standing and smiling at some of the soldiers standing around the mat. "Alright, anyone who had more than thirty seconds, pay up." She walks away from me laughing.

They were betting on my pathetic performance. Rage ripples through me. Tatum hasn't left the mat yet. Before I know what I'm doing I'm behind her, shoving her to the floor. She lands on a knee and spins around to face me and her face has contorted into fury that almost puts a crack in my own anger. She's on her feet in less than a second. I put up my fists.

She moves toward me but I swing before she gets the chance. At the last second, she moves her head and I miss. This leaves me vulnerable just long enough for her to take full advantage of my exposed side. She hits me. Twice.

I step back, cradling my side, and when she spins around turning her back to me, I think she's finished but then her elbow comes out of nowhere and connects with my face. My nose is fine but she's busted my top lip. Instinctively, my tongue checks for missing teeth. They're all still there. I swing again but this time when she moves out of the way she also grabs my arm.

I pull but her strength outweighs mine. Her knee flies into my stomach and I double over. The wind is knocked out of me. I gasp and she shoves me to the floor. "Stay down this time," she snarls.

I lie on the mat trying to regain the ability to breathe.

Tatum and the others at our mat move on to watch other sparring matches at different mats.

My eyes find Commander Garrith looking at me from one mat over. He quickly looks away. I get up and walk toward him.

"Have you nothing better to do than observe others misfortune?"

I can only see his eyes but I think I surprised him by speaking to him.

"It's my job to observe. I report to General Pinnell. He needs to know where our weaknesses are." He looks me up and down.

"Are you referring to me as one of those weaknesses?" The annoyance is clear in my voice but he doesn't look at me. I've said only a handful of words to him but he already seems bored of the conversation. I don't know what compels me to poke the bear, but I can't help it. "I don't see you out there. Or do you believe you are above sparring? Are you so arrogant to assume you have no weaknesses?"

His eyes cut back to mine. "I train. But you aren't wrong. Training among your squads is far from a challenge." Then his attention returns to the sparring mat.

He's so reserved, it makes him such an obvious target for my curiosity. "Will I ever get to *observe* your weaknesses?"

He doesn't look at me but he says, "Maybe if you clean up your footwork and learn that none of your attacks carry weight without a solid foundation."

"That's great advice. Or I think it would be if I knew what any of that meant." This time he turns, shoulders and all, to face me.

"Okay." He takes a breath. "Get into your defensive stance."

I don't trust that he's actually about to give me pointers right now. I'm sure skepticism is painted across my features. He rolls his eyes so I lift my fists and spread my feet, my left foot way ahead of my right. Garrith's eyes fall to my feet. His mouth is covered but by the wrinkle that appears next to his eye, I'm sure he's sporting a smirk. He taps the side of his chin. "Hit me. Right here."

I'd like to knock the fabric right off of his face. I don't waste any time and rear my right arm back, then send my fist hurtling for his face.

He moves with lightning speed, appearing almost fluid. I miss his chin and he lightly shoves my shoulder. There is minimal force behind the shove but it sends me toppling over.

I spin around with anger and embarrassment simmering under my skin. I'm becoming too familiar with this feeling. Several eyes have come to land on the spectacle we are making ourselves into. He holds out a hand and I ignore it.

I stand up ready to try again. I get into position but this time he walks around me to stand at my back. "The wind alone could blow you over," he says to the back of my head. His right hand slides around to the front of my waist while his other hand spreads out across my back. He pushes me forward and pulls me back, "See how wobbly you are? Even if you manage to land a punch, it will only have as much power as your stance will allow."

His foot moves to the outside of my boot and he knocks my foot until the distance between my feet is just a tad wider than my shoulders. "Now." He tries to wobble me again. Even though I move, I can tell that my stance is much more stable and controlled. A smile spreads across my face and I turn my chin and tip it up to look at him.

His eyes lock with mine and I think he might be feeling the same excitement that I am. This was a tiny learning moment but I'm already eager to get back out on the mat and see the difference it's made. His hands are still clasped around my waist. The realization hits him and though he's already wearing a mask, a mask of disconnection slides over his exposed eyes. As quickly as his expression changed, his hands and body are suddenly several feet away from me.

"Am I ready to spar with you now?" I tease him. But this time his attention has moved on and it's clear he has no intention of continuing this encounter.

He doesn't look at me as he walks away and says, "You've got a long way to go before that will ever happen."

I stand at one of the mats trying to absorb the tactics that the soldiers are using when Reid appears next to me. My adrenaline from sparring is starting to wear off. There's a throbbing in my side, and my lip is tingling. I reach up to feel where it's swollen.

"I heard about Tatum," Reid confesses.

"She's tough." I don't know what else to say. I thought I was more capable because of my time in the Arid, but it's clear I still have a lot to learn.

Reid looks around. "I hate to tell you this, but since you lost today, you have cleaning duties this afternoon."

"Cleaning duties?" He nods.

"There are several chores to choose from but everyone else has already claimed the kitchen and med wing. You're also pretty low on seniority right now, so they're leaving Training Quarters to you." His eyes seem apologetic so I don't argue with him.

He shows me the bucket, soap, and sponge. All the blood on the mats has to be scrubbed off and the floors mopped. There are at least twenty mats in here and Training Quarters is a huge room. This will take hours to mop when I get done scrubbing mats.

"I'll meet you in the mess hall for dinner when you're finished here."

"Okay," I say, and start heading to fill the bucket with water.

"Jemma," Reid stops me, "steer clear of Commander Garrith. He's one of the occupants here that has a second agenda. Moria doesn't normally let potential traitors stay here, but he's earned his way." He stops to look over his shoulder then leans in. "Just promise you'll keep your distance, he's not a soldier to put your trust in."

I nod, even though his warning is unnecessary. It will be a long time before I put my trust in any of the soldiers here.

My head hits the pillow with more force than I intended. My muscles ache and my brain is foggy from exhaustion.

There's a knock at the door. They can wait until tomorrow. I'm still in my uniform. At this point I'd let it become my new skin before I get up to peel it off of me.

There's another knock. I lift one eyelid to look at Jo. She shrugs and gets up to unlock the door. "Hi Reid. Can we help you with something?"

Shit. It can wait until tomorrow, whatever it is.

"Jemma needs to shower before bed and I have a tonic for her." I hear Jo widen the opening of the door.

"Yeah, good luck with that. She hasn't even unlaced her boots."

I felt another weight sink down into the edge of my mattress. "Jemma, I know all you want to do is sleep, but tomorrow is going to be just as bad as today. You need to take care of your muscles. I have a tonic that will help and a shower will keep you from feeling like death for the workout tomorrow."

"No," I grumble. The weight on the mattress disappears.

"She's stubborn," Jo comments.

"We can work with stubborn." Reid lifts one of my legs and starts unlacing the boot. The relief when it slides off my foot is divine. He removes the boot from my other foot and the already heavy fatigue grows more persistent. "I'll send for someone to strip her bed in the morning. Good night, Jo."

And he's gone.

～

And he was right.

Jo is still asleep and when I check the clock we've got two hours before breakfast. Everything hurts. And I stink. I try to lift my arms and my muscles scream. I need water and out of these clothes.

I grab another uniform, towel, and toiletries and hobble out of our room and to the showers. It's empty in the cave as well as in the washroom. I leave my clothes on the stool outside the shower curtain. My undershirt and pants have molded to my skin in the worst way and taking them off is difficult.

The hot water thaws my rigid body. I have two hours to be good as new and ready for another beating. I stretch and attempt to loosen every tight muscle. Once I'm certain I've worked out as many kinks as I can, I shut off the water. I wring my hair and hear a step echo down the shower room. Someone else might be an early riser today. I reach through the curtain for the towel, eager to dry, dress, and get back to my room. I wrap myself in the towel and tuck it snugly around my chest. Another sound echoes off the walls.

Whoever is here is trying to stay quiet. And my daggers are in my room. Idiot.

Idiot!

My resources are limited. Another step, closer this time. I unscrew the hose of the shower head. It's pretty long and the stainless steel could do some damage. This curtain is the problem. I don't know where they are or how many people are out there. I need an idea. I pick up one of the little shampoo bottles and throw it at the wall across from the shower. I look for feet under the curtain. A boot comes into view. I plow through the curtain and throw the hose around a neck, still turned toward the source of the shampoo explosion. His dagger swings toward me but I leap behind him putting us back to back and pull on the hose that has bunched around his neck. He swipes the blade behind him and grazes my hip through the towel. He presses me up against the wall but I get my feet up and use the hose as leverage to walk my body up the wall where he can't reach me with his blade.

His frantic dagger jabs can't reach me tucked up against his shoulder and they get weaker every swing. All of my weight is resting on the hose, cutting off his airway. He tries to roll me off by bending over at the waist but when I flip over his shoulder, the hose falls into a more effective angle on his neck. I kick the blade from his hand and he claws at the steel hose.

My attacker falls to his knees. I circle back behind him and press my foot into his back. His airway has been cut off for too long now. His attempt to get fingers under the hose is wasted. His hands fall slack at his sides. I pull until I know that the release of the hose won't allow him to gain consciousness.

I pull.

I pull.

"Jemma." I hear Reid's voice but can't pull attention from my attacker.

"Jemma," he whispers. "It's okay." His hand rests on top of mine on the hose. "It's okay." My vision is blurry and I wonder where this moisture is coming from. "I've got it from here." Reid grabs onto the hose with one hand and caresses my fists with the other. I let go. What I thought was fog turned out to be tears and my vision finally clears as the salty water falls from my eyes.

"I killed him," I whisper. "I killed him. He's dead."

"Better him than you," Reid says to me before turning his head toward the shower hall entrance. "Garrith!" Commander Garrith comes into view. "Clean this up and I'll get her back." Garrith nods. His eyes shift and I follow his gaze to my hip. His eyes snap back to Reid who is wrapping an arm around me and rubbing my arm with his free hand. Tears continue to spill over onto my face and I can't get them to stop. I wipe them away only to be met with a bigger lump in my throat and cloudy vision.

Reid guides me out of the shower hall and instead of turning to my room he directs me up the stairs to the door of his own. People have gathered at the showers. They look up at me about to enter Reid's room and I am immediately sobered. I still wear only a towel. And it's amazing. I killed a man wearing a towel that somehow never came loose. Extraordinary.

He ushers me through the door. "Reid, is this fabric magic?" I reach down to feel the towel and notice that down my left hip the white fabric has stained red. He grabs my hand and pulls me into his own personal bathroom. "Your hand is so warm. How do you get your own bathroom? I want one. Maybe then I won't have to kill people so I can wash my hair," I joke.

"My hands aren't warm, yours are just freezing. And you're in shock." But I don't feel like I'm in shock. He motions to his sink. "I need you to clean up while I grab your clothes. I'll stitch you up once you're dressed. Unless you'd rather be naked while I play doctor," he teases.

"I'll clean up," I quip.

"I'll be right back." And he leaves, shutting the door behind him. I drop my towel in his shower and look in the large mirror over his sink. The cut isn't bad. I couldn't actually feel it until now that I'm looking at it. I dab it with a wet cloth; the bleeding has stopped but it is a large gash.

There's a knock at the door and it opens just enough for Reid's arm to extend holding my uniform. I put everything on but don't button my pants so that it doesn't rub against the gash.

"Ready for me?" Reid asks but he's already opening the door to come in. He brings in a stool that sits a little lower than the bathroom counter, a stitching kit, and a glass of water. He pats next to the sink. "Hop up here where the lighting is good. And drink this tonic." He hands me a glass with clear liquid inside it.

I do as he says and let my legs hang off the counter. The tonic is bitter but my attention is pulled from the taste when he folds up my top and tucks it into the bottom band of my bra then rolls down the waist of my pants. "Lean back." I stretch my arms out behind me and lean back until my head is touching the mirror. He sits on the stool and starts disinfecting the skin around the gash, then rubs a numbing agent over my skin.

His gentle touches awaken a burn deep within me. He starts with the needle and thread. It should hurt but I'm more focused on keeping this blush from devouring my whole body.

I study him from under heavy lids. His focus, and the way his lips are pursed in concentration. "So you went to the showers with no weapon and still came out on top against an armed attacker. Sounds like a win today. No one will be making you clean the sparring mats this week."

I'm not sure if it's the adrenaline or shock wearing off but the lightness of the conversation doesn't seem possible anymore. "Do I call it a win or did I just become a killer?"

"Either, both are true." I don't want to talk about it. I want to look at the way his hair glows under these lights. And I want to watch his light eyebrows come together in focus to tend to my wound. His skillful fingers cinch my skin back together. He ties the final stitch and places a bandage on it then stands to weave a tighter wrap over the laceration. He stands up and positions himself between my legs then leans over me to bring the wrap around my waist. Instinctively I want to move, unsure if it's to get away or to accommodate whatever he's trying to accomplish. I start to squirm. "Be still." He brings the wrap back around and then returns to sit on his stool. He measures out excess fabric then brings the roll to his teeth and tears.

I am warm. A fire has sparked in my chest and it's engulfing my organs. I want to put it out. My skin is buzzing. After he ties the fabric he looks up at me and moves his mouth. His beautiful mouth. And his eyes are so bright blue. He holds me in his gaze. Reid is a trap. He's a trap and I don't think I'd mind being caught.

"Jemma?" he says. And suddenly I'm aware that he might have been talking to me. "I asked if that feels okay. Do you want to get up and move? Make sure that it's snug and secure. They aren't going to go easy on you today just because you had an eventful morning."

I stand and take a few steps then stretch. It feels fine so I button up my pants and roll down my shirt. "I'm good." I try to sound strong like I didn't just kill a man and then eye fucked Reid to cope with it. But my voice comes out strained in awareness that every decision I've made today has been the wrong one.

He holds open the bathroom door and I enter his bedroom. It's much bigger than mine and Jo's room, even without taking into account that he has an attached bathroom. His bed is ornate with beautifully carved posts at every corner. "So from now on why don't you just stay in your room and I'll walk you and Jo to wherever you need to go? This way you don't have to worry about anyone following you. I can escort you to showers every evening and then to breakfast every morning."

I know his intentions are good since I was just attacked in the shower hall. But the mention of needing an escort makes me claustrophobic. "I mean, sure I was attacked but I learned not to go anywhere without my daggers from now on," I press. There's a lot I have left to learn about this community and I don't know how much information I can uncover with a constant escort.

I take a step toward the door and he comes with me. "I need to go check on Jo, she's probably worried by now." I bend down to pull on my boots that he's placed next to the door and wince when it pulls on the stitches.

Reid crouches down and slides his fingers behind the back of my calf while pulling the boot onto my foot. He looks up at me again. "Please promise me you'll be careful." I nod and he laces up my boot and moves on to the other. When he's finished he opens the door for me and says, "I'll see you at breakfast."

CHAPTER 13

"Find me, find me," she taunts.

Her voice is louder now. I know I'm getting close.

Mom holds her favorite mixing bowl to her stomach and vigorously mixes what I'm sure will be a new favorite dish. She smirks and tilts her head to the lower cabinet.

Little fingers peek out from under the curtain covering our pot cupboard. Pots and pans usually put away, are scattered across the counter. And I'm sure Mom is eager for me to find Ray so she can return her kitchen to its fixed order.

I lean against the counter's edge, trapping Ray in her hiding spot.

"I've looked everywhere!"

"Clearly not, if you still haven't found her," Mom goes along with my antics.

I exaggerate a great ponder with extra loud hms. "You know what, I forgot to check under her bed!" I stomp away from the cupboard and creep back to await her reveal from behind the curtain.

A giggle escapes from the cupboard and her face emerges, giving Mom a gleaming smile of triumph and baby teeth.

"Got ya!"

Ray squeals and tumbles from the cabinet, taking off to flee through the back door of the kitchen. I'm on her tail and she knocks into Mom's legs.

It happens too quickly, too chaotically. The mixing bowl breaks into pieces at our feet. Shards of white and teal scatter across the floor.

Mom's deep breath in would imply that she's about to yell. At least, for someone that doesn't know her.

Mom doesn't yell. Mom never yells.

But her silence is just as loud as any raised voice.

This mixing bowl belonged to her grandmother.

She bends down to collect the pieces and whispers, "Take Ray to the market. Get something that will be easy to make. Shillings are on the dining table."

I nod. "Let's go, Ray." In one hand, I hold the bag of shillings, in the other, Ray's tiny fingers wrap around mine.

"Jemma," I look back at Mom, "Do not lose her."

"Before we share today's sparring lineup we need to address squads." General Pinnell has everyone's attention. "We do have a new member and this provides a good opportunity to change up some of the squads." There are a few groans scattered around the room. "I know some of you are comfortable in your squad. This is not a punishment but a chance to discover leadership qualities and chemistry among teammates that we haven't seen work together before." It goes without saying, the team that has me will not be excited about it.

I want to go back to this morning, sitting across from Reid

in the mess hall while eating breakfast. It isn't common for me to feel moments of bliss, but eating bacon while watching Reid's beautiful lips share with me the details of today's plans can't be far from it.

Snap out of it.

Snap. Out. Of. It.

I indulged today. I'm a domino of distractions. And Reid is a good one. I wanted distance from my dreams and he was such an easy focal point. But it never lasts.

The memories are always there.

Do not lose her.

But I did. Ray is gone.

I can bend all my reasons until putting her on that wagon is justified. But I'll know. I always know. I chose wrong and it cost everything.

My center of balance tips at the glimpse of my raw heart.

The beats hurt.

All the company around me and no one can see my chest bleeding.

Patch it. Push it down.

Mummify this part of me.

General Pinnell calls names, placing soldiers into squads. I ignore the relief on each member's face when their squad is complete and my name has not been called. I want to be invisible. I want to take my chances in the Arid. Squads are split into groups of five, one member being the squad leader. There are only ten of us left not moved into a squad. Five more are announced together before those of us left have no choice but to accept that we've been placed together.

"Reid Cerastes, leader of squad ten. Tatum Langley, Enon Pettigrove, Cynrad Pettigrove, and Jemma Shayde." I look at the squad I'm in and the solace I find in having Reid as our leader allows my breathing to be more manageable. However,

Tatum is as scary as she appeared on the sparring mat and has already proved that she can kick my ass. Enon and Cynrad are nearly identical. Definitely, twins. The only difference being that Cynrad has dyed his hair jet black which causes immense contrast between his skin and hair. There's a black ring, a piercing in his eyebrow. There's no denying it, he is terrifying. It's amazing how much softer Enon appears just from deciding to wear his natural, light brown hair.

Reid gives me a reassuring smile before addressing the group as we come together. Cynrad glares at me and I almost jump out of my skin when Enon says, "Hi Jemma!" He extends his hand, "I'm Enon." So they're identical twins yet opposite in every other way.

I take his hand and my voice doesn't carry the same booming enthusiasm when I respond, "Nice to meet you."

"This is my brother, Cynrad. He comes off as a dick but he's actually a big softy." Cynrad rolls his eyes and decides not to acknowledge me. Enon moves his attention. "And this is Tatum. Who I'm pretty sure you've already had the privilege of meeting." Tatum doesn't look at me for several seconds.

"Nice to me you," she smirks, "Jemma." Everything about her taunts me. Her smile, her tone, her stance, all of her is trying to provoke me. If ever an army of cloaked creatures were chasing us, I would trip her. "Don't worry, I'd never fight with you off the mat. Especially not when they've assigned your bodyguard as our squad leader. How convenient for you."

Despite Enon's warm welcome, peace and comradery among this squad is unlikely. Enon claps his hands together. "So, anyone up for an icebreaker?"

Cynrad groans and Tatum turns around completely, ignoring the squad. Though his greeting was refreshing, Enon's eagerness to put trust in this squad only makes him appear naive. His tenderness will get him killed. Everyone must be thinking the same thing. But if he knows how we feel, he refuses to show it. "Okay, you guys don't like icebreakers. What if we set a real challenge? I'm sure everyone here is up for some healthy competition." He looks around at all of us. "Right?"

Tatum raises an eyebrow. "What kind of competition?"

Enon is quick on his feet, "Our squad member, Jemma, was attacked in the showers. The first person to solve the assassination mystery gets..." Enon taps his chin and turns to Reid. "Squad leader, provide us with some incentive, please."

Reid quickly overcomes his surprise and says, "Winner is exempt from a month of chores. Their rotations will be covered by the rest of the squad."

My attempted murderer's motives have officially been reduced to a month's worth of chores. I've always known I was insignificant, but to hear it out loud is something I never planned on being present for.

General Pinnell takes his place at the front of the room again. "I hope you are all well acquainted with your squads," he says. "Tomorrow you will be going outside with them. You will have their back as they will have yours. We never know what's going to come above ground. I know many of you are slow to grant trust." For a split second, Pinnell's eyes connect with mine. "But I would recommend that you learn to lean on one another, starting with your hand-picked squad members. Enemy armies grow closer every day." Does he know about the cloaks?

We are dismissed to go to our sparring lineups. Today I'm placed against Reid. Go figure. I get the feeling that all the steps I make are directly into a footprint carved out just for me. It's unsettling. I want to break away from the path that King Amos and the council must be laying for me. I know I'm playing into all of their games but I have yet to decipher their edge.

Reid goes easy on me when we spar. He knows I'm not present. All his moves are slow, allowing me to counter him unconsciously. I need to take it in. Play nice and see what they're trying to accomplish. Do as expected until eyes are no longer on me.

I will come to know every nook and cranny of Moria. Even if that means abiding by their rules.

~

"Free meals treating you alright?" I spin around quickly. Too quickly. So quickly that my intruder knows I've been caught.

At supper I took my time, waiting for almost everyone to dismiss to their sleeping quarters. I didn't go to my hall. Instead, I went into Corridor One, a tunnel I hadn't yet mapped.

And I'm caught.

So much for flying under the radar.

I don't respond to his question. He comes into the light of the lit torch on the cave wall. This corridor is much narrower than the rest, with torches farther apart, leaving too many blind spots in the tunnel. I take in my intruder's face. He's familiar, several years my senior, and the light does little to disguise his deep wrinkles.

"Are you lost?" His voice is gentle but I detect the trap.

"I got turned around and I'm not yet familiar with the layout here." The truth mixed with a lie.

He smiles and the shadows cast by his wrinkles create a most menacing expression.

"Do you think we want you to know the layout of our home?" A councilman. I remember him from my meal in the dining room. He sat further down the table but he repeatedly roamed with his eyes. He was also, no doubt, a bloodthirsty witness to my display of survival instincts against the wolf.

He takes another step forward and I take one back, ready to sprint in the direction I came.

"I don't wish to alarm you." He moves his arm forward, gesturing for me to take it. "Let me escort you back."

To uphold pretenses and any chance that he hadn't caught onto my sneaking, I place my hand in the nook of his elbow and he clamps his over mine. Hard.

I still when he moves down the hall, not in the direction of my room.

"I think I'm supposed to be going the other way." I pull away but the grip he has on my hand is a cuff of iron securing us together.

"You really must be turned around, this is the way you want to go." I stumble as he pulls me along beside him, fright rising in my veins. My curiosity of what might lie down this tunnel vanishes. The more steps we take, the more certain I am that this is not where I want to be.

"Where are we headed, Mr. Gray?" Reid's voice echoes from behind us. Excellent.

Reid walks to us with purpose in his step and confidence in his shoulders and I'd give anything to emulate such leadership. He is calm and collected as he awaits a response. Regardless of circumstance, just seeing him brings me relief.

Mr. Gray opens his mouth but utters nothing as he likely decides on a lie. He smiles and says, "Miss Shayde was quite curious this evening. I was giving her a tour."

Reid nods. "I see." He takes in my face and says, "But it is late. I was about to head to Corridor Two if you'd like to join me."

"Now," Mr. Gray objects.

"Thank you, Councilman, I can take her from here." Mr. Gray's shock is evident when I'm suddenly able to slip my hand from his grasp. Reid doesn't offer me his arm the way the councilman did and I'm thankful. I'm definitely touched out for the day and only want to get to the showers where I can fully wash the sweat of his palms from my skin.

Once around the bend of the cave, Reid looks at me, a grin plastered to his face.

My shoulders fall and I grumble, "What?"

"Exploring the councilman's bed chambers are we?"

"Oh God. Is that where Corridor One leads?" I thought it might hold secrets or something useful, a secret exit perhaps. I have never seen anyone enter or exit when we eat in the mess hall.

Reid's laughter is musical as it bounces off the walls. The mess hall is coming back into view and I'm eager to put as much space between myself and Mr. Gray, and anyone else in Corridor One.

We enter the mess hall and I dart for Corridor Two where the company is still questionable, but at least I know what I'm up against. I notice Reid who stands a few paces away and makes no move to follow me.

At my hesitation he says, "I still have some meetings I have to attend tonight. I'll see you tomorrow."

I nod.

"And Jemma, if you have any questions about Moria, or you're interested in a *map*," he smiles, "all you have to do is ask."

CHAPTER 14

We have to be up at three in the morning to prepare for today's exercise. It's two right now. Close enough. I get ready without waking Jo. I'm not normally a morning person but the anticipation that I'll be above ground and seeing more than the Arid today was making it difficult to sleep. I've paced the room and stretched and I've run out of things to occupy my restlessness.

I open the door enough to peek into the cave. No one is out yet. I make sure all of my daggers are secure and start down the stairs. I skip the last step and turn to go to the mess hall.

"Couldn't sleep?" Garrith's voice breaks the silence and nearly sends me into cardiac arrest. I hold a hand to my heart and attempt to catch my breath. He's leaning in the doorway of his room twirling a knife between his fingers. And as always, he's decked out head to toe in black, leaving me with only his eyes. Not that I'm complaining. He has extraordinary eyes. But I am surprised that, even at 2:00 a.m., he's still committed to his headscarf.

"I suppose you couldn't either." I'm still breathless and shift my weight to try and contain my excitement for today.

"You're in the room directly above mine. You've been pacing for the last ten minutes. So yeah. I guess you could say I can't sleep either." Smug. I want to tell him off but guilt does tug at my chest that I woke him up.

"Sorry." I would stay and bicker with him, as I do enjoy the 'What Expression Is He Hiding' game. But I need to cool it with these jitters. The illogical need to walk off the nerves so I can turn around and walk several miles today doesn't make sense but it's what I've got.

He pushes off the door and walks toward me. "You're showing too much."

"What, skin? Because all you can see are my hands and face."

"No," he starts, "your excitement is evident from every angle. You're vulnerable. And you're too naive to know it. You're going above ground with fifty other soldiers, most of whom want you dead. Show a little restraint."

"Since when has a little excitement hurt anyone?" Maybe I will bicker today. The way he talks to me always rubs me wrong. Every word he sends my direction is condescending.

He rolls his eyes. "If you have to ask me that question, you're more naive than I thought." Smug asshole.

"Would you prefer I hide behind my headscarf? I'd rather be excited than a coward. You hide your face, your emotions. Your mask doesn't make you scary. It makes you scared." My jitters have gone and I feel steady on my feet.

"I'm not scared," he grumbles.

"Why cover your face?" I take a step toward him and he rolls his eyes. He turns away from me heading back to his room. "It's a mole, isn't it? You probably have a huge mole on your nose. I bet it grows hair."

He looks at me. "Good luck above ground today, Shayde. I hope you don't get yourself killed."

"Aye, aye, Commander Mole." I spin on my heel and begin down the tunnel. It would make me a happy woman to know that he's irritated. But I don't turn around to find out. Even if I don't get under his skin the way he gets under mine, I can't be knocked down today. I'm going outside.

The mess hall is empty, but I guess that was to be expected so I have a seat and wait for the breakfast shift to arrive. A crew of ladies is supposed to get us fed and packed with food for today's journey.

I sit at one of the tables and accept that all I can do right now is have patience.

❧

"So, have you figured out who wants you dead?" Tatum's question pulls me out of my mind. Everyone has clustered in the mess hall, eating breakfast with their squad. It's not a secret no one in my squad wanted me, which only adds to my surprise when Tatum speaks to me.

"Um," I chew on a corner of toast, "no, I haven't sorted that out yet."

"Pity." She turns her attention back to her breakfast before thinking better of it and drops her fork. "You know they're going to try again, right?"

"That's why we're doubling the security rotations." Reid walks up to our table. He looks delicious, dressed in various shades of ivory. It's more believable that he's an angel rather than a human. "And I've started escorting her personally."

I smile up at him. As claustrophobic as the idea of being on someone's metaphorical leash started as, it's been a real treat to get to look at him more often.

Tatum pulls me from enjoying the view. "Is that enough for you, *Jemma*?" She's taunting me.

"Yes. I believe Reid is on the side of keeping soldiers safe."

Tatum holds my gaze, a storm brews in the blue hue of her eyes and they appear more gray today. "Well that's amazing!" Her tone is sickening as she exaggerates my opinions. Enon and Cynrad join the table. Tatum looks at them while gesturing to me. "Just what I thought, a duck."

"Excuse me?" I'm not sure what she means but I do know it's offensive.

"A duck!" Tatum slams her hand on the table. "If it walks like a duck and looks like a duck, it's probably a duck. And you are exactly what you seem. Someone tried to *murder you*. And what's your great plan? Sit back and let Reid protect you?" She stands and looks at Enon and Cynrad. "This isn't a warrior, she's hardly a soldier, and she's going to get us all killed."

Tatum stalks off. I won't look at Reid. I'm embarrassed enough without the thought of our audience.

"She's an acquired taste," Enon says with pity embedded in each syllable. "We'll figure out who orchestrated the attempt on your life. And I have a feeling when she sees you make them pay, Tatum will regret her words."

"Good morning!" General Pinnell walks out of Corridor One and thankfully pulls the attention away from me. I bite back the need to dwell on Tatum's words and focus on what today will bring. "Is everyone fed and ready to take on the Ocean Trek?" The room erupts in whoops and hollers. I'm not alone in my anticipation for today. All company is giddy as we make our way out of the mess hall.

Our squad is last in line traveling deeper into Moria. I recognized the tunnel that leads to the throne room and we passed by it. I haven't mapped this part of the city yet. Calm pours into my chest as my mental map of these underground tunnels grows with new information. We leave behind the mess hall, sparring rooms, dorms, and throne room and delve further. The tunnel narrows until it's a tight fit, even moving single file. The torches that light the cave grow apart in distance leaving us in near total darkness occasionally.

I focus on Reid in front of me. Any potential light reflects in his hair. He is a glowing beacon of guidance.

I get anxious wondering how long we will be walking through such a narrow pass when the cave opens up. The walls around us turn from bleak caves to intricate canyons. The natural phenomena of caverns scattered around us create a hum of excitement in the group. The temperature grows warmer with every step I take. The faint sound of soft horse whines drifts into my ears, and goosebumps erupt on my skin. The scent entering my nose is fresh with notes of salt. It takes everything in my being not to spring ahead of everyone and drink in the freedom I feel must accompany being above ground

Reid's silhouette goes dark as the light of dusk pours in behind him. He takes another step forward and the sun's warmth falls on my face. Every muscle in my body relaxes and I breathe in. I could stay in this spot forever. I close my eyes and revel in the bright red backs of my eyelids. At this moment, I'm back at the oasis.

Fingers lightly wrap around mine. Reid stands before me and his grin allows me to notice my mouth turned up toward the sun. I'm light as a feather, I want to sprout wings and fly from this cavity in the ground and just keep flying until the sun swallows me. I can't think of a better way to end my journey in this world. Reid softly tugs me to keep moving.

Steps are carved into the ground bringing us up, up, up. More light floods into every nook and cranny. The line of soldiers walk under a long archway and the steps disappear into a slight incline, and when the shadow of the arch falls away we are outside.

The breeze is warm and sends sand colliding with my face. I'm a fool for ever being irritated with the constant dancing dust above ground. I pull the fabric from around my neck and tie up my shemagh until only my eyes are visible. General Pinnell has retrieved a brown horse somewhere. I guess that they're kept somewhat in the canyon maze just below us. He circles us shouting orders and we fall into sequence. Squad one sets the pace as we head East. I wish our squad was first. The dunes here are less common. In the Arid, Jo and I would climb the tallest dune we could find just to look in any direction and be met with miles and miles of sand.

I've missed the blue sky, void of clouds. There's so much possibility in the sky. If I could have looked out from her perspective onto the Arid, I could have told Jo and myself what direction to map in, instead of discovering more and more sand. I respect the sky for her commitment to her secrets. I don't think I could personally watch Jo succumb to the end and never provide a vital clue. I doubt she notices us. And I wish that she doesn't. I wish there were so many other things, outside our tiny oasis, that we never held her attention. I wish the same air I breathe is carried from here to a million other places filled with beauty and possibility.

Wishing puts a small crack in the armor around my chest and I quickly box it up and pretend the dust still sits on that mental box. Pretend I don't, from time to time, blow off the dust and inspect my collection of wishes.

Cynrad blows out a sigh close behind me, clearly discouraged by the expanse of sand. Walking long distances doesn't bother me. It's walking long distances without the reassurance that something is to come that has regularly gotten me down. For too long I've taken steps without any idea if I was closing a distance or creating a larger one. It's refreshing to know that every step I take today brings me closer and not farther from something, anything. I've never seen the ocean, and that in itself, makes it magical.

Mile by mile the dunes get smaller. The sun rises higher in the sky. Sand hues here are cooler in comparison to the warm-toned sand that surrounded our oasis. Ahead there's a movement just above a peak. Rustling palms come into view. I squint through the mist of dust that never tires to dance. Green. The color green sends my pulse into overdrive. This is the first tree I've seen alive since the trees started drying up around me and Jo. Thank you, God for the color green.

The pace has sped up as if the tree sighting has physically made our bodies lighter and easier to carry. The wind whips the fabric ends of my scarf around my face. The smell has shifted and I swear the air has started to taste faintly of salt. We've passed several trees and it takes all of my restraint not to stop and introduce myself to every one of them. The groups ahead of us break from our formation. I look at General Pinnell in the distance. He makes no move to organize the sudden chaos. I run to catch up with the group.

Under the sound of squeaking my boots make with every plop into the sand, I can hear a distant crash. Repeated crash-ing. Over and over. I tune my ears for the crashes. I climb a dune and my excitement has me tripping over my own feet and my hands sink into the sand. I reach the top and the rest of the soldiers come back into view. But I can't focus on any of them because behind them stretches miles and miles of water as far as my eyes can see. I stumble toward the crash of waves, of water.

Groups of soldiers are stripping their shemagh, and tunics, and unlacing their boots. Reid appears next to me. I can tell he's smiling even before he starts pulling the scarf from his face. I move toward the water; watch it rush the land then retreat. The sand here is heavier. Dust doesn't blow and get trapped in my lashes. My footprints are more defined, leaving more details than the normal foot dent I make in the dunes. I glance back at Reid. He's placed his sword, tunic, and head-scarf in a pile. His undershirt is snug and I can make out the taught muscles he conceals underneath. I'm not sure how long I spend taking in his appearance. The only thing that pulls my attention is the splashing of soldiers running into the water. They have stripped down to only their undergarments.

Alarms go off inside my head. I wish to experience the water, but I will not become bare to do so. Reid reaches down and pulls up his undershirt. The sun is high in the sky and it's beaming off Reid's porcelain skin. He doesn't have a flaw, a blemish, a scar. Insecurity smacks me in the face. My body is lined with trails of near-death encounters. My scars reach, twisting up my throat and gripping my windpipe. Air comes in and leaves my lungs too quickly to use.

Reid pulls down my shemagh, exposing my mouth. It doesn't allow me to breathe any easier. Concern has taken over his features and his finger tips my chin up trying to understand my distress. He's talking to me but my hearing has retreated in the sounds of waves. And as always, I'm a walking contradiction. I want to escape into the waves and shield myself with the water. Yet it's the act of going into the water that's terrifying me. Just like I yearn for the Arid, to hide among the dust. Yet the Arid has almost killed me multiple times.

Reid pulls me down to sit on the sand. "You don't have to go in. We can just sit here and look at it." His words are meant to comfort me but it's all wrong. I want to go in. I just can't bring myself to ditch the layers concealing my scars.

Tatum rushes the water. She wears the same black sports bra and boyshort style underwear that must be in everyone's bureau. She looks beautiful. Her short hair whips around in the wind. I've never seen her hardened face appear so soft. She dives under a wave and comes up and her joy calms my racing heart.

General Pinnell comes up behind me. "Your dad used to be a hell of a swimmer." I squint to look up at him. He nods at Reid, who removes his pants leaving him in nothing but black shorts, and takes off toward the water.

"Sam would tell your grandpa he was staying at my house, and I would tell my parents I was staying at his. And the whole group of us would take a trip to the water and camp on the beach."

"I have a hard time believing that. Dad never took me to the beach."

A crease formed between General Pinnell's eyebrows. "Yes well, the last time I even know of him going was when he convinced Trish to come with us." I remember Mom and Dad talking about Aunt Trish. She died before I was born. "When Trish drowned, he never went back."

I suddenly feel ill. My parents are dead but the betrayal from their secrets and stories untold to me still stings.

"It was difficult to watch your dad, once so full of life, turn into a shell. Things got better when he met your mom. And even better when he had you. His eyes held happiness again."

My eyes are wet but I will not cry here. "I guess I'm just trying to say that even though you've endured terrible things, you are still capable of experiencing greatness and freedom. You can build it yourself, the way your dad did, little by little. At least I hope that didn't die with Sam." And with that, he walks away. As much as I want to voice my frustrations and get to the bottom of every story and sense that everyone in Megara knows more about me than me, now is not the time.

Right now there's an ocean in front of me and the moments

I have with it are limited. I pull my shemagh completely from around my head and place it in the sand. Then my daggers, and my boots, and my tunic, and my pants, and my undershirt. I dive into the water, not for sanctuary, but for happiness. I don't know how to swim but the waves are gentle enough not to steer me. I make large strokes bringing me closer to the blond boy giving me all of his best smiles.

I know my scars gleam in the sunlight. I know the map of places I've been and battles I've won are shining where everyone can see. A permanent stamp. But today I won't wear them like they're ugly. I wear them like they are proof of my strength. My armor is etched into my skin.

Today my scars are a warning to all the soldiers around me that despite every battle I've faced, I always win.

CHAPTER 15

Moria is quiet as we make our way back to the mess hall. My body is exhausted but I'm not ready to go to bed. If I fall asleep the day will come to an end and I'm not ready for that.

We swam for hours then let the sun dry our skin. It was nearly dark when we finally reached Moria's entrance.

The sound of footsteps and hushed whispers echo down the tunnel walls. I can smell food before we round the corner to the mess hall and my fatigue is replaced with excitement for the meal ahead. Reid's hand grazes the small of my back when he guides me to my seat at the table.

We've played a quiet game of light touches all day. I notice every single one. I can't not, as they send goosebumps across my skin every time. I try to keep my head level. Romantic games do not hold anything close to priority on my list of things important to me. But I can't deny that a little change of pace is refreshing. It feels good to have entertained other thoughts.

And it might be just that, silly little thoughts of mine. Reid could just be a naturally affectionate person who reassures those around him with gentle touches. As much as I know better than to indulge in these circles of romantic curiosity, the consequences of things going wrong in a relationship seem so much smaller than the consequences of anything else in my life going wrong. Low stakes are comforting and Reid's touches are becoming too tempting.

Tatum sits down across from me at our table, "I thought for sure today was going to turn sour. I spent all morning anticipating another attack on Jemma, just for her to run out into the ocean without any idea how to swim."

The lightness of her comment takes me off guard. After breakfast, I thought all she had for me was hate. But her tone almost makes me forget the things she said. "I shouldn't have gotten so mad this morning. But for all of our sake you need to learn to look out for yourself," then she adds, "and to swim."

A blush creeps up my neck. "I thought I did okay." Perhaps my movements in the water did not translate into the grace I was feeling.

Cynrad scoffs, "For a newborn deer learning to swim for the first time, yeah you did okay."

Reid rubs my back. I shut out any ideas of his hands on me. But every circle he makes on my back sparks excitement in my mind. I know I'm delusional. His touches mean nothing. He's just affectionate.

He's just affectionate.

I force my attention back to the arguing at our table. The banter between Tatum, Cynrad, and Enon is a good distraction from the blush that threatens me every time I glance toward Reid. I do wish I wasn't the butt of most of their jokes but I can't complain. I'll take jokes over attacks in the showers any day. I also appreciate the camaraderie, like maybe I could find peace among my teammates.

"You two are worse than my brother," Tatum fires back from the constant antagonizing comments made by Cynrad and Enon.

I can't help that curiosity gets to me. "I didn't know you have a brother."

"He's at Megara. I don't get to see him often, he's about to age out and then he'll be sent here to be another dedicated and honorable soldier." With just a few words from Tatum, I'm reminded just how much I don't know about my new quarters.

"Megara?"

This time Reid steps in. "Everyone under age eighteen lives in another portion of the kingdom. They have classes kind of like Fundamentals back in Audun. Over half of the Kingdom lives in Megara. It's south of here and closer to the ocean. Moria's position puts us between Megara and other threats. We're like the first line of defense." I noticed that the age group here didn't have much variety. Everyone looks to be between eighteen and thirty. I suppose I should have asked where the children and elders were.

Everyone seems to be thinking about the time they resided in Megara. Tatum speaks up first. "I miss it there. Being underground takes its toll on a person."

She has my undivided attention. "Megara isn't underground?"

"Nope. It's all the kids accompanied by anyone deemed old enough not to be a soldier. It's so much better than here. It's like they show you how wonderful life can be while you're still a child so that once you're sent to Moria, it's your goal to survive as a soldier and be granted retirement in Megara." I can't read her tone and it's hard to tell if she's being sarcastic or genuinely wants to go back. "We're underground here in case the Howlers move south and start in on Megara territory. We're hidden and so are all the entrances, making it easy to counter an attack." Interesting. I wonder where the other exits are. Wonder how sealed the exits are. The desire to touch the ocean again is already a stubborn itch I can't wait to scratch.

"Well, I should turn in." Tatum is the first to rise from our table. And she isn't wrong. We have been here a while. There are very few other soldiers still occupying the mess hall. "I hear Garrith is going to help with training tomorrow. So I'd recommend you all get to bed soon as well. Who knows what kind of ass-kickings he has planned."

In my peripheral, I can make out Reid stiffen at the mention of Commander Garrith.

Tatum is right, it is late. Jo is probably asleep but in case she's not, I would still like to share with her the details of today. I stand and Reid follows. "I'll walk you." Yes, please.

We walk in silence. It's so quiet in our wing that I feel like we're sneaking. Or maybe it's the guilt of wanting to melt into the warmth radiating off Reid that makes me feel like we're sneaking.

"I probably won't be there at the start of tomorrow's training." That revelation disappoints me more than I'd like it to.

"Prince duties?" I ask.

"Yeah, something like that. I can arrange for someone to escort you in the morning."

"That's okay," the stairs to my room come into view, "after today, I think my scars were enough to create some distance between me and the other soldiers."

We round the first step. Instead of seeing me off here, he follows me up the stairs and to my door. Every step he takes up the stairs with me makes his presence heavier. He's all around me. His scent of mint sends my mind swimming. I want to swim in this moment. We make it to my door. "You looked beautiful today." Heat ignites in my chest. I'm at eye level with his mouth and even after the stunning scenery I witnessed today, I still can't think of a better view than this one. He takes my hand and rubs his thumb over the scars that thread in my skin.

He pulls my hand up to his lips and kisses my knuckles. "Goodnight, Jemma." And then he retreats down the stairs.

I escape into my room and lock the door behind me. I was fully expecting Jo to be asleep at this late hour. But instead, she's sitting on her bed wide awake with her hand over her mouth. "Oh my god. Did he kiss you?"

I let out a half sigh, half laugh. "No. Well, he kissed my hand."

"That's sweet," she trails off, trying to gauge my reaction.

"He's nice." I don't want to think about it but I can't help it.

Ideas are pouring into my mind.

Reid's lips. Reid kissing me. I don't know how it works. How can I fantasize about something I don't understand?

I shake my thoughts off. I have priorities here and a boy can't be one of them. Jo was exactly what I needed to pull my head from the distraction that is Reid. I get ready for bed and try to ignore the dread that comes with knowing I won't see him tomorrow.

CHAPTER 16

There are five active sparring mats out, two squads at each and Garrith is rotating from one mat to the next to correct and disgrace those on it. Anxiety grabs me by the throat when his attention falls to Tatum and a boy from squad Nine sparring on the mat in front of us. Garrith stands at the edge of the mat, arms crossed. He doesn't have to speak or move for everyone to be aware of his presence. His attention alone is enough to make even our most confident and capable soldiers squirm where they stand.

Tatum throws her opponent down on the mat. I feel for the boy from nine. Tatum is a fierce competitor. I wish her accomplishments would grant her safety, but even the winners are under harsh scrutiny.

Commander Garrith steps onto the mat. Tatum is an expert and always has absolute control of her face. To anyone else, she looks focused and determined, but I can see the slight movement in her throat. She is nervous.

Garrith looks at her and nods.

I let out a breath as Tatum leaves the mat. The boy has just been beaten and now Garrith will drag out the humiliation. Garrith instructs him to get back into the position he was in before Tatum was able to throw him down. Garrith's voice is unique. It's so deep that we can all feel the rumbling, proof that he is speaking. But he keeps it so low that we can't make out the words he's sharing with the soldier. I feel sympathetic for the boy. Who knows what condescending "advice" he's receiving?

He tries a move that Garrith deflects, then Garrith uses the boy's surprise to shove him to the floor.

The boy is instructed to get back into the position he started in. He tries a different move but plants his foot too close to Garrith's reach and Garrith swipes his foot out from under him. He lands flat on his back.

Again, Garrith tells him to get back into the original position. Again, the boy discovers a new way to fail. He's thrown to the mat again. Again. Again. Again.

He's knocked to the ground over and over until sweat is rolling off the boy's skin. Sweat is dripping off his nose before Garrith eases up and gives him a pointer. This time the boy's fist makes contact with Garrith's ribs. Garrith doesn't show any sign of pain. The boy's eyebrows reach his hairline in surprise but his feelings of triumph quickly turn to panic that Garrith will retaliate for the shot.

He doesn't.

"Congratulations. You learned something today," is all that comes from behind Commander Garrith's shemagh. The men start to walk off the mat. Garrith walks. The boy limps like there isn't a muscle in his body not screaming.

"I haven't forgotten about the competition." I hadn't heard Tatum come up behind me. I arch an eyebrow at her. "You know? The asshole that tried to kill you? I think I have a lead." I was sure that was all for theatrics. I didn't think my squad mates would take it seriously.

Determination rests heavy in her eyes. "What do you know?"

"Nothing solid, but the man that tried to kill you, his name is Dax Anderson. He was a member of squad Seven. His closest friend was also in his squad, Bellamy Gray. I haven't gotten very far with him, he keeps to himself. Be sure to steer—"

Several heads whip around toward the entrance and Tatum's voice trails off. I follow their gazes to find King Cerastes. He always looks happy. But he's not the right kind of happy. He's a sick type of happy; his smiles are forged in blood and he's so pleased with himself for it.

He holds his hands out. "Commander Garrith! Lots of progress today, I'm sure." He walks to our mat and takes in the state of many soldiers before returning to Garrith, standing at the edge of the mat. "I would have thought there would have been more," he ponders his words, "injuries. Yes, some incentive. Big things are coming. How are our soldiers to understand the severity if we don't dish out the occasional broken bone?"

Garrith doesn't answer but I don't think the King ever expects a response. He seems to only be interested in his own voice.

"I think we can turn it up a bit. Why don't you put yourself in the lineup, Commander?"

This time Garrith doesn't choose silence. "If I spar, you'll be weakening your army by placing them in the med wing."

"Oh, I have the most confidence in our med wing. They have a way of getting our soldiers healed and back on the mat at an unbelievable turnaround time." I can tell there's another conversation just below the surface of this one. Garrith and Amos communicate without speaking. The intensity of their eyes makes me feel spared for not having to know what discussion they are keeping quiet.

Amos doesn't look away from Garrith when he yells, "Jemma Shayde, you're up!"

God, no. A fifty-pound weight lands in my stomach and nausea rocks through me. Cold sweat is beading on my skin. How am I supposed to spar with Garrith if just moving my feet to the mat is an extreme sport?

Take a breath, square my shoulders, say goodbye to the tiny amount of dignity I have left, and step onto the mat.

I feign confidence and smile. "Did you think we'd be sparring so soon?"

Garrith doesn't mind silence. He lets silence grow. I think it's a tactic. He likes to make people squirm when they talk to him as if at any moment he could decide you aren't worth a response.

"No. You are not ready." He looks away. "But I don't make the rules around here."

Amos claps. "Let's get on with it!"

I take a defensive stance with my fists up. I try to circle Garrith but he seems bored and doesn't counter my movements. He stands completely still even though I'm moving around to his side. It's a trick. It's a trap and I'm walking right into it. There's hesitation in my movements but I get close enough so that I'll be about to kick his knees out from under him. Maybe once he's on his knees this will become a more even fight.

I move to hit my mark but his once relaxed stance disappears. In less than a second he's turned to face me and diminish the space between us. He's fast. Too fast. And my terror makes me slow. I can only watch as the consequences of sparring against Garrith unfold in front of me.

His fist hits me deep in my stomach. I double over. He steps back, allowing me a moment to catch my breath. I stand back up. He looks to the right of me. I can never seem to hold his attention. Anger ripples through me. I will not be an irritant chore for him. I will not be dismissed so easily. My hesitation and terror are replaced.

I charge forward, swinging my right arm, then my left, then my right again. He deflects all of my punches. I try kicking him in the side but he catches my leg and spins me until I'm facing away from him. I know he could do considerable damage from this position, but instead, he pushes me away from him.

I stumble but manage to outrun my fall.

Embarrassment clings to my skin. I spin around to face him. He looks to the right of me again. I follow his line of sight. He's looking at the King like he's consulting with him. Like he's confirming whether or not he's put me through an adequate amount of pain. Amos looks annoyed.

I face Garrith. His eyes are calculating. I run forward, plant my feet, and send my fist right for his face. He veers to the right and turns to grab my arm. He continues his spin until I'm stuck behind his left shoulder. And as I realize his left elbow is hurtling toward my face, it makes contact with my nose. Pain shoots up my nose and tears spring to my eyes. I take a disoriented step back and bring my hands to my face.

Blood seeps through my fingers. Is it broken? Is my nose broken? Tears might be streaming down my face. I feel like my brain is flowing out of my nose. Garrith comes up to me and grabs my face, his thumb touches my nose and I flinch. He sighs, I'm not sure if it's in relief or annoyance and says, "There wasn't a crack. It's not broken." And then his attention falls back to Amos, no doubt questioning if he's hurt me enough to release me.

It isn't fair. The realization hits me and I see an opportunity. I reach up and grab the fabric covering his face.

It may as well have been the last thing I've ever done.

The room moves too quickly, everything is a blur. The right side of my face smacks the mat, the noise echoes through my ear, and I can't tell whether or not my eardrum has ruptured. My equilibrium is nonexistent and dizziness rakes through my body.

I lay flat on my stomach. Garrith has both my wrists gathered together at the bottom of my back as I'm pressed further into the mat. "Okay!" I yell but my screech hurts my head. The smack in my ear has done a number to my equilibrium.

Garrith lets go and backs away from me. I roll over and lean back on my elbows. I want to apologize for my attempted invasion of privacy but no words come to mind. His knees are on the mat and he's sitting back on his ankles. Only when he places his hands on his knees do I register that he's breathing heavily. "Do you even want help? Do you wish to learn anything?"

The hum of soldiers around us pricks the shame in my ears, neck, and cheeks, but it doesn't leave half the impression Garrith's disappointment brings. His disdain is a heavy cape that I've tied too tightly around my throat. He doesn't wait for my response.

Garrith leaves the mat, and the soldiers who witnessed my ignominy move on to greater things than me.

I have to leave training quarters. I don't realize where I'm planning to have a breakdown until I'm turning the corner.

Holding my still bloody hands out in front of me, I make my way down the auditorium steps. I can't find sanctuary quickly enough. I sit on one of the steps and lean against a seat.

Should have left them in the desert.

What skillful addition?

I have no arguments for them; the only reason I'm grateful they picked me up in the desert was because it saved Jo.

I'm shocked by how much being an outcast is bothering me. It shouldn't matter. It doesn't matter.

If only I could just get my body to stop revealing my embarrassment every time a soldier lays me out on the mat.

As uncomfortable as I am in my own skin, I can't help but see their side. I am an outsider. I'm an outsider who hasn't been trained in hand-to-hand combat. I suppose I can't blame them for their indifference toward me.

I take a breath. My eyes have adjusted to the darkness of the room.

I make the remaining trek down the stairs until I'm floor-level of the wolf den.

Here is where I was shoved into a cave with a wolf, which was expected to be an entertaining execution. Here, I surprised the King and his council. Here, I started climbing the metaphorical Moria ladder.

Killing the wolf earned me a place among the soldiers. I earned sleeping quarters. I earned the right to train. I earned a good meal every day.

It dawns on me that even though I killed the wolf, I have yet to earn the respect of the soldiers. From the looks of it, success in sparring might be the key to my ability to thrive here.

Starting early tomorrow, I will begin earning again.

CHAPTER 17

I'm in my last lap around training quarters when Tatum finally shows up.

I've been up for an hour. There's only so much training I can do on my own so I started running. My irritation is evident when I walk up to her.

"I'm here aren't I?" And she's right. I asked her to work with me this morning so maybe I can stop embarrassing myself on the mat. Tatum's skills are refined while mine are limited and I have a much shorter timeline to get caught up.

"Alright. Let's get started." We start toward the sparring mat when Tatum grabs my arm. "What are you doing?"

"I thought you were going to show me how to spar."

"Yeah, first we're going to talk about it."

"What's there to talk about? Wouldn't it be easier to show?" I gesture towards the mat.

"We have to get you in the right head space before we can do anything on the mat."

"I'm ready. I'm focused. And we don't have a ton of time so

I'd rather not spend it talking." My voice does a lousy job of hiding my agitation.

"Your mind isn't right. And you should never go into a match with your emotions out of line."

I cross my arms.

"No one wants you on their team. I don't want you on my team. But you are, and I'm not going to die because you didn't know how to handle yourself on the field. It's not just you at risk if you don't get your shit together."

"Then go appeal the lineups." I'm out of line and I know it. But I can't help the offense I take from feeling unwanted. It was one thing to assume it, it's another to hear it out loud.

"With your emotional chaos always making an appearance, I wouldn't dismiss the chance that you could get more than your own squad killed. We have a community here. You don't have to like everyone. They obviously don't like you. But you *will* adapt. Or we are all doomed."

She isn't going to budge and stands in front of me for ten, eleven, twelve seconds before she decides I look ready to listen. "It's good to have emotions. It's a good thing that your feelings are as strong as they are. That means you have something you're fighting for. But when you spar, your feelings take over. It keeps you unbalanced and wild. You feel anger and start acting out in anger. Your feelings should push and motivate you; they should not control you."

"Okay, so how do I push down the feeling that I need to choke out Garrith when he's taunting me?"

"First, Commander Garrith doesn't taunt you. He's trying to teach you. But you're always so busy *feeling* that you don't grasp any lessons." Instinct tells me to argue with her but I realize that might be a part of my problem. "Jemma, why do you fight? Why do you get up? Why do you continue to try when no one else is getting thrown around as much as you are?"

"I didn't know that avoiding the mat was an option."

She rolls her eyes. "You are a fighter, Jemma. What are you fighting for?"

"Jo." It's instinct. It's the only constant in my life. Jo is the driving force behind every choice I make.

"Exactly. You need to quiet your brain. Get familiar with your priorities and then simplify them. Any anger inside you needs to create a barricade around your priorities. Turn your anger into protection and focus."

She makes sense but doubt plants a seed in my mind and tells me her advice is easier said than done.

Today I will ride a horse. There was still a small handful of soldiers not acquainted with riding, me being one of them. I'm familiar with camels, goats, and other animals weighing less than half a ton. But I've never known a horse. Only the wealthier company in Audun had horses.

Our squad is guided down a tunnel to one of the entrances where we will retrieve our horse. I fall into step with Tatum, rolling my shoulders and stretching my back. No matter how much I tried to "find focus in my anger" I continued to "be controlled by my feelings." And as a result, Tatum tossed me around.

A lot.

I'm sore and we'll be riding horses today. Squads one through three were taken to the stables just below the East Entrance. Squads four through seven went to the North Entrance. And we are joining squads eight and nine at the stables at the South Entrance. I try to force every detail to stick in my brain. I'm only familiar with the East Entrance since we exited there to go to the beach. The ceilings are lower here and the hall is only wide enough for two bodies to stand next to each other. Except for Garrith, whose hulking frame nearly takes up the entire space. He's several feet ahead of me but he's hard to miss as he towers over anyone else in the tunnel.

Tatum grabs my attention. "Have you seen Reid today?"

"I haven't. I knew he wouldn't be around yesterday, but I thought I would see him today at breakfast. He usually walks me and Jo." Jo did whine that she wouldn't get to admire his nice hair.

"He probably already has one of the best horses. I guess today's exercise wouldn't be essential for him." She's right. But I still miss his presence. His father is the King, but I often find myself forgetting he's the prince. He just seems like Reid to me. Reid with hair as bright as the sun and eyes as blue as the sky.

Sunlight streams into the tunnel and I watch Garrith's head duck and then climb up. Everyone shuffles forward until it's my turn to take the steep steps into the outside air. I bring the fabric of my shemagh over my nose and mouth and take the final leap from Moria. Like last time, it takes some time for my eyes to adjust. I pull my shemagh down slightly to cast a shadow over my eyes.

Moria's South Entrance isn't much more than a hole in the ground. I keep walking to get out of the way of the rest of my squad. I turn around to look back at the entrance and if it weren't for the bodies rising from the ground, no one would ever suspect the entrance to an intricate underground city is only steps away.

General Pinnell guides us South on foot until we are face-to-face with an enormous block of sandstone. It glitters as we move and the sun reflects on the tiny particles. Jo and I have slept in the shallow caves of many similar structures. I've been waking before her lately so I can start training earlier; even losing the few minutes we have together in the mornings makes me miss her. Tomorrow I should skip morning training.

The closer we get to the sandstone, the bigger it seems. It casts a shadow at least a hundred feet long and I have to crane my neck to look at the top. Once enveloped by its shadow, I see the wide opening at the base. We follow Pinnell who marches forward, into the belly of the rock.

Inside, torches are lit down the wide cavern. I pull away my shemagh, my eyes adjust to see long rows of stables, and I notice many horses have turned their heads to take in their guests.

I've seen horses before. But in my corner in Audun, there were far more goats walking by than horses. The sheer size of their heads alone is intimidating. I will ride one today. Everyone from my squad breaks off to greet their horse. Four of us remain without a horse, a girl from eight and two boys from nine. General Pinnell waves his fingers, summoning us to continue toward him down the stables.

He turns around and waves to the dozen stables closest to us. "Alright guys, time to socialize."

The girl from eight says, "You want us to socialize? With horses?"

"You do intend to ride one don't you? Trust me, you want your horse to know who's on their back, lest they buck you off." At this moment the girl reaches out to pet the nose of the nearest gray, spotted horse. Its teeth snapped, attempting to bite her. I back a step away from the closest horse, the path between seeming smaller now. We continue down the path. The other soldiers stop hoping they find compatibility in the most prestigious stallion.

In the last stall, a head does not hang from the opening so I turn to head back to the other horses.

But I hesitate.

Just to be sure, I peek into the stall. Backed against the far wall stood a brownish-red beauty. Its mane is the same color, rich chestnut. It turns to look at me. A long white stripe runs from its forehead to its muzzle. The same white color decorates all its legs, appearing like stockings. I lean in to get a better look. It turns its head away from me to continue staring at the wall only inches away from its face.

I unlatch the stall door. "I wouldn't." I almost yelp in surprise when Pinnell speaks up from behind me. "This mare lost her foal a few months ago. No one rides her. She does enough not to whither. She eats, drinks, and moves, but her mind isn't right. Her heart isn't right." I look at her. The stunning beast stares straight ahead into the wall. My heart breaks for her.

"Come on, I'll get you a good one."

General Pinnell helps me onto the saddle of another brown horse, this one with a black mane, named Gideon. He guides us out of the stables and into the sun to join the rest of the squads. Even walking, the motion feels alien. Adjusting to the body and learning not to fight the sway of the horse as it moves is not as easy as I thought it would be.

Despite my discomfort, another feeling leeches in. Anticipation festers. There's a swell sweeping through me, I recognize my excitement, a sensation I haven't known in a long time.

Gideon slows to a stop, following Pinnell's instruction.
Pinnell shouts, "Gideon Up!"
Gideon, up.
Giddy on up.

I'm about to roll my eyes at the ironic name but before I can start, Pinnell slaps his hand across Gideon's rear. Startled and full of a sudden burst of adrenaline, Gideon takes off.

I grip the reins. No one gave me instructions. How do I stop? How do I slow down? My muscles are rigid, resisting every bounce on the saddle. I've never known such speeds. The rest of the group falls behind me. We barrel over dunes so steep that I'm looking directly into the sun on our ascend. The fabric around my head and shoulders comes loose and is soon lost in the wind behind me.

The might within this beast is astounding. I unlock some of my joints, give into the motion, the repetition, and glide effortlessly through the sand. After some time it feels less like jostling and more like a dance. It is a dance of speed and the skill of putting distance behind you in record time. I look around and find Tatum on her horse several dunes away.

Tatum is a natural and her white horse is angelic. I've never seen such a smile—Tatum's teeth gleam. She is the image of freedom as she lets out a high-pitched, long yelp. She gets closer, her horse closing the distance quickly, then pulls ahead of us.

My instincts take over. This is indeed a competition. I wave the reins up and down, urging Gideon. He meets my request with larger strides and we match paces with Tatum. She laughs; the sound is simply musical. The laughter echoes. Joy and freedom come out of my mouth in loud spurts, mimicking Tatum.

I am laughing.

I laugh. I howl. I close my eyes and trust Gideon. And there's never been a feeling known to man.

Tatum and her horse slow down. I pull on the reins and somehow Gideon understands. I pull them to the left and he turns until we face Tatum. She whips her chin back in the direction we came from.

It's time to return to the stables.

As we pass Tatum I smile and cheer Gideon forward. We take off in another race.

It's exhilarating. And I think maybe Moria isn't so bad. Maybe Megara isn't the Kingdom I thought it was. Maybe this home is better than no home.

Gideon slows to a trot when we see the other soldiers grouped at the entrance to the stables.

Tatum's horse beat us by a long shot. I gather that Gideon might have more years on him. When I look closer, I see that he has white hairs mixed in around his eyes. I dismount from the saddle and wish that no one is watching. I have never been blessed with grace, especially when doing something new.

I stretch my legs and back as I guide Gideon. I never realized how many muscles riding such an animal would take and I'm certain of a sore start tomorrow.

Once the horses are back in their stalls, our squads start the trek to Moria's entrance. I'm just about to go with them. And I know I should. But I have to check on the mare. I check her stall and she is standing with her head in the corner, her rear to the door. I want to do something, help her somehow. But I'm without the means, I haven't any treats or time. Today I will leave.

Next time I will try.

It isn't long before I come up on the opening to Moria. Immediately I spot Reid. He's wearing different shades of cream and his shemagh is wrapped snugly around his head and face. His light-colored attire almost matches his natural lightness. He is the sun in man form. His slim frame leans against a sandy boulder with his arms crossed.

I flash a smile at him. He doesn't move and I'm assuming

he doesn't see me so I pick up my pace, eager to share today's experience.

The rest of my squad is already standing with him. Enon and Cynrad have their heads tilted toward one another. They rarely look like twins, but at this moment, they share the same expression. And despite their obvious contrast in style, they are every bit the identical duo they refuse to acknowledge.

The closer I get to the group the louder the conversation. Tatum's arms are crossed while she listens to Reid question the man hidden behind him.

The man steps away and I see that it's General Pinnell that's got everyone's attention. When he sees me he says, "Ah, Jemma. I'm glad you're here. I was just telling your squad about the most recent change in leadership."

"Change in leadership?" I eye Tatum but her face gives away nothing.

"Yes, we are moving Prince Cerastes to squad six where he will be their new squad leader. And Commander Garrith is stepping in as leading for your squad ten." No. God, no.

Reid looks at General Pinnell. "Did my father tell you to make this change?"

Pinnell does not falter under the pressure of Megara's prince. "The king trusts me to make the necessary decisions when it comes to training."

Pinnell considers this the end of the conversation and begins to walk away. "She's still green. She needs an ally in her squad," Reid argues.

For the first time, something about Reid doesn't sit well with me. I would prefer having Reid over Garrith as a squad leader, but when he spells it out as being for protection, something in my gut ignites. I don't need protection. And I don't need Reid using his prince card to *protect* me. I know that being defensive over this is foolish but it doesn't stop my mouth from reacting, "Reid, it's fine."

General Pinnell looks at me and nods before moving on to other duties. Reid's face is stamped with concern. "I'm certain my father would not have approved of this. I'll be sure to bring this to his attention tonight." He finally looks at me. "This will be fixed by tomorrow, I promise."

"I meant what I said. It really is fine. I like my squad mates. And as much as I don't want to work with Garrith, I'm sure I could learn a lot from him."

"How kind of you," a smooth voice travels over my head. Garrith stands behind me. Lovely. "We appreciate your concern, *your highness*. But I think we've got it from here. Let's go, Shayde. We've got work to do."

I guess Garrith's taunting isn't reserved only for me. It seems he's comfortable getting under the skin of everyone. Reluctantly, Reid finally leaves to get acquainted with his new squad and I follow close to Garrith. Our squad is probably at training quarters by now and Garrith is in a hurry to get there. One of his strides is two of mine.

Once I'm within a few feet of him I say, "You don't have to antagonize him." Garrith turns to look at me, his eyes slightly wider than normal, like he wasn't expecting me to speak to him.

He turns his head back and continues walking before responding. "I don't know exactly what protocol was with your previous squad leader, but from now on, don't speak unless instructed."

"Excuse me?"

"What a surprise, Shayde already breaking protocol." Imperious ass.

"I'm pretty sure you can provide efficient guidance without being an ass. General Pinnell is proof."

This time he stops walking and faces me head-on. It's much easier to talk to him when he is walking away, but when he stands at attention and there's nowhere to look but at *him,* words seem to get caught in my throat. I want to be stronger, and less easy to intimidate, but Garrith has consistently been my Achilles. "Then go complain to him about it, but I can guarantee that appearing entitled will do little to gain you any respect around here. Just look at your precious prince, do you think the rest of your squad will respect him when he complains to his dad to get his spot back?"

He doesn't wait for me to say anything before he takes off again and I'm left to catch up. "Reid is an excellent squad leader!"

"Sure if you're in the market to be coddled. I think Pinnell made the right decision today, it was becoming a bit too obvious that no one was being pushed in this squad."

We're nearing training quarters and I let the quiet fall between us. He has a point. He's smug and sarcastic and arrogant, but he's also a little right. Reid was a fine leader but we did plateau under his command. That doesn't make listening to him show disdain for Reid any more enjoyable.

Enon's reach is too much for me and his shin makes contact with my torso, sending me flying. He's on top of me in an instant, both arms, both legs, completely out of commission. His knees rest on the outside of my thighs, his legs holding my legs in place while his hands take my wrists, trapping them above my head. I release a sigh of defeat.

Enon crawls off of me while Garrith steps onto the mat.

"Alright Shayde, I'm going to be brutally honest right now."

"When are you not?"

He doesn't acknowledge my remark and continues, "You will be knocked down—a lot. You're lacking the training that your fellow soldiers have had access to for years. There's no question, you are going to be compromised."

The thought of a cloak with its spindly fingers wrapped around my neck chills my blood. For once, I close my mouth and listen.

"We need you resilient in that no matter how hopeless your situation may seem, you have to fight anyway. You have to get out of it anyway. You have to be ready all the time. So that when the moment arises, and your opponent has let down their guard, you can strike."

I wipe the sweat from my brows and get back into my stance.

"You're not going to start there this time."

My face must give away my confusion so he explains, "Get back into the position you were in when you gave up. Then get out of it."

I lie on my back and put my hands up above my head. Enon moves back onto the mat, trapping me once again. There's no chance of moving, no shot at escape, while in this position.

Garrith comes up next to us, plants his knees on the mat, and leans back on his feet. Even kneeling, his presence is menacing. "Alright, Shayde. Get out of this."

I can't. I know I can't.

I wiggle my legs, try to push my body up, try to shake my arms from his grasp; Enon is too heavy and too strong for either. And when I look up at his face, there is no anger or fight, he isn't even trying. Somehow his lack of fire is insulting and I shrink to the size of a pea. All I survived in the Arid, to be reduced to the lowest of competitors. Enon might as well squash me in his palm.

"Shayde." Garrith's voice is miles away, down a tunnel. It sounds almost soft, an encouraging whisper. "He's beating you at his game. Don't play his game. He's big and strong. You've faced opponents bigger and stronger. What was your game? And when you figure it out, play it." Garrith gets up and instructs Enon, "Stay there, do not let her up." The softness in his voice disappears and he's back to his normal self.

Garrith walks away. Tatum and Cynrad are standing together at the edge of the mat, their heads tilted like they're sharing secrets. Enon looks down at me and says, "Sorry about this."

"It's all good." I continue to wriggle but it does nothing but waste my energy. I push against Enon looking for weaknesses but in doing so I'm exerting too much of my remaining strength. Garrith is right, I'm not playing my own game.

I relax and try sensing the opportunity.

"So what's their deal?" I refer to Tatum and Cynrad and their exchange of secrets.

Enon scoffs, "Who knows this time."

"This time?"

"There's definitely something there. He's my brother. I know when things are going on. I just can't ever figure out what it is when it comes to them."

Very slightly, he relaxes, still not enough for me to try anything. "Are they together?"

He goes on, "I think so. Not publicly. Cyn's been acting different for about a year now. When he's happy, he's the happiest I've ever seen him. But when he's down, it's beyond what I can do to help. And it doesn't make it any easier that he doesn't talk about it."

We both turn our heads to look at the maybe-maybe-not couple. Cynrad says something that puts a deep crease between Tatum's eyebrows. She sighs and walks off. Cynrad also blows a gust of air out of his mouth as he watches her go. Then he looks at us.

Not at us.

At Enon.

It looks like a tiny plea, a moment of vulnerability. Cynrad, normally dark and broody, looks like he needs a hug.

I feel the shift in Enon. He leans forward slightly.

The opportunity. In one swift motion, I push my left foot flat against the mat, pushing my hips up. Enon leans back to recover his balance but with my other foot, I kick it up into the air to the right of his back, bend my knee, and wedge my ankle under his chin.

Then I stretch.

Straightening my leg back out, I take Enon with it, pulling him away from my chest. He loses his grip on my wrists and goes sprawling out on his back. My leg windmills around spinning me on my back as I roll off the floor.

Enon is still gasping for the air I knocked from his lungs when I stand above him. His hand lays atop his chest. "Christ," he breathes.

A slow clap ensues from behind me.

Garrith stands, his hands clasped together. "Your game, Shayde. Good work today." He turns on his heel and walks away.

Pride grows. If I were stripped down to my skeleton, I'm sure it would be glowing. We walk to the mess hall for dinner. Or I supposed, Enon, Cynrad, and Tatum walk. I am borderline skipping down the tunnels.

"You'd think she just defeated an entire army of Howlers," Tatum snorts.

Enon chimes in, "There's only so many times you can lose before someone has to let you win." Cynrad giggles.

Their words bounce off of me. Amazing things happened today, I don't want this day to end.

We fall into place in the food line. Garrith is here, standing at the wall speaking with General Pinnell.

I turn to look up at him as we pass.

His eyes are already trained on mine. I know I shouldn't say anything. I hold in my words like I'm holding my breath.

He raises one eyebrow.

I go against protocol *again*, smile, and say, "Thank you."

Garrith doesn't call me out for speaking without being instructed to. Instead, he says, "You're welcome."

Garrith looks over my head. His eyes narrow.

I whip around to understand what has captured his attention.

Reid is storming out of the mess hall and down our dorm cave. I've never seen him move with such hostility. Anger is etched into his skin, into his posture.

Something terrible has happened, I'm sure. Before I can recognize that it's none of my business I'm already following him down the cave.

CHAPTER 18

I throw my hand out to catch Reid's bedroom door before it latches closed. I've seen warm and welcoming Reid. I've seen goofy and charming Reid. I've never seen this brooding Reid. His shoulders have settled high around his neck like his own, personal armor. These are new waters and I'm not sure what kind of ocean I'm stepping into when I follow him into his room.

"Reid." My voice is stern but curious.

"A little space tonight, Jemma." Rude.

"Have I done something to upset you?" I venture farthing into his room. He removes his sword and places it on his desk. He still hasn't turned to face me, and from the look of his rigid stance, he doesn't want to.

"No," he sounds annoyed. "You didn't do anything. I'm just requesting a moment alone."

"Are you sure? Maybe we should talk about it." He doesn't turn around but I swear his eye-roll is audible.

"Typical," he scoffs.

"Okay. You're grumpy. I'm only trying to figure out why. Maybe I can help."

He finally turns around. There is no warmth in his gaze and his patience is long gone.

"*Typical*, Jemma. I told you to leave. I told you I need a moment to myself but you're still here." He sighs and runs a hand into his hair. "I told you not to engage with Garrith. He's unpredictable and manipulating. He's already trying to provoke you and you're falling for it. But do you listen to me?" His palms are out in front of him and his gestures keep getting wider. His voice grows louder. "No! You don't do what you're told. You don't listen!"

"I listen! But I am capable of making my own decisions and I won't feel guilty for taking your words as recommendations instead of orders."

"Watching you ride off, without me. I can't protect you this way."

"Have I not proven myself capable of staying alive?" I try to lift some of the weight between us. This moment is heavy and I want to pull him out.

"You shouldn't have to kill. You shouldn't have to live with the guilt of taking a life to save your own." He's talking about the attempted assassination. "And Garrith is not the company you need; he's only going to convince you that it's okay to draw blood first and ask questions later." I don't tell him that guilt isn't what I felt when I knew my shower attacker was dead. I don't tell him that pride is what blossomed in me that day. I don't tell him that defeating my attacker gave me a sense of belonging. I want to stand among the strong, and I know in my heart that death is going to come with that.

He's silent. His shoulders relax and he brings both hands to his forehead and rakes them down his face. His fingers reach his chin and reveal his incredulous smile. He chuckles and leans back to rest against his desk. His hands grip the edge as he lets go and laughs. The sound is nearly musical. He *sounds* pretty.

Is pretty. So much about him is pristine and perfect.

I'd love to join him in this delirious state; it is truly inviting. I just can't seem to ignore my confusion.

His head is thrown back and his laughs continue from deep in his chest. He's gone mad and I want to go with him. I want to laugh with him, cry with him. Reid is showing me every corner of him; I want to turn on all the lights and inspect all the pieces.

He gathers himself and wipes the tears from his joyful eyes. He sighs and looks down.

Looks up.

His eyes are endless reservoirs and I'm drowning in them. "I didn't like it."

He's mesmerizing. It takes me a few seconds to register that he's spoken.

"Like what?"

"I knew better. When I cried out while you fought with the wolf. I needed to get you out, make you safe. I didn't know you yet but I knew. I knew I was in trouble. I'm in trouble because I *want* to protect you. I want to keep you safe, and that became more difficult today when I was removed from the squad." He ponders his words and I realize that watching him think, wonder, breathe, blink is my favorite pastime. "I am a reasonable man, and even though the events of today would have concerned me, I would not have been so angry. I only would have reminded you to keep better company. Trust me, Garrith's intentions are never good." He's not making sense. But he's so handsome that his nonsense is okay with me. His words come out low, "Would you like to know what sent me into a blind rage?"

Everything is so cryptic and I've seen more variety in his emotions in the last five minutes than in all the time I've known him. He has a way of keeping me perplexed. I can only nod.

"You seemed quite chummy with Commander Garrith." Another sigh. "I didn't like it."

All of the pieces start falling into place. "Reid Cerastes, are you telling me you were jealous?" I tease him. My faltering confidence is nowhere to be found in my voice.

His stance is relaxed now. He chuckles. "I guess I am." His smile makes my chest swell and when his eyes meet mine again there's something in them that's different. His eyes aren't warm and inviting but they aren't angry either. His mood changes are giving me whiplash. He pushes off the desk and walks toward me. "It's a difficult pill for me to swallow," he starts again. "Jealousy. I rely so heavily on logic. And today my feelings were far from logical."

I understand this look. I understand this feeling.

He likes me.

He likes me and he's closing the space between us.

He likes me and it's not anger in his eyes, it's hunger.

Reid is going to kiss me. I feel outside of my body.

All of my insecurities, my lack of experience, I have no idea what I'm doing; nervousness should be taking over. Instead, my anxiety goes quiet.

There's a hum of excitement between us. Only desire flows in my blood. I don't know how this works or what to do but I want to do it. He's close enough now.

His hand wraps around my wrist and pulls it to his chest, pulling me into him. His other hand reaches for my face.

I'm showered in warmth. In this space I am content. My eyelids close to revel in this comfort when his lips brush mine.

A jolt of something unknown erupts from my lips to my knees, lighting up the rest of me on its way. I can feel every joint in my body. Every cell, every particle is buzzing.

I reach out to grip his tunic and something in him shifts. My lips still tingle and I'm already craving another brush of his against mine. His hand swiftly weaves around my waist and he presses me to him. I gasp and he covers my mouth with his, swallowing my surprise.

His mouth moves against mine and it's the most delicious dance. I want more.

More.

More.

I reach into his hair and his groan vibrates my lips. I feel him everywhere. It's too much and not enough. It's overwhelming; I'll surely split in half. A splotchy mess of desire is marking my skin.

Reid is a fever I don't want to break.

I've never been held this way, kissed this way.

His tongue finds mine. His hands find the skin under my tunic. I melt into all of his touches. And he is giving me all of his touches. He is delicious. I want to taste him. His lips, his cheeks, his neck. I'm not sure where the thoughts come from. I've never felt this need to know someone so thoroughly with my lips. I shock myself.

He pulls his head back long enough to look into my eyes. "Stunning," he murmurs and his mouth is back devouring mine.

His hand at the small of my back starts trailing down my spine, pressing us impossibly closer. I feel his hip bones collide with mine. The friction between us is heavenly.

He feels incredible.

Incredible.

Incredible.

Incredible. But it's so much. Too much.

An alarm sounds in my head. Bright lights blink behind my closed eyes. He feels my hesitation and pulls his face from mine. All of the humiliation I ignored earlier comes crashing down on me. My blood runs cold.

No. No. Push these feelings away. But it's too late, my head isn't right. I'm already retreating. My body rejects this moment and I've never been so frustrated.

I'm acting on instinct. I'm acting without thought.

But acting recklessly feels so good.

"My apologies," he breathes. Reid takes a step back. His hair is jutting out, evidence of my hands running through a moment ago.

I'm so angry with myself for ruining this. "There's nothing to apologize for." Even my voice is strained like I just ran a mile in record time. Or I just experienced one of the best kisses to ever go down in history. I curse myself for my hesitation. I want to ask that we pretend I didn't ruin it with my freak-out and try again. And again.

I don't realize I'm smiling until Reid sees it and smiles too; relief is written on all of his features. I get it now. His laughter was justified. I feel wild and raw and laughter is only a hiccup away.

I want to tell him it's okay and I liked it but words are caught in my throat. I walk to him. He's smiling but prac-ticing caution. I place both my palms on his stomach and slide them around his sides until he relaxes and hugs me back.

He welcomes my embrace and nestles when I tuck my face into his neck. He kisses my forehead.

I don't know what to say. I only whisper, "Thank you." I

could have thought of something better but I need him to know how much I appreciate this moment.

He chuckles and leads me back to the door. "Let me walk you back to the mess hall. You must be hungry, a day horseback should always be followed by a good meal."

He walks with my hand in his. I'm a walking contradiction. Because as good as it feels to walk with Reid. A specific set of eyes lands on our clasped hands and unsettles my stomach.

CHAPTER 19

It's incredible how often the highest points in life are followed by the lowest. The moment before I walked in on Mom coughing up blood for the first time, Ray had said my name correctly. She always called me Yemma. But that day I sat with her for an hour, bribing her with candies to pronounce the J. I was so excited to tell Mom.

Every light and happy moment only reserves a spot for a moment of tragedy. I swear off hope and forget that I did. I swear off dreaming and forget that I did. Heartbreak always waits for you to be off guard. I forgot to remain low. I forgot living content brings chaos. I forgot that rising will always bring falling.

Idiot. Forgetful idiot.

"Jemma," Reid is taking my hand and pulling me into his arms, "I'm so sorry. She's in the mess hall. It's time to tell her goodbye." No.

No.

She's too young to be in Moria.

She needs to be taking classes.

She should be in Megara with the other kids her age.

This isn't forever.

You'll see her soon.

None of it is sinking in. Even as Sondra explained why, my mind wouldn't wrap around it.

We have to send Jo away.

None of this makes sense. Jo and I are a unit, a package deal, we would never split up. I should do something but I'm too deep down the hallway in my mind. I can't find the door. I can't find the surface. I can't find the place where I have control of my words, my body, or the ability to burn this kingdom down if they even think about moving Jo away from me.

Do something! Do something!

Do what?

Reid's arm is thrown around my shoulders. Sondra walks ahead of us, guiding us to the mess hall.

My feet are moving. When I look down I can see that I'm putting one foot in front of the other. I can't feel myself using the muscles to move my body. Reid rubs his hand up and down my arm but there's too much numbness in my limbs to be warmed by him. I can't focus on anything except the ringing in my ears.

How did I not notice the ringing before now? It gets louder every step I take towards Jo.

Something festers under all the ringing.

Light pours out of the doorway to the mess hall. We move in that direction but I simultaneously fall deep into the hallway of my mind.

None of it is real.

In a couple of seconds, my sweat and distress will pull me out of this dream.

I haven't had a nightmare like this in some time. I also haven't missed them.

Wake up.

Please wake up.

I can taste blood. It's my own. I think I bit my tongue. Ignore the possibility that I bit my real tongue. That will hurt later.

I've come to terms with this dream. I must have pushed myself too hard on the sparring mat today. Exhaustion got the best of me. Plus, dinner tasted funny last night. It must be giving me a wild imagination, a colorful palate for this terrible, terrible dream.

The ringing is almost unbearable, and I'm certain that if it doesn't quiet down it will split my head in two.

Wake up.

Reid turns me around the corner and the mess hall opens up in front of us. King Cerastes is talking to Commander Garrith. Garrith throws a bag over his shoulder. And there's Jo behind him, dressed like she's ready for travel.

Her eyes are huge and full of tears.

This is not a dream.

They all turn to look at me. The ringing comes to a stop when my eyes zero in on King Cerastes. He smiles. He did this. He organized all of it, and not for the reasons that Sondra gave me earlier. He is toying with me, turning me into his lab rat, and he has all the tools to rearrange this maze. He will keep moving the pieces, keep trying different injections, and keep altering my surroundings. Now he's taking Jo away from me.

I've cut the distance between us in half in less than a second.

I will rip the skin from his face.

I will shatter his teeth.

I will rip his heart from his chest with nothing but my

hands. Tear it apart with my teeth, I want to taste his blood. If only for the sole satisfaction of knowing he is dead and I've killed him.

A hand wraps into my hair, suspending me from any more forward movements. Garrith turns me toward his face, his grip on the back of my head pulling me away from the King. It's like cold water has been poured over me. I'm a swirling sandstorm of arms and legs and hatred.

His words are husky, "You will play nice, or you will never see her again." Betrayal stings but at what point did I ever think he was mine to be betrayed by? I want to fight. I claw at him. Claw to get closer to Amos. "I promise." He steadies me again and tilts my head up, my feet are barely making contact with the floor. He pulls me back to his gaze, his grip on my hair wrapped up to my scalp. "I promise. Just tell her goodbye. Don't make it worse. Put away your rage, and I promise you will get to see her soon." He releases my hair and I push away from him.

"No!" I walk up to King Cerastes. He doesn't back away, even when I'm close enough to make out every pore in his face. He's expecting this. He wants me to make a mistake. My anguish is his triumph.

I push away the urge to rip him apart and say, "This was not a part of the deal." My voice is steel and cuts the cold air between us.

He grins. "I made an executive decision. Soldiers train here. This is not an environment for Jo." He turns his attention to Jo, "However, my offer still stands to let her earn a spot among our soldiers." Eyes back to me. "We have the wolves."

"She's not going into that cave. And she's not being taken away from me. If you send her to Megara then I'm going with her."

"That won't do either. You have to train here. War will be

upon us sooner than you think. And you agreed to train and serve on our side." His lids are heavy and his eyes move toward the door. He's clearly bored of this conversation. His smile fades and I'm dismissed when he waves Reid over to us. I don't wait for him to use Reid as a middle ground. So I turn away.

I take in Jo's face; she's wearing horror and confusion and it's ripping my heart from my chest. I walk back to Garrith. My voice is small when I say, "Will she be okay there?"

"Yes. I wouldn't take her there if it wasn't the safest place for her."

And somehow, I know he's telling me the truth.

Garrith packs the bag back over his shoulder and leaves the mess hall.

I'll play nice today but I still glare at the King. This is not the right time to kill him. And though I'm not one for dramatics, I want to make his death as extravagant and ironic as possible. I can't wait for that day.

My thoughts sober me. I've never known such rage, and I ignore the curiosity tugging at what else I keep bottled up.

I walk to Jo and tuck her head under my chin. She whispers into my collar, "You promised. You said we would stay together." I can't stomach her pain but she needs my brave face right now.

I've swallowed a thousand razor blades. Deep breath, strong voice, I have to remind myself before I allow any words to escape my throat. "It will be okay." She cries into my chest. We've never been apart, not in seven years. It's been me and Jo ever since the day I found her half-dead in the Arid. A six-year-old Jo was such a treasure, as was every age since then. I smooth a hand over her curls while tears stream down my face. "We'll see each other again soon. Even if I have to sneak off to Megara, I will always find you."

She leans away from me so I can look at her. I dry her face

with the sleeve of my tunic. Her beautiful face. This face has looked to me for every tough decision. For seven years I've been the answer to all her questions. I've been her sturdy ground and structure, and I'm letting them take her away. ~~It's Ray all over again.~~

"Commander Garrith is getting Tiago's horse ready. We should go." Sondra ushers us out of the mess hall.

"Who's Tiago?"

"The Commander's right hand, he stays above ground." Oh.

It's happening now. They're going to put her on a horse with a stranger and leave.

I keep my arm secured around Jo while we walk through the tunnels. We are going to the West Entrance again. I assume there is another entrance but I have yet to find it. I will be sure to add that to my mapping task list.

We start climbing the steps that will take us outside. With every step, the hole in my chest grows, along with the grip I have on Jo. Sunlight falls on her skin. At least she gets to go outside.

Her caramel skin is stunning and sparkles under the sunlight.

She will be okay.

I watch her breathe in deep, the smell of outside fills her lungs as the separation settles heavily on her chest.

She will be okay.

We are completely outside. Garrith finishes up by strapping Jo's belongings to the horse.

She has to be okay.

She turns to me and all I want to do is comfort her but I don't know how. She reaches out and wipes a tear from my cheek that I didn't know had fallen.

"I will be okay."

She hugs me tight around my waist. I lay my cheek on her springy hair and let more tears continue.

"I love you," she says into my neck.

"I love you," I can't manage anything more than a whisper. "Be safe and kill anyone that thinks about harming you."

She giggles and her small frame shakes in my arms.

She looks up and I kiss her forehead. "I'll see you soon."

Jo leaves my embrace and walks to Garrith and the horse. A man mounts the horse—Tiago, her guide to Megara. He must speak to her, as she nods and moves her mouth to respond.

Reid and Sondra keep their distance, closest to the steps that descend into Moria. We all watch as Garrith lifts her onto the saddle. I watch them ride off until the dust they leave behind covers their retreat. A piece of myself runs away and I'm not sure what I'm supposed to do now.

Jo knows my promises are empty. She knows that the word soon could mean anything from next week to next year. But I know, I will see her soon even if I die trying to get to her.

CHAPTER 20

I won't make a peep.

Silence and invisibility are my friends.

I will drift in shadows. At least until I'm in my room. When I am alone I will shatter.

I'm not there yet.

Don't stop moving.

Keep to the edge of the caves. They say my name.

Retreat.

Retreat.

I'm so close to my room.

I want to be the same burnt orange color as the walls and flow easily from one location to the next. I don't want eye contact. Once the glossiness of my eyes is discovered, I know there will be no holding back my tears.

The lump in my throat grows and even though I continue to close the distance to my room, that distance seems to grow.

Do not cry.

Do not cry in front of these people. Some of them want me

dead. Show no weakness. For Jo. Even though the thought of death sounds comforting, keep going.

"Jemma!"

Keep going.

"Jemma, wait!"

I can see the door to my room.

I can imagine the satisfaction of my bedroom door clicking into place.

That sound. It's so close. Privacy is so close. Once I'm behind that door I can fall apart and succumb to my guilt and thoughts of Jo.

No. Do not think of Jo. Not yet.

I'm not there yet.

Don't break. Don't break.

I round the stairs to my room. Two, three steps at a time.

Almost there.

I get to my room, our room, and immediately collapse on the floor.

There should be solace here. This is a safe place.

But her bed is still unmade.

Crying will help. Just cry. But there are no tears, only pain. A noose around my neck, tightening the longer I look at the room I no longer share with Jo. I will sleep in here without the sound of her light snoring. I will come here after training every day and she won't be here to ask me about it. Just cry, maybe it will help slip the boulder from my chest.

The door creaks. Perfect. Someone to witness my breakdown.

Reid.

He steps toward me, slowly awaiting my weeps.

I expect tears and sobs but I can't find enough air to do either.

I look up at Reid. The concern is written in his features as he picks up on my desperation for air. I gasp but air will not enter my lungs. My hands fly to my throat.

Reid comes up to grip my shoulders. I'm hyperventilating. The realization should assist in my ability to get control, but it doesn't. Reason has flown out the window. Reason is a lost cause. He tells me to 'just breathe'. But my mind can't decipher logic and his words may as well be gibberish.

My hands begin to shake.

I focus on my shaking hands as they fall into my lap. How are they sitting in my lap?

Reid has scooped me up. One of his arms falls behind my back while the other catches the crook of my knees. The color of the cave whooshes past me. He doesn't jostle me and I can't tell if his movements are that efficient or if I am so out of touch with my surroundings that everything appears foggy, gentle, smooth.

I melt into his warm chest despite my suffocation. I'm thankful to have found such warmth and solace in my death.

This comfort is short-lived as I'm dumped into frigid water. Air finally enters my lungs.

Reid stands in front of me while the cold water from his shower soaks through my tunic. My breaths are quick and sobering. It doesn't take long for the water to spread and I'm quickly drenched from head to toe.

I take a moment to breathe. Everything is crisp and fresh. The pain in my heart is still piercing but the chilled water introduces clarity.

Jo is capable. We have been fighting for years. She can handle a village of children. And I'm not helping anything by crying about it.

I reach out and turn the shower nozzle to warm. Soon the water in my boots heats. Reid stands before me. I focus on his mouth.

Reid's lips move but his voice sounds distorted. It sounds like he's in a tunnel, a mile away from me. He steps into the water with me and pushes my back against the tile behind me.

"Jemma!"

The water is collecting in his light lashes. They look like crystals around his eyes. So much of him doesn't seem human. Too beautiful.

More words echo into my brain. "She's vacant." A sigh. "Should I just give her time?"

"There's no time for that."

That isn't Reid. This voice puts cracks in the tunnel walls. This voice isn't gentle and demands transparency.

"If Jo could see you now." Shame settles under my skin. Someone turns off the water. Commander Garrith stands in front of me. "At least we know one thing for sure, Jo is doing a lot better than you are."

I don't know how long I spent hyperventilating or sobbing. My throat hurts. I whisper but the syllables pour salt on my raw throat, "Shut up."

"Is that what's going to pull you out of your pity party? Jo isn't here. That sucks. But if you want to see her again, you can't sit here and wither away in the shower." I meet his gaze. It's not fair that someone who's only shown me a tiny portion of their face gets to know so much of me.

He sees the anger filter in and out of my face. Without a word, he leaves the room. Reid comes back into view. "Here's a towel. And some night clothes are sitting here on the counter. I'll be outside."

I peel the fabric from my skin and grab the towel to dry. The clothes left on the sink are not my own. A long-sleeved tee and matching pants. They're basic, soft cotton, and loose-fitting. No undergarments are provided but it's the least of my worries right now. I put them on and I'm swimming in extra length. They must belong to Reid. I roll the waistband a couple of times. I can't ignore the comfort I find in them.

I stall, a hand outstretched toward the bathroom door.

Today I checked out.

And Reid was a witness to it. Again.

It doesn't bother me that Garrith saw my cowardice for some reason. It isn't like it's the first time he's seen me at a low point. And under his mask seems a safe place for my secrets.

But Reid matters. Reid shouldn't have to see such a broken side. Have I not seen tragedy enough to contain myself, to conduct myself, as a person who has a threshold for pain? I want to deserve him. I want to be as together as he is.

I want to.

I want to.

I will be.

Block it out. Box it up.

Deep breath.

He's sitting on his bed when I swing the door open. So I plaster a smile on my face and find my voice, "Hi."

"Hey." He stands. "You had us worried."

"I know, I'm sorry. I just haven't been without her since I found her. And that room was just a reminder that she won't be with me anymore."

"I assumed. I've made arrangements and they're bringing a cot in here for me to sleep on if you want to stay here, they can also move your belongings if you're not ready to go back in there yet."

"Oh! No! I couldn't put you out like that. This is your space."

He crosses the room and takes both my hands, holding them together. "Jemma, the idea of you suffocating in that room by yourself is killing me. Let me be here for you."

I'm probably wearing out my welcome. But I agree. The

thought of being in that room without Jo brings feelings I'm not ready for. Those feelings I'll save for another day.

~

Reid lays on the cot, placed at the foot of his bed. I can't deny how comfortable his bed is. I guess being a prince grants you a few privileges in Moria.

I try to sleep, but the sound of his breathing is too much, too intimate. Sharing this space with him has planted awareness in all of my nerves. My roots are alive and thrumming with the consciousness of Reid. And he's not sleeping either. His breaths are just as uneven as mine.

Reid rolls from one side to the other. Then he rolls back. Sighs. I think about the adjustment he's making from his normal, luxurious mattress to the cheap cot.

I push the blankets down and place my feet on the floor. Reid sits up in alarm.

"I'm sorry," I say. "You can't sleep. That cot can't be helping. Please take your bed back." I stand and Reid is up.

"No." His hand presses into my hip. Pushes me lightly back toward the edge of the bed. "You've had a shit day." His expression is unreadable and the lack of light in here makes it more difficult. "I'm ashamed of my thoughts. You're here. You're here and you're in my bed and I can't—"

"I know." I know exactly. "I'll go. I'm sorry." My feet move forward but he's blocking my path and gets a better grip around my arms to hold me steady.

"Jemma, no, I'm sorry. That's not what I'm trying to say." His hands loosen and start sliding up to my shoulders. "You've had a terrible, terrible day. And I should be here to support you; I should be tending to you. But I listen to you breathe and I—" He trails off and his fingers become restless, finding their way to my back. "I can't do anything but think of you. I think of touching you. I think of your lips." He presses his forehead to mine and I can feel the crease that's formed from his internal battle. He's right that today will go down as one of my worst. But giving into his desires sounds like the much-needed distraction I've been searching for.

I fist his hair and pull him into me. Pull his lips to mine.

A perfect distraction.

Our bodies melt together. I feel hot everywhere. There's fire behind my closed eyelids and smoke coming from my brain. But this is an inferno I wish to be engulfed in.

Reid is gasping and slipping his hands under my shirt—his shirt. I whirl in this fire that grows with every touch. Reid stokes these embers and my bones are less solid than they were moments ago. Every cell in my body is identifying as a liquid. My head is plopped onto a pillow and I've lost his mouth but find it at my neck, at my collar, and he's pulling on the hem of this shirt.

Warning flashes in my mind again. But this feels amazing and I don't want to wreck it again. I don't want to remove my shirt but I'm not ready for this moment to end. I want his lips on mine. I pull on his neck with one hand and still his wandering hand with my other.

He obliges and lies next to me. His withdrawal is slow. I know I'm putting up walls but I want to express to him that this isn't all or nothing. I want him to know that just because I want my shirt on, doesn't mean I don't want him to kiss me. But I'm not sure how to discuss that. There's a shift in the mattress and I know that I'm losing him. Panic rises. I'm going to mess this up again.

I grab his arm and whisper, "Stay."

He understands. Thank God he understands. He kisses my forehead. Kisses my nose, my eyes, my cheeks. He's smiling and so am I. He reaches over my side to rub my back and I nestle into the crook of his neck. Our bodies settled together is a sliver of heaven I didn't know existed.

After a few minutes, our breathing synchronizes and tiredness finally stakes its claim. I'm on the edge of consciousness when Reid murmurs, "Goodnight, Jemma."

CHAPTER 21

Anger and anguish propel my fist with more force than I'm used to tapping into. Drive starts in my stance, moves to my torso, and continues down my arms. Each swing of my arm, of my leg, is carried with a momentum pulsing from a deeper feeling. The access, the control, it's all addicting once you fall into focus.

Tatum is meeting me block for block. It's a dance. It's beautiful and violent and I don't want it to end.

We create a rhythm, block, duck, swing. I spin again to send an elbow her way but she catches me this time and sends me sprawling onto the mat.

"You're becoming repetitive. You're landing impressive shots and your footwork has come a long way, but you can't be predictable. You have to adapt. Become something your opponent can't anticipate."

She's right. I was enjoying the dance too much to recognize that I was following a pattern of movements.

"This is a good place to stop for the day." Tatum has been training with me in the mornings before breakfast or sometimes we take a late supper so that we can keep at it after training quarters clear out.

"I just want to know it already. Everything about hand-to-hand combat, that is. I want my mind to know it, my body to know it. I want to be ready."

Tatum nods with understanding. "It takes time. And focus. But you've come a long way in a short time."

Tatum's words are encouraging. I never expected to be a witness to this side of her. "Enough to take on Garrith?" I ask. I know the answer but the question still slips from my lips.

"That's ambitious." She laughs. "Everyone here would love to see Garrith unleashed. He's always so careful. Even giving only ten percent he can take anyone here. Blindfolded with a hand tied behind his back you still wouldn't stand a chance." The respect for Garrith runs deep in Moria. Even those who hate him would sell their soul to be him.

Tatum chugs water while I do my cool-down stretches. After, we make our way to the mess hall. It's nearly empty. We head into the kitchen where the remaining food is. Our late arrivals have become so common that the lunch maids have been holding our plates on the warmer. There's only a handful of people remaining in the hall. I recognize them from training but have yet to learn everyone's names.

Tatum sits across from me while we eat in silence. Her head snaps to the entrance of corridor two and I follow her gaze. Cynrad is walking out of the cave and passing through the mess hall. His hair is wet like he just got out of the shower. I turn back to my food but notice that Tatum is still following him with her eyes. She watches him until he finally exits the room.

I open my mouth to speak but she beats me to it, "Jemma, would you like to come out with me tonight?"

"Come out where?"

I'm still not sure that Tatum and I are considered friends. We train and we talk, but there's so much about her that I still don't know. For instance, the company she keeps that I'm only learning about today.

Tatum leads me to one of the corridors behind the throne room. The area is small, only as wide as my room but twice as long. Ornate sofas line the walls. Seated on them are other occupants from our corridor. A dark-haired girl throws her arms around Tatum. "You made it!" Her words come out long and relaxed. She turns to me and says, "And you brought a friend!" The scent of alcohol is heavy on her breath. My first instinct is to express that I'm tired, that I need to get back to my room. But Tatum looks at me and written in her expression says,

stay a while,

live a little,

have some fun.

And I think, yes. What would a little indulgence hurt? Jo isn't here. As much as it pains me to acknowledge, she isn't here. Suddenly my feeling of purpose disappears. What am I doing if I'm not busy protecting Jo? A voice from the other end of the room says, "Tatum, who's your friend?"

I don't want them to think I'm a mute so I speak up, "I'm Jemma."

There's a chorus of *Jemmmmma* and I find myself moving forward to take a seat on one of the couches. Tonight, I decide, I will just be Jemma. Whoever that is.

At first, I only accept drinks from Tatum. She gives me a glass of something sweet. And the more I drink, the better it tastes. I'm anxious and certain we aren't supposed to be here. Tatum tells me it's wine and refills my cup. I drink it, unsure what else to do. Any ounce of tension finally eases, leaving me relaxed and warm. My mind quiets down. The warnings ringing loudly in my head turn to distant whispers.

I accept another.

Tatum throws back two small glasses of liquid, one immediately after the other. "Rough day?" Jaxon asks.

"Cynrad broke up with me this morning. For the last time." My eyebrows shoot to my hairline.

"I didn't know you were dating Cynrad," I say.

"Yeah, well," she starts, "apparently that was the problem. I was trying to keep it all *a secret.*" She uses her fingers to put air quotes around it. A scowl takes over her face. "Whatever is wrong with a little privacy?" The more she talks the harsher her voice becomes.

"How long have you been together?" I can't help it. I've been talking to Tatum every day for weeks, and not once did she mention Cynrad or hint at any relationship notions.

"A year." In an instant, Tatum looks like she's a million miles away. In her mind, I know that she is far away, at a time when I wasn't here yet. "We had been friends for a while. But it wasn't until the evening that I pierced his eyebrow that we first kissed."

I can't imagine him without the metal in his face. The piercing in Cynrad's eyebrow creates a new possibility of injury when sparring but the level of intimidation he acquires with the ring evens out any potential risks.

Tatum tells us about how they had been sneaking around for six months until Cynrad decided they needed to be honest and stop hiding their relationship from everyone and they've been off and on ever since. "It's no one's business but ours anyway." She rolls her eyes. "I guess he got his way though. Everyone knows about us now," she laughs, "and I don't even have him." Tatum keeps her voice light, like her turmoil isn't current, like it's an old, funny story. But her voice breaks on the last syllable.

All the curiosity I had swirling around my head about Tatum seems tiny now that I know. Tatum is still a girl completely in love with a boy. As icy as she seems, she is human. And for humans, heartbreak is inevitable.

It's late when I finally get to Reid's room. I'm holding a full bottle of wine that Tatum insisted I take, "In case of emergencies." Suddenly the idea of being caught with alcohol makes me regret accepting her offer. I make it to the end of the cave and run up to my room to hide it in the back of my dresser before I cross the hall to see Reid.

When I open the door to his room I try to be as stealthy as possible but the remaining alcohol in my system makes all of my movements larger and sloppier than normal. I try to inch the door open slowly but I trip and the door goes flying until it smashes into the wall behind it. I squeeze my eyes closed. Everything pinches and my shoulders shoot up to my ears. I open one eye expecting to have startled Reid. But he's sitting on the edge of the bed already, his fingers intertwined in his lap.

He's been waiting for me. Maybe he missed me. Maybe he couldn't sleep without me. The idea plants a lazy grin across my lips. I saunter toward him expecting his face to crack into a smile mirroring mine. I move forward, standing between his knees, and run my hands into his hair. I tip his head back but there is no smile on his face. I'm thankful I stopped to get rid of the remaining bottle.

I do my best impression of his face but I know I only

formed a deep frown in my features. I stand there mimicking his grumpy face until giggles bubble up and out of my throat.

"Why are you drunk?" There isn't any ounce of warmth in his voice.

"Why are you grumpy?" I counter. I can't help it. I take both my pointer fingers and plant them in the corners of his mouth, trying to bring the corners up. I want so badly to see him smile.

He gathers my hands and brings them between us. Still, he does not smile.

"I've been worrying about you. You never came here and you weren't in your room."

"I was with Tatum. She's been updating me on the underground dramas and theatrics." I ignore the way theatrics come out as a long slur and so does Reid.

"Who else was there?" His voice is so pushy, so demanding.

Again I mimic him, this time by deepening my voice to match his, "*Who else was there?*" I ruin it by giggling again.

Finally, there's a crack in his armor. Finally, he smiles. "Unlace your boots. Let's go to sleep."

Reid gets under the covers while I strip down to my shirt and underwear. I expect a kiss goodnight when I crawl into the bed but find that Reid is already lightly snoring.

CHAPTER 22

King Cerastes thinks we're getting too comfortable in our squads. At least that's what General Pinnell tells us. Today I'll be working with a boy from one, Lincoln, and a boy from seven, Bellamy. I swear I've heard of Bellamy. I introduce myself to them which they do not return a warm welcome. Maybe I have gotten too comfortable in my squad.

General Pinnell will not be joining us today but tells us that he's sending Commander Garrith, who seems to be the most capable man in Moria. His leadership is admirable; no one has ever questioned him. The taste of my jealousy is bitter. It isn't fair that he's a prick *and* has the authority to tell the rest of us what to do. I try to shake my irritations, not wanting to feel anything regarding the commander.

We enter the stables level. Today we are exiting from the North Entrance. It looks similar to the East Exit that's closest to our living quarters. The stables here are underground and lead to a ramp that brings us above ground. Once I exit, I turn around and look to the entrance that has seemed to disappear.

If camouflage is what they were going for, they've hit the head on the nail.

Pinnell told us that today we are mapping because, in the future, we need to be able to navigate the lands easily. My trio is handed a scroll with several instructions for finding a relic. This is a treasure hunt, and the first group to bring back their relic will win today's expedition.

I read the instructions. It seems easy as I am a good gauge for distance. The instructions are ripped from my hands. Lincoln. He looks at the scroll and shows my other teammate, Bellamy. Teammate is probably too strong a word, but for today, we will work together; even their aversion to me can't keep me from being excited about going above ground again.

"So," I sound as much like the naive child they think I am, "once we get outside, it looks like we need to head West for one mile. And then once we—" I gesture for the map, but I'm cut off.

Lincoln says, "Do you think we don't know how to read a fucking map?"

Lincoln and Bellamy mount their horses and start West. Once I'm on Gideon and secure the shemagh around my face, I take off after them.

We've gone too far. The scroll said to shift directions and face North once we saw the split tree one mile from where we started. We've gone a mile. I look behind me at the tree, split down the middle. I know that's it. We need to go North.

"Guys." They ignore me. "Guys! We've gone too far; it's time to turn."

This time, Bellamy stops and looks at me. "We know where the relic is. We also know where another group's relic is. It's just four miles West of ours. Their scroll sends them South first, so we have plenty of time to retrieve both. We already have a deal with them. If we bring back both our relic and theirs, they cover our chores for a month. And if they bring back theirs and ours, we cover their chores." Of course, there's more to this.

"I wasn't notified of this exchange." I'm intrigued by the challenge but it would have been nice to have set my terms.

"Fine. Run back to Moria and tell them you quit. Or you can get in on this bet and have chores done for a month." There's always been parts of me that rejoice in the face of competition. The feeling of besting those around me pumps adrenaline into my veins.

I follow close behind the boys, taking in landmarks. Nothing here is familiar. I never ventured back into Audun after I left, let alone the lands beyond Audun. The sand here isn't nearly as mobile. Much of the ground we cover is hard. I miss the dunes surrounding the oasis. They changed daily, recreated by wind.

The boys come to a stop, and I come up alongside Bellamy. He pulls his shemagh down to expose his nose and mouth. His chin is slightly scruffy; he must be young, too young to grow a full beard. "So our relic is two miles that way, wedged between two boulders, one resembling the tail of a scorpion," he gestures to the northeast of us, "and the other's is two miles that way." Northwest. "I can go retrieve the other while you and Lincoln grab ours." Bellamy and Lincoln exchange a look. Suddenly, being so far from Moria with them doesn't feel right. An unease is flowing in my blood. Despite the hot temperature, the hair on my neck stands. "I don't trust you to get our relic yourself, so you can either come with me or Lincoln."

"I can get ours." I won't take my shemagh down. My face would definitely expose my distrust. I do not want to be alone with either of them. "I know the Arid. I can get it and meet you back here in a half hour."

"No, you'll cost us the challenge if you don't make good on your word."

I need to be away from them. "I'll have the relic and be back here before both of you."

Lincoln's eyes float to Bellamy before he speaks up, "Fine. You better be right here in a half hour."

I'm done talking to these assholes.

I'm off. Gideon soars. After some time, I look behind me to see if I can spot Bellamy and Lincoln but I've put too many dunes between us.

Wind penetrates the fabric covering my skin and the cool air swirls in the gaps of my clothing. It's cool and crisp and my lungs suddenly possess the ability to inflate to twice their normal size.

My heart beats.

Freedom.

Freedom like this is something I won't take for granted. My limbs seem longer, my body lighter. And I think if Jo wasn't in Megara right now; if she were here with me, gliding through sand, I would keep going. I would go all the way to the ocean. We would map everything to the left, and then everything to the right. We would make another oasis out of someplace beautiful. And I would tell her that I'm sorry.

I would tell Jo it was my fault we ended up in Moria. I would apologize for not choosing another direction. I would hold her little hands in mine, and tell her everything will be okay now.

But I can't do that. Jo isn't here. Jo is in Megara. And it's my fault.

An iron door closes on my freedom. The air that whooshes past my ears and cools my body is not mine. This scene does not belong to me. Miles and miles of sand surround me and I might as well be underground.

I could go. I could go on my own and leave Jo in Megara. But life anywhere without Jo would be worse than any prison.

So I will find this relic and continue chipping away the moments until I see her again.

Just as the map described, there is a rock formation similar to the tail of a scorpion, roughly two miles from our meeting spot. I hop off Gideon and pull him to the structure. Where one boulder collides with the other, something glitters within the seam. I reach in.

My fingers wrap around the hilt of the dagger.

I bring it out into the sun. Gold shines from where it is encrusted in the handle. It's old and delicate, the sheath appears to be that of an old snake skin. I pull the dagger from its sheath, careful that it does not fall to pieces into the sand. As ancient as the piece first presents itself, the blade within shows no signs of wear. The curved blade is as bright and razor-sharp as the day it was forged.

I wish for the opportunity to marvel at its beauty when we get back to Moria, but now I am on a time restraint. Gideon does not protest when I urge him to return quickly to our meeting spot.

The boys aren't back yet. I wait.

I wait and wait and wait.

To the West, the sun is sitting low, hinting at the approach of nightfall.

I slide off the saddle and pace. I will wait ten more minutes. If they don't return, it is safe to assume they went back to Moria on their own.

I hear faint hoof beats. To my left, Bellamy and Lincoln are barreling toward me. For how close they are, they make little noise, the soft sand always swallows loud sounds.

They approach, close enough now for me to see their eyes. "Did you get the relic?" I yell.

They don't respond.

Their horses are fast, faster than Gideon. They fly past me, leaving me in a cloud of dust. I pull my shemagh back over my nose and watch them disappear over the dunes. They're heading for Moria's entrance.

I expect they found the relic. They're definitely assholes but, after this challenge, we won't have chores for a while.

Something tugs at my instincts. Cold sweat beads under my clothes. Bellamy.

Bellamy Gray.

Tatum told me, "The man that tried to kill you, his name is Dax Anderson. He was a member of Squad Seven. His closest friend was also in his squad, Bellamy Gray."

Foolish, stupid girl.

Gideon whines from behind me. I turn away from my fleeing teammates and go to console my horse. I need to mount. I need to get back to Moria. His legs won't stop moving. I grab his reins and try to put him at ease.

That's when I see them.

Two wolves as large, if not larger, than the one I fought in the cave. They cut through the sand flying from the same direction Bellamy and Lincoln rode in from. I try to calm Gideon enough to get back on the saddle.

But the wolves are upon us, hairless and gray, with black capes flowing on their backs.

Not capes.

Cloaks are riding the wolves.

Gideon won't cooperate as he bucks again and takes off for

Moria. I have ten, nine, eight seconds before they will be here. Two dunes away. One dune away.

I trip over my thoughts. Every worst-case scenario is here. It's here.

It's here and I'm spending more time dwelling on its severity than I am preparing my escape. Two more seconds.

Three more seconds and the shock wears off.

Gather myself.

Collect my bearings.

My fingers fumble as I unsheathe the dagger. It glitters in my hands. I stand at the ready.

They are here.

Yellow eyes are everywhere. They close in on me but there's a barrier. Their speed has ceased. They no longer move through the sand. It looks as though they are stuck in it. The air is too thick for them to move faster than the pace of an elderly snail.

It must be my own shock.

I look down at my hand holding the dagger. When I hold it up to my face, it moves with no resistance.

Shock has seeped into my brain, muddling my perception.

And I think.

I think.

I think.

I think I must already be dead.

Dead enough for my mind to play such tricks on myself.

I look up into the nearest yellow eyes. The cloaked figure and the wolf have the same grotesque gaze. I get hold of my dagger.

I've done this before. I can do it again.

I step around my momentary lapse. Their speed commences. The dagger hilt rests comfortably in my hand. I am ready.

The nearest wolf lunges for me at the same time the cloak flips off of its back. I lean away, my dagger slicing at the wolf's open mouth. I pull the blade until I've cut the corner of its mouth half a foot open toward its skull. The skin flaps open to reveal the back teeth, only ever been seen by those digested by the beast. Its initial whimper quickly becomes a growl of rage.

The curve of the dagger is drenched in blood. I face the cloak and eye the wolf.

Face the cloak. Eye the wolf.

I'm split without enough defenses to protect myself. All the while there is another cloak still on its wolf circling us.

I abandon my fear. The fear that I will die today has become a reality. But I will not go down without bringing them with me.

Just as I step, ready to attack the cloak, I hear the familiar gallop of a horse.

"Jemma!"

I risk the look. I risk a moment spent with my back to the cloak to identify Reid. Relief sweeps through me at the same time the cloak's fingers wrap around my neck.

But I don't have any time.

I don't even have time to panic before the cloak's arm is cut clean off, its hand still gripping my throat. Garrith. Garrith is here, head-to-toe in black, riding a horse as dark as night. He is swift, an inky blur, sword drawn leaving only a trail of destruction.

I can't evade the feel of those fingers against my skin. Blood seeps from its arm onto my clothes as it dangles still attached to me. I can't feel my hands as I pry myself from its unnatural hold. I trip away from the cloak as Garrith sends its head soaring beyond the nearest dune.

A firm arm grips my bicep and I'm pulled against the warm chest of Reid. I allow my leg to sling over, onto the other side of his horse and we ride. I didn't understand the speed Gideon was lacking until I am on a horse in its prime. We pull away from the commotion quickly, effortlessly putting distance between us and the cloaks. Unease settled in my stomach.

"What about Commander Garrith?" I shout at Reid.

"He's got it taken care of," Reid dismisses me and continues straight, back to Moria.

"He's outnumbered!" I exclaim. "Two cloaks, two wolves, he'll be dead in a minute if he isn't already!" Hysteria works its way into my vocal cords. "We must go back!"

"Jemma!" I can tell by Reid's tone that he will not allow this conversation to continue. "Garrith can take care of himself. We have to get you back." His horse rides on.

When the entrance of Moria reveals itself, Reid takes us to the opening. He says into my ear, "Get inside and wait for me. I'll be there in just a moment," and helps me slide off the horse.

I run down the steps taking me further into Moria. I never imagined I would find such solace in every step I take into the underground kingdom. I pull the fabric from my face and frantically try to put soothing breaths into my lungs. As soon as the steps fade away and I'm standing on level ground, I throw my hands out against the narrow cave wall and heave. I retch and sob but nothing comes out. I let this continue until the adrenaline finally releases its hold on my stability. In one exhale I allow exhaustion to spread into my limbs. I press my back to the wall and suddenly even holding myself up by my legs is too much and I slide down until landing with a thud on the ground. My body shudders again, recoiling from the events that unfolded.

Bellamy and Lincoln tried to kill me.

This was a setup.

And I realized it too late.

I don't know where Gideon ran off to, if Garrith is alive, or what is to come for my treacherous teammates.

Just then, Reid comes bounding down the steps. His hands wrap around my shoulders as he crouches in front of me. He rubs his thumbs in soothing circles over my shoulders. "Hey." I want to melt in his words, so strong and reassuring. "How are you?"

I nod, unsure how to react appropriately to another attempt on my life. He moves his hands down to my arms and rubs his hands up and down on my biceps. I realize he is mistaking my shaking for being cold.

Maybe I am cold.

I can't tell.

"I'm sor—"

"It's not your fault." Reid is quick to prevent my downward spiral. "Someone is working against you. It's not your fault. But I promise. I will find out who it is."

"Garrith," I croak. "Tell me he's okay."

Reid brushes me off. "He's always okay. What can I do for you?"

I want to see Commander Garrith. I want to be sure he's okay. I don't know how long it will be before he comes back— if he comes back.

I don't know how to tell Reid that his lack of concern for the commander bothers me. So I tell him something he wants to hear, something he can handle. "I'm cold." He nods. "And I'm a little hungry."

Reid takes my hand and guides me into the depths of Moria.

We get to the mess hall where he offers me a plate of food. I push it around, mimicking the act of eating without ever putting more than a pea-sized amount in my mouth. It's completely empty here, and the usual amount of lit torches is cut down to less than half. I wonder how long I sat in the entrance tunnel. My grasp on time at the moment is useless. It could have been thirty minutes. It could have been three hours.

I don't know why I said I was hungry.

I'll be lucky if my appetite reappears before next week.

But getting me food was a task Reid was more than happy to oblige to.

My mind is far away.

A mile away, in the Arid, with Garrith and my attackers.

Reid tells me that I need to tell Amos, tell the king, about tonight. I can't conceal my disdain for any conversation with the king. "Jemma, you were there. He needs to know. We must go tell him now."

"You know what happened." My voice is stronger now than it was moments ago. "Why can't you go tell him? I'd like to go to bed now."

Reid looks torn. I can tell that his restlessness is due to wanting to tend to me and my needs but also following the expectations of his father.

I stand from the table. "Go tell Amos. Tell him what you saw and that I am fine. But I am going to bed."

Reid nods. I thought he would report to his father at once, but his kindness keeps him near. "Let me walk you. You've had an eventful evening."

"No!" His eyes widen at my outburst. "Sorry, I'd just like a moment alone. Please." I lean down to kiss his cheek. "I'll see you when you come to bed."

I walk in the direction of our dorm tunnel. When I turn around, Reid is exiting the mess hall.

I give it a moment, standing in the doorway of our corridor before I cross the mess hall and turn down the other way. Back to the entrance, back to the stables. I'm out of line but I have to know. I have to know if he made it back.

The sand is lit by the light of the moon. It must be getting close to midnight by now. I follow the trail to the stables.

Only a few horses stir from their sleep while I creep between the stalls. I've made two passes before I accept that the black horse Garrith was riding has not returned.

If he's dead, Moria will have lost one of its finest soldiers.

If he's dead, it will have been my fault.

I shouldn't have waited so long for Bellamy and Lincoln. I should have returned to Moria with the relic as soon as I found it.

A horse whines loudly from outside the stables. And then there's another. I'm at the end of the cave with no way out and no permission to be here. I slowly open the door to the last stall. The still mare has her head facing the wall again. I can only pray she is sleeping. I peek over the stall door.

At the entrance, Garrith appears. He's walking, not only his black horse but two more horses behind him. He ties the two up and walks the black horse to a nearby stall. Behind me, the mare grunts.

Definitely not asleep.

I press my body to the wall, eager to get out of here.

I saw what I needed to. Commander Garrith is intact. His death will not be something I'll have to live with. I crouch down and hide, waiting for Garrith to leave.

The mare blows out a loud breath. I face her, ready for any sudden moves. There's a thud on the door that shares a wall I currently have my back pressed against. I look up to find Garrith's hands clasped together, his forearms resting on the top of the stall door. "Hey Winnie girl." His voice holds such a softness. It's a foreign sound on his lips. I resist the urge to stand and make sure it is, in fact, Commander Garrith. He clicks his tongue. The mare, Winnie. Does not respond.

He clicks again.

Then there's a creak as he starts to open the stall door just to my right. I grit my eyes closed. Squeeze my fist. I open one eye slightly and see the toe of his boot coming through the opening.

In one moment I was crouched in the stall, the next I'm being held up by the back of my tunic with a dagger to my throat.

Anger and the instinct to kill swirl in the eyes of the commander. "What the fuck, Shayde?" he hisses.

He removes the dagger and carries me out of the stall by the handful of tunic. My feet barely dust the floor and I'm struggling to get air in my lungs from my hanging position. He tosses me to the ground and shuts the stall door. "Can you do anything as you are supposed to?"

I have no words. No excuses. I sit up, my mouth wide open with an explanation I can't find.

"Just go."

I stumble to get to my feet. On my way out of the stables, I inspect the horses he tied up and familiarity hits me in the face. "These are Bellamy and Lincoln's horses." I look back to Garrith. His frame is rigid and he says nothing. "Where are Bellamy and Lincoln?"

"Just. Go."

I don't. I stand at the other end of the stables awaiting answers. I await an answer but I have bad feelings. I have a feeling I won't see Bellamy or Lincoln again. Their horses have been returned to Moria without riders. My stomach twists.

Finally, Garrith approaches, his strides full of purpose. He unties one of the horses and begins leading it to a stall, "Why are you even here?"

I follow him. "You were out there. And outnumbered. Two cloaks, two wolves, and Reid and I ran away." He latches the door shut on the horse and goes to put the other away as well. I keep following him. "I thought maybe they killed you. I came to see if your horse was in its stall, to see if you had made it back."

He steps out from the stall and latches the door. All the horses are put away and it's just us. Garrith stands a foot from me, likely enjoying the way he towers over me. He looks at me, in me, through me. His eyes give me nothing, his eyebrows shadowing any hints his iris' could provide.

He tilts his head to the side as if trying to read me or see me in a different light. Seconds tick by. He shakes his head and looks out the opening, into the night. "Just go." His voice is gravel. "Go back underground. Don't stop in the mess hall. Don't stop for anyone. Go straight to *your* room. Go quickly. *Go now.*"

So I do.

And I follow almost all of his directions. But I don't go to *my* room. It hasn't been my room since Jo was sent away. I go to my comfort. I go where I can sleep. I go to Reid.

CHAPTER 23

"This one," Reid whispers as he traces the scar stretching from my shoulder blade to my collar.

"Some of the last occupants of Audun caught me scavenging. A man charged me with a dagger but I had a sword. At the time I was just defending myself. But I think he was trying to protect his son. His son did this." I gesture to the scar. "He was behind me, too weak to lift the sword a second time. I realized what I had done, and walked away." His horrified expression when he noticed the fallen body of his father behind me left a larger scar than the swing of his sword.

"These?" I lay on my side facing away from Reid and blink away the tears surging to my eyes. He runs a finger over my side, littered with short, jagged lines starting at my thigh, running up to my hip, and across my back.

"There used to be a group that lived a few miles west of mine and Jo's oasis. We had only lived there for a month. I still didn't know her very well. Every day I would go out to map and hopefully bring back animals and food. At the time, goats and pigs were still scattering around Audun." He lifts my hand

and inspects my palm where the same scars are engraved deep into my skin, the bottoms of my feet are nearly numb from the same lacerations. "One day, I came across three of the men. I tried to fight but I was outnumbered. They tied me up and took me to their camp. There were two women. And four more men when we got there. I realized they were cannibals when one of the women, who appeared to be in the later months of pregnancy, called dibs on my thigh because she was eating for two."

Reid's hand freezes. I want to put the words back in my mouth. I feel dirty and beneath him. I feel like the scars are only scratches compared to the traumas strangling my soul.

Only Jo knows the hardships we faced in the Arid. But Jo isn't here to bear the experiences with me. More words tumble out and it's horrifying and freeing and I can't stop. "I was put in a room with no windows, bed, or light." They were going to save me for a few days since they apparently had leftovers that would soon go bad. People, they were eating people and I nearly went insane anticipating that I would soon be their meal. I watched from a crack in the door as they ate and drank around a fire at night. I could see a fence that likely wrapped around the perimeter of their camp. But the door to my room was stopping me from ever reaching the fence.

"There was a large, wooden latch on the outside of the door. I knew my death was close. I tore the bottom of my tunic and thanked God that my fingers were long and slender enough to reach out and reel the fabric back in the crack of the door under the wood slat. My vision was limited and I could only see three people sleeping around the fire. If anyone was awake and paying attention, they would have seen me shimmy the wood up away from its latch." When I got out I realized the fence did run around the camp, only stopping at a hut, lit with torches. At the first sight of movement within their hut, I ran to the back side of the shelter they'd stored me in.

"I was out and the only thing between me and freedom was the fence. It didn't look too terribly tall so I ran for it. But my eyes adjusted too slowly to the darkness cast by the hut's shadow. I was already falling into the pit when I noticed the gleam of barbed wire collections and who knows what else. I landed on my side, it got the worst of it. I was bleeding and afraid to move. Afraid to make it worse. I leaned off my side and started crying as it cut into my back, I tilted my head to look at the fence. And she was there."

Reid's gentle hand transforms into a full-body embrace as convulsions rack my frame. "It hurt. It hurt to be still. It hurt to move. And Jo stood there terrified and unsure what to do." I knew that when they found me, they would find her too. In that moment she wasn't just Jo, she was Ray too. I blocked out the pain. I stopped crying. I needed to calm her. I needed her to think. "She threw me a rope. It was only a couple of feet away. I couldn't feel the cuts growing in my palms when I pushed myself up. I made it to the rope and managed to stand on top of the jagged metals. I mangled my feet as I walked through the carnage, and scaled the side of the pit. One piece went clear through my foot. I didn't realize it until I made it over the fence."

He still holds me tight. And I'm surprised by my even breathing. "You are strong. You are the warrior everyone wishes they could be." I am not. No one wishes to be this. I think something broke in me that day. Because we went back to the camp a week later, still mummified under my clothes, still limping from my wounds, and slit their throats in their sleep. Jo took out two of the men. I took out the rest. And the two women. Even the pregnant woman.

Jo and I didn't speak of it. I was acting on fear, not honor.

Fear that they would find Jo. Fear that they would find anyone. I think I've been scared ever since.

"You don't ever have to worry about that again," he tells me. And I'm confused by how he can be so sure. Especially, when his father continues to stress that war is coming.

"What war are we preparing for?"

Reid leans away from me, surprised by my question, and sighs. "Groth. It's the land many miles North of here. Supposedly our ancestors used to occupy the land until they were forced out. Now there's some kind of magic in those mountains. The cloaks you encountered in the Arid, they're from Groth. And they're called Howlers." Just hearing about them makes my skin crawl.

"And we are supposed to be going to war with them?" I press further.

"It's nothing you should trouble yourself with now. We have plenty of time to prepare. Where they surpass us in height and reach, they are handicapped by their simple minds. You shouldn't worry."

But I do. Jo and I faced death because of one *howler*. Dread spreads farther from my chest with every heartbeat.

And Reid isn't worried.

And I'm afraid that what is broken in me, is still unscratched in him.

Reid still breathes evenly in his bed when I gather my belongings for the showers. He possesses the ability to remain unconscious no matter what jostling is going on around him. I chalk it up to how late it was before we fell asleep last night.

I'm jealous of him. I wake at the sound of a pin drop caves away. But he has never known the Arid like I have. He sleeps deeply because he can. He's experienced his version of loss. Everyone has. But sometimes I think his version was kinder. At the very least, his sleep was spared. I move on and grab the clothes I'll be wearing today. If I look at him, deep in his slumber, for too long, I'm afraid of the temptation to shake him awake. I adore Reid, but panic is a feeling too familiar to me and too foreign to him.

I tossed and turned all night. His steady breathing should have put me at ease, but it was a reminder of how little yesterday's events affected him. I can't pinpoint what's unsettled me the most: the attempt on my life, the assumption that Garrith disposed of my conspirators, or the confusion left swirling around my head after every encounter I have with the Commander.

I throw the rest of my things into the bag and sling it over my shoulder. I could use his personal bathing room, but I'd hate to disturb Reid's *slumber*. I swallow the bitterness seeping into my senses and head for the showers.

I told Tatum to be up early today for extra training. I can tell I'm getting better and seeing my improvement on the mat has only encouraged me to train harder. I shut the door behind me and pad down the stairs.

Garrith is leaning against the cave wall next to his door, sharpening one of his daggers with a flat stone. Of course, he is.

His eyes meet mine but quickly fall back to his dagger.

I step down to the ground and say, "Good morning." I try to get a gauge on whether or not last night is put behind us or if I'm in for another angry talking-to.

I've seen glimpses of Garrith's eyes holding warmth. I've been sure the fabric on his face was concealing a smile from time to time. But today, there is no warmth. He takes up so much space. His body alone is massive, but even that doesn't measure just how large a presence he is. The air around him belongs to him and molds to his attitude. Today he is cold, and when I pass him to go into the washroom, I swear I can smell annoyance.

"Getting comfortable here?" His voice isn't loud but it still startles me.

I look over my shoulder at him but he's still focused on his dagger.

"Getting comfortable with people trying to kill me? I suppose." I hold onto my bag of toiletries slung over my shoulders with a firm grip. I never know what I'm getting into with Garrith.

"Looks like it."

This time I turn around completely to face him. "What does that mean?"

He sighs and keeps at work making it clear he does not intend to answer. I stand my ground and refrain from taking refuge in the washroom. I cock my head when he releases a sigh. Finally, he goes on, "You've gone from terrified and being attacked in the showers, to being devastated over Jo, to what? Disregarding danger? Sleeping with the prince?" His movements become sharper and more forceful. But he doesn't look up.

"I missed where my personal life was any of your business." He won't get a rise out of me today and I ignore the tug of defiance in my gut when he rolls his eyes.

He tilts his head up against the wall and looks at me under heavy lids. "It's not. I was merely sharing an observation."

"Unless you are advising me on the mat, maybe you should keep your observations to yourself." I'm proud of my steady voice. I'm happy that for once, Garrith's attempt to rile me up falls short.

"I just wonder," he pushes off the wall, and puts away his

dagger, "if Jo is as comfortable without you as you are without her." With that, he walks off.

Unbelievable. What an arrogant, smug, assuming prick. And I am moving. I was going to stay calm. I was going to let his words bounce off of me like rain. His words were going to pool at my feet until they flowed down the drain. But I'm a poor excuse for an umbrella. The rain got through and soaked my clothes. I'm a shivering, shaking ball of rage while he is weightless as a cloud.

I hate him.

I shove his back and try to ignore the fact that he doesn't budge. Doesn't do anything but freeze.

"You think you know me? You think you know anything about me?"

He turns around slowly. His eyebrows rest heavy over his eyes. I wish there were something else to look at other than the intense green of his eyes. Today they are a shade darker. "I know your own foolishness landed you here. And I know Jo has to pay for your errors."

"What right do you have to accuse such a thing? I'm doing my best! There's nothing I can do for her from here and it's killing me! What is the harm in finding ways to cope? Finding a way to make the days pass with a little less torment?" He's won. He's gotten to me and I'm spewing the proof all over these cave walls.

"There's plenty you can do from here!" He yells and his outburst appears to have rattled him because his voice is quiet when he speaks, "Jo isn't gone forever. You're acting like you lost her. And you're leaning on the wrong people for comfort."

"I'm not leaning on Reid."

"But you are," he accuses. "And of all the people underground, he's the last one you should rely on. His own blood is the reason you don't have Jo with you to begin with."

"He didn't make that call. It was his dad, Reid had nothing to do with it."

"Are you sure?" Garrith steps toward me. I'm breathing heavily, suddenly tired. Garrith is planting insecurities in my head and I don't have time for it. He whispers, "Shayde." Another step. "Are you sure?"

Of course, I'm sure. Reid cares for me. Garrith is manipulating me. He's trying to plant doubt and paranoia in my mind. Reid told me he would. But if that were true, would my eyes glisten right now? Water is collecting in my eyes so I tilt my head and blink the tears away. I will not cry. I pull my emotions back in and adjust my grip on my shower bag. "Have you any other hobbies Commander? Or is sticking your nose in other people's business your favorite pastime?"

He steps back but doesn't respond so I go on, "I am flattered. Really. To be the center of your *observations,* but I'm sure you could find more promising entertainment than where I'm sleeping." I spin and start walking back to the showers but not without telling Garrith, "Have a great day, Commander, I hear there might be some exciting drama surrounding Tatum and Cynrad if you want to maintain your position as Moria's official gossip queen."

CHAPTER 24

"Shayde! You're with me; let's move," Garrith booms across the sparring mats. I spent all of breakfast ignoring him, but now that we've started training for the day, he's not having it.

I ignore Reid's gaze. Without turning to face him, I know his eyes are hot beams attempting to melt holes into Garrith's back. Garrith gives notice to none of it and leads me down the rows of mats before stopping at one and turning to me. I can't help it when I say, "Couldn't stay away?"

He rolls his eyes. "I know you've been getting up early for additional training hours. I want to see if any of that time has paid off."

"Or maybe you just want to piss off Reid."

"The little prince's feelings are of no consequence to me. I need your best today, Shayde. I need to know where you require the most work. We have to minimize your weaknesses and we don't have a ton of time to do it." His words are cryptic but it's clear that he knows something.

"What's coming?" I say quietly. He looks around, but his eyes give away nothing.

And then he looks at me.

I won't break the eye contact this time. I watch him contemplate my expression. Watch him absorb every piece of my face. Watch him decide if he trusts me or not. He has zero reasons to trust me and a thousand reasons not to. One of those reasons being that I don't trust him. He lets out a sigh. I can't see his mouth but the movement in his shoulders says that he's letting down his guard the tiniest bit.

He steps toward me but trains his eyes over my head on any possible audience behind me. "I don't know any details yet." His eyes scan. "But I'm sure we'll be in a war soon." Soon? Reid said we had time.

"Groth?" He nods. What does this mean for Jo? Will I be fighting? Am I ready for that? "When?" There's a hollowness to my voice.

Garrith's eyes snap down to mine, hearing the fear in my voice. "Less than a month. The king is on his way to Megara as we speak to update the councilmen there."

My blood drops a few degrees. I can't fight in a war. Less than a month, and I could be dead. Less than a month, and Jo could be completely alone. Jo, wasting away in Megara, with no one to save her.

"Don't do that," Garrith says, pulling me from my spiral.

"Don't do what?"

"Premeditate your failure. It does nothing but lower your chances of survival."

"Stop acting like you can read my mind."

"Stop wearing all your thoughts on your face."

Maybe I should wear my shemagh at all hours like Garrith. I don't understand his commitment to covering his face.

"Alright, Shayde." He stands five feet from me, appearing

relaxed. Not at all like he just told me we'll be in a war with howlers in a matter of weeks. He throws his swords and daggers to the edge of the mat and gestures for me to do the same. We get back into position. "Attack me."

I've been here before. I've been humiliated here before. I've gone about it wrong but this time I know better.

Garrith is bigger than me, stronger than me. But I will have patience this time; play the long game.

I start to circle, and he mimics me. It's a slow walk around the perimeter of the mat. I smile at him. "So do you come here often?"

He rolls his eyes. Garrith is a man coated with armor. Nothing catches him off guard. He's made his disdain for me abundantly clear, yet occasionally shows me pieces of himself. And I think, what if under all that power and skill, is a man?

"I *really* am sorry about last night." We continue to circle one another. "I was just worried about you." I slow down my voice and attempt something sultry. He remains steady. I stop rounding the mat and take a slow step toward him. Then another.

The closer I get, the higher I have to look up to see his face. I keep my head level but allow my eyes to rise, feigning innocence, creating the best doe eyes I can muster. He cocks an eyebrow. For once he doesn't look so serious. Pride blossoms in my chest that I've managed to take him by surprise. I take his hand. Look at it while I rub a thumb over his knuckles. "It bothered me," I look back up into his eyes, "to think that you might be dead." Not a lie, but also not because I have anything remotely close to feelings for him. I had to check on him to make sure his death wasn't on my conscience.

His chest rises and falls at a quickened pace. "Shayde," his whisper feels like a warning.

"I've been trying to talk to you for weeks. I've been waiting for the right time."

He slides his other hand up my arm, stopping at my elbow. He cradles it while tilting his head down. "Tell me," he whispers. Something flutters in my stomach. It isn't right. I'm in control here. I'm supposed to make him lower his guard. And yet, heat is coursing through my veins.

"Not here." I look at him from under hooded eyes.

He squeezes my elbow and pulls me toward him. "Come with me."

The second he turns away, exposing his back, I lunge.

I try to get my arm under the crook of his neck, but in the moment I spend in the air attempting my attack, he spins.

I'm met with a hard forearm knocking the wind out of me. I'm tossed to the mat where he doesn't bother to pin me. We both know I've lost. I look up at him from the mat, on my back with defeat etched into my skin.

"It was a nice idea, Shayde. Next time use it on someone who's standards are low enough to consider your advances."

"You, *fucking*, asshole."

He's already walking away, unaffected by our encounter. Rage courses and I kick a leg out and wedge it between his feet when he tries to step. My leg goes taut against his resistance, but from this unorthodox vantage point, gravity is finally on my side. Garrith lands with a loud thud.

When I expect him to regroup and seek revenge, he only lays there looking at me. First, his eyes shine with bewilderment; then they melt into satisfaction and respect. He finally nods, gets up, and continues on his way.

I'm dusting myself off when Reid grabs me by my arm.

I look up at his bright eyes, they almost bring me back to my knees. "Hey," I say with a smile.

"Are you okay?" Reid inspects me.

"Yeah. Did you see it? I—" I start to share my moment of triumph but he cuts me off.

"I saw the whole thing."

"Yeah, I tried to be tricky and throw him off. It didn't work. But I still managed to trip him." I look behind me to see if I can spot where Garrith went off to.

Reid squeezes my arm, dragging my attention back to him. "Jemma, you have got to be more careful. Whatever game you thought you were playing with Garrith, trust me, he's ten steps ahead of you."

I can't help the way my eyes narrow. Obviously, Garrith is trained beyond my grasp, and with his dislike for me, I meet it with an equal hatred for him. But if working with him makes me more capable of defending myself, I have no choice but to do it. "Reid, I've got this," I try to sound earnest but it comes out as annoyance. He releases my arm.

I regret my tone immediately. Reid is here trying to look out for me and I dare to perceive him as a nuisance. I backtrack, "I'm sorry. I know that your intentions are good. I'm just surrounded by soldiers stronger than me. There have been two attempts on my life since I got here. I would like to be equipped to defend myself."

He nods. His hand slides up to cup my cheek. I lean into it and smile. "You amaze me," he whispers.

His hand still rests on my cheek when he takes half a step back to leave me, then thinks better of it. He brings his foot back to me and his other hand joins in cradling my face. Quickly, he plants a kiss. I should have seen it from a mile away. But a kiss in the middle of training quarters seemed an absurd thing to predict. He releases my face and walks away. I check my surroundings. I check to make sure no one saw the display of affection.

Reid goes to regroup with his squad. He makes my instincts

muddy. I like him. But kissing me in front of my peers is too much. I don't know how I can tell him that.

I have no right to feel this way. He is the prince. I'm lucky to receive such attention from him. But I know it's moving too quickly.

I decide that I will sleep in my own room again. I'll tell him I have to train early tomorrow, even though my early departures have never woken him this far.

The thought lifts a weight off my shoulders. Though I enjoy our touches and our exploration of one another's bodies, the idea of slowing us down makes me feel sharper, and my reflexes more refined.

Besides, I need my instincts ready, as Garrith so graciously shared with me, disaster is coming.

We're lined up for sparring match-ups against other squads. I wait for the announcement with my teammates. Normally morale among the group is decent, but today it's full of tension.

I look at Cynrad. Look at Cynrad look at Tatum. Tatum is ice. She gives away nothing, not in her expression, not in her stance. I want there to be a chip in her armor for Cynrad but she is too strong, too stubborn. If she hadn't told me herself that he broke up with her, I would have no idea the turmoil of her heart. She's hurt. She's angry but she shows nothing.

Cynrad, who craves invisibility, has turned into an open book of despair. The dark hair he normally hides behind is pushed back exposing his round eyes. Round eyes, full of sadness and regret, incapable of looking away from Tatum. If asked a month ago which brother I would classify as puppy-like, I would have said Enon. But today Cynrad is the puppy and none of us can ease his misery.

I have to turn my attention elsewhere. Their conflict isn't mine, I remind myself.

"I think I have some good news," Enon says from behind me.

I cock an eyebrow. "Oh yeah?"

"Some councilmen have been dismissed. Their rank was stripped, and they were sent back to Megara yesterday. Councilmen Anderson and Gray." The names sound familiar and I look at Enon's expectant eyes. Exasperation flails from his hands. "Jemma! Dax *Anderson*. Bellamy *Gray*."

My shower assassin and my Arid deserter. "Oh."

"Oh's right. I think they orchestrated the attempts. And the king figured it out."

That doesn't make sense. When did the king become interested in justice for my sake? Perhaps he only wants the attempts on my life to be on his terms. And I'm so sick of his terms.

"Jemma!" For once, I'm grateful for the call. Earlier I dropped Commander Garrith on his ass. And for once, sparring doesn't seem like a death sentence.

I'm pitted against a girl with long, brown hair that she keeps in a braid that reaches the backs of her thighs. She's a few inches shorter than me but sturdy, easily fifty pounds of muscle heavier than me.

Our match lasted only a few minutes. I got in several good shots, the blood trickling from her nose proof of it. But still, I managed to get pinned. I know my key to success is going to be staying upright. I do not possess the weight or muscle mass to escape once caught. I know I need help, and for a moment I choose to be thankful because I now have the resources and the people to grant me that.

After she gets up from pinning a boy twice her size, I try asking Tatum for pointers. For a minute she seems engaged and provides reasonable advice. But her eyes keep drifting elsewhere. Cynrad is sparring a couple of mats down. It's a relief to see that she is affected by the storm brewing between them. I want to be there for her but I also need to know what I'm doing wrong. I snap my fingers in front of her face.

She looks at me appalled. "What the fuck? I'm listening!" She rolls her eyes and crosses her arms. She's fiery today.

Enon sneaks up behind us. "Come on Tatum," he says. "Jemma's looking for guidance and you're looking for remorse in my brother. So let me save you the hassle. It's there. Trust me. He and I shared a womb and now we share a room. He is in pieces." Enon sighs. "So since we're all caught up, you can rest assured that your friends are here to talk it through." I elbow him in his ribs. "*And* Greenie is eager to be criticized for her performance today."

Tatum rolls her eyes.

Enon tsks at her. "We love the sass, really. But Jemma is merely an innocent bystander. She needs correction, not dismissal." Enon's dramatics are an easy distraction. He is a master of keeping spirits up and entertaining. "Besides, she gets enough eye rolls from our exasperated squad leader."

Tatum whips her head my way and flashes a smug half-grin, Enon's distraction proving effective. At this, she speaks up, "My eye rolls don't come close to Garrith's." Enon joins in laughing with her. They take turns imitating the commander.

Tatum stops Enon. "You're doing it all wrong, you have to sigh first! Like this—" Her mocking gets more exaggerated. And I want to quiet their giggles before someone overhears.

I whisper to cue them in on our growing volume, "What's Garrith's problem with us anyway?"

Enon looks at me incredulously. "Us? I've never been

honored with such an eye roll. Until you showed up, I had never heard him speak."

Tatum piques up, "Jemma just has a way of bringing out hostility in those around her." She pokes me in the ribs.

Other squads begin moving out of training quarters. We fall in step behind them. While Tatum and Enon continue with their antics, thankfully pointing them toward a victim other than myself, I can't help but wonder what it is that I've done. Garrith's patience always seems to be much thinner when it comes to me. Regardless of the little moments that he treats me like a person, hate seems to always flow off him, knocking into me. Not knowing why plants a seed of irritation. I try not to let it grow.

CHAPTER 25

I've tossed and turned in my bed long enough so I finally get up. It still hurts to see Jo's bed empty. After the show of affection Reid put on during training, I told him I thought I was ready to sleep a night in my old room. I told him I planned to get up extra early for training and didn't want to risk waking him. He didn't question anything, he just told me he would miss me and kissed me goodnight.

The truth is that I need space. Today it became clear that things between me and Reid have progressed quickly. I'm not sure I have room in my heart to get wrapped up in the dramas of what a public relationship with him might entail. Jo is gone and it seems my only options here without her are loneliness or suffocation.

I lace up my boots. Maybe a midnight run will exhaust me and I'll be able to sleep the second half of the night. As I reach the bottom of the staircase, Cynrad is coming out of the shower hall. His eyebrows are pinched together and his eyes appear to be several shades darker than normal. He shakes some of the water out of his dark hair. I'm heading down the cave but slow down to fall into step with him

"You couldn't sleep either?" I offer.

"No." He sighs. "Thought I could shower off all my ideas." I smile. "But it doesn't matter how much water I waste, things still won't make sense."

Having just listened to Tatum's side of the story, I feel I'm cheating by hearing out Cynrad.

I want to explain that Tatum is my friend but he cuts me off.

"She doesn't get it." Cynrad is unraveling. "I didn't want to break up. But I also don't want to keep at this back-and-forth bullshit. On and off. I'm in it. I want commitment. But I can't keep putting myself out there for her if she won't meet me there. I have to protect my heart too."

Cynrad is gutting me. Tatum hadn't shared too many details of their most recent separation. She's private about her relationship. I now realize that her grasp on privacy might be part of the problem.

Something doesn't sit right knowing that two amazing people who love each other, aren't making it work. On paper, love should be easier than this. So I say, "Love should trump pride, Cynrad. For the both of you. You should tell her what you told me. And her need for privacy shouldn't be what separates you." I think that suggestion is sufficient. I have no right to be giving out relationship advice. I'm still not sure how relationships work if I'm being honest. All this time I've spent in the desert, my only thought process ended in keeping Jo safe. I've never considered one day knowing Reid, and now that the day is here, I'm lost trying to navigate it.

Cynrad sighs, resigned, and I'm about to take back what I said. Maybe he doesn't love her the way I thought. And then he does what I thought was the impossible, and *blushes*. "I'm sorry for unloading all of this on you. Tatum is the person I tell everything. I guess I just had a lot of things built up that I couldn't say to her. But I needed to vent. So maybe you're right. As much as I don't want to have this conversation with her, if we're going to save this, we need to have it out."

I nod, not comfortable voicing my unsteady opinions. Cynrad's room is near the opening to the mess hall; I'll leave him and get back to outrunning my problems.

As we near the opening, I can hear Reid talking. I didn't know who I was even looking for while out this late until I could listen to his voice. I regret trying to sleep in my room. It made sense earlier today when I thought my plate was too full. But now it's midnight and I'm walking the halls of Moria, unable to sleep. Though it was just for a few hours, I missed Reid.

I quicken my steps to intercept him sooner, but Cynrad touches my arm. His face is weary. He squints his eyes and motions for me to quiet down. Reid's voice rings clearly down the corridor. I give Cyn a quizzical look.

And then I hear another voice. King Amos must be back from Megara. I understand Cynrad's caution. The conversation we're eavesdropping on is clearly a hushed topic. The king whispers while Reid's outbursts are annoyed and defensive.

"I don't know why!" Reid bellows at his father.

"I thought you were making progress," Amos hisses.

"Maybe she had a bad day. I don't know. But I'm not worried about it. I'll talk to her tomorrow." Reid's footfalls sound down the cave.

He's nearly in view when the King says from behind him, "Get a handle on your project son, or I'll have to assign someone else to Miss Shayde."

There's a brush against my hand. I forget Cynrad standing next to me.

Assign someone else to Miss Shayde.

Get a handle on your project.

My lungs deflate and shrink and refuse to expand beyond half their capacity.

Reid comes around the corner. The shock on his face mirrors that of my own. He opens his mouth but says nothing.

I swallow but my throat is dry and it hurts.

Reid extends his hand, and moves forward. "Jemma—"

"Your *project*?" I spit the word at him. He freezes. I have been reduced to an experiment. Or I suppose that's all I've been. This whole time, I was nothing more than a series of data.

I run.

I run out of the cave.

Through the mess hall, past the King. I will not look at him. None of it was real.

I try to swallow the lump in my throat. But it's dry, it hurts.

It was all an instruction. I've been sleeping in his room.

I'm a fool. He's never been mine, he's only the Prince of Megara. I was a fool to think any of his loyalties resided in myself. I expect tears, but I'm out. I cried the last of my tears when they took Jo away. I won't give them anymore.

My shoulder collides with Tatum when I barrel down a turn in the tunnel, eager to get to the wolf cave. I've knocked her into the wall.

Tatum pushes against me. "Shayde, what the fuck?"

"Are you in on it too?" Anger wedges itself between the tears falling down my face. "Are you just a pawn, instructed by the King? Were you ever my friend?"

Tatum eyebrows rest higher on her forehead than usual and she reaches out to touch my arm. I flinch and pull away.

"Jemma, what are you talking about?"

"I know it's a setup. Reid has been taking orders from his father. He was instructed to befriend me, he was expected to form a relationship with me." Hearing it out loud hurts. Until now, there was still a sliver of myself eager to believe what I overheard was a misunderstanding. But saying it out loud, I know it is the truth.

Tatum blinks. "And you think I was told by the king to become friends with you? So I can what? Tell him you're somewhat of a shit soldier and spend a little too much time in your feelings?" Anger flashes in her eyes. "And why would the king want Reid to get close to you?"

"I don't know." My shoulders slump. Exhaustion settles in my bones and I want away from the dramatics of today. I want a nap long enough to soften this betrayal.

Tatum's eyes soften. "Hey." She wraps her arm around my frame and starts walking us back to our dorms. "You're my friend and I am yours. Not because the king or anyone else told me to be. You're fierce and loyal and I know that if I came to you with a problem, your instinct would be to help me. That's rare, especially here. Everyone seems to have second agendas and trust is hard to come by." I know she means it. Tatum is not built to reassure anyone, but right now she is, and I know it's because she cares about me the way I care about her. She smiles. "Why is the king orchestrating this? It's not like you're anything special."

I whip my head to face her and she's already cackling.

I leave Tatum at her door and drag myself to mine. Exhaustion has settled into my muscles and the twelve stairs leading to my room might as well be fifty. I round the bottom of the staircase and sitting eye level with me is Reid.

He appears crushed, like a lost puppy. I wish he would wipe it from his face. He's an actor, a puppet of the king. I intercept him when he opens his mouth to speak, "Your explanations will have to wait. I'm tired." I step around him and open the door to my room.

He follows me. I sit on the edge of my bed and begin unlacing my boots.

"No! I have to tell you! Jemma, I love you! It wasn't a game for me. Tell me you know that this love is real." He's never told me he loves me before.

Love. The sound of that word could make me vomit. I pinch the bridge of my nose. I know there will be a time to sort this out, but it's not tonight. "You should go."

"Jemma." Even the sound of my name on his tongue sounds wrong. The betrayal is too fresh and I don't want to sort through the logistics of it tonight.

I get up and walk to the door. I swing it wide and the hinges creek. I only wanted to provide Reid with the opening to leave. Instead, I find Commander Garrith standing outside.

He takes in my startled face and quickly explains, "I could hear yelling."

I look back at Reid who has yet to take a step toward the door. "We're fine," I reassure. "The prince was just leaving."

"Jemma," Reid says. Desperation is wedged between every letter of my name. I don't want to hear him say my name. Not now. Not ever.

I sigh. Don't look at him. I repeat myself, "*Just. Leaving.*"

I won't look at him. I keep my eyes on the ground, on Garrith's boots in the space before me. I hear the shuffle of Reid's feet as he walks past me. I feel his gaze, begging me to see him. But I can't. Not tonight.

Garrith's boots move out of the way so Reid can finally leave.

I look up to find concern etched into the green of Garrith's eyes. For a moment I think he cares, before I realize this look is *pity*. I've taken part in an orchestrated relationship and everyone knows. "I'm fine, Commander." He stays still. "Just dramatics." I couldn't make my mouth stop talking if my life depended on it. "A misunderstanding. Everything is fine. Thank you for checking." My voice cracks and I can tell tears aren't far behind. The adrenaline earlier was able to ward off such an emotional reaction. But I'm tired now and the dam is going to break. As much as I don't want to cry, the privacy awaiting me is too tempting for my feelings.

Garrith goes to speak but I cut him off. "I appreciate your concern but I promise, it's all good here. I'll see you tomorrow," I rush and before he can get a word out, I shut the door.

Twenty-six, twenty-seven, twenty-eight seconds pass before I hear him start down the stairs to return to his room.

Once alone, I take in the expanse of my tiny room. Aside from my attempt earlier tonight, I haven't slept here in weeks. Loneliness creeps in. Tears begin to flow. I know time will heal this feeling of rawness, I just wish I could sleep through it.

And then I remember a bottle I stashed away. A bottle of wine from a night out with Tatum is still tucked away at the back of my dresser.

I hold the bottle up toward the bed opposite from me, Jo's bed, and cheers to everything good always seeming to be ripped away, just out of reach.

CHAPTER 26

Gideon doesn't stay in the stables at the West Entrance. The stables here are smaller, hidden away just underground before we break the surface. I'm supposed to ride a different horse, and suddenly the entire idea of a late-night expedition sounds ridiculous.

During dinner, I asked Tatum what she thought of sneaking out tonight. I couldn't sleep in my room again. I've spent two nights back in my own quarters now and all I've been capable of is staring at the ceiling. Rest was an old luxury I took for granted. I was without Jo. I've been made the fool by Reid, who I've refused to look at, let alone speak to. I felt restless, and reckless, and feared insanity if I lay in my bedroom alone with my thoughts. Tatum was the right person to ask.

"Here, you can ride this one." Tatum knocks on a stall door. When I look over the wall, the depressed mare, Winnie, stares back at me.

I give Tatum a weary look.

"Garrith has been working with her, she's doing much

better. She's eating more, and allowing riders."My side eye encourages her to continue. "Well, she's allowing Garrith to ride."

I step into the stall. At first, Winnie resists. I try and soothe her. Her coat is richer than the last time I saw her. She's been tended to, brushed, and polished. More light shines from her eyes. I run a hand down her neck. When I slide the saddle over her, she does not oppose.

I guide her out of the stables, out of Moria, and into the night. She allows me onto the saddle without a hiccup. I'm in awe of Garrith's ability to restore a disconnected mare. We fall into pace with Tatum.

Just being somewhere outside of the schedules and squads makes it easier to breathe. The weight on my chest is lifted, and the only tightness remaining is knowing that this is only temporary. And completely against the rules. For so long, I haven't been managed. It's just been me and Jo. And now there are levels and levels of management above us.

We head East toward the beach.

At first, we travel in at an even trot, but it quickly turns into a race. Tatum's horse is fast and I expect it when she pulls away. Tatum and Garrith have the two fastest stallions, at least that's what Enon told me.

I don't push Winnie, afraid of asking too much of her. But at the sight of Tatum flying far ahead of us, she speeds up.

Little by little, she kicks the frost off of her bones, her joints.

She speeds up.

And up.

And up.

When I think her rate of speed will plateau, she persists.

And I realize I've never known such wind. I've never known

the feeling of traveling such a distance in record time. Winnie is lightning, and I'm no longer guiding her. I hold on for dear life.

We fly past Tatum. Winnie glides through the dunes. I'm almost certain she doesn't leave tracks. This horse does not touch the ground.

I've missed this. Here, there is never true darkness like what I've found underground. Here, the stars go on forever. The moon lights up the sand and instead of the usual hues of orange, the dunes appear in shades of blue. The sand holds its own sky of stars the way the moon reflects and creates glimmering constellations that move with us. The dunes are as endless as the waves I saw when we last visited the ocean. But here, the waves are still and calm. Nights in the Arid must be one of the most beautiful pieces of nature.

And I think Winnie needed this too.

I want to share this with Jo. I don't know where exactly she is or what she's doing. And I'm supposed to trust that she is okay. My heart breaks for her feelings of isolation. I crave hope. I wish to know that she is well and happy. But I know better than to hope. She too, is away from all we've ever known; and here I am, selfishly claiming more freedom for myself. I have to block out the thoughts. The guilt grabs hold of my throat and sends tears pricking behind my eyes. I am indulging tonight. And if I want to enjoy tonight, I need to leave guilt underground.

Distances don't seem as vast the way Winnie soars. It took half a day to make the trek on foot, but with Winnie, we've closed the distance from Moria to the ocean in just over an hour. I spot the first palm tree and an overwhelming eagerness overtakes my senses. We slow down and let Tatum take the lead. The sound of crashing waves just ahead propels us forward. I'm buzzing with excitement when Tatum turns her head back to look at me, the same enthusiasm glowing in her eyes.

We reach the peak of the final dune between us and the sea.

Dark shadows fall upon us.

Tatum is thrown from her horse.

I whirl my head to follow her cream tunic as she is sent several feet to the left. She crashes on her back creating a cloud of sand and dust and two Howlers fall upon her.

Winnie tries to back up as a Howler appears to my right and I lose my hold on the reins. She rears back as my hands try to find the reins that I let slip. I slide off her back. My hands fly to the daggers I have secured at my thighs.

I roll backward over my shoulder and palm a dagger in both hands. The Howler that knocked Tatum, then sent me flying off Winnie, advances. I can see two more closing in on me. They come from the direction of the beach. I rush to the side of the beast in front of me. Though he wins in size and reach, his movements are lagging. I try to slice his middle but I don't get close enough.

I want to think with strategy but all I can come up with is shame and embarrassment for thinking this was a good idea. It seemed like a brilliant idea mere seconds ago. And now I'd give anything to rewind time and stay in my room.

I check to see if Tatum is up and the two Howlers that were there before have turned to four. She's a blur of white fighting against too many looming shadows.

And there are too many.

Too many.

Too many.

I run to Tatum. I know my presence will bring the three Howlers on my tail with me. But first I need to support her. If we keep each other's backs, we might have a chance. I slice through a creature's side just as he reaches for Tatum's neck. His long hand quickly covers his wound and blood seeps from between his fingers.

I get to Tatum who's managing to keep the Howlers at bay with her sword. One of them is missing its hand.

She's tough, but there's too many.

She's skilled with her sword, but there are too many.

I swipe past a Howler making contact behind its knee and its once hulking height comes down to eye level with me.

There are too many.

Keep moving. I make it to her back and we move clockwise taking in the circle of cloaked Howlers around us.

There are too many.

Every time Tatum lunges to attack one of them, two others close in on us.

Too many.

Too many.

We are too outnumbered for us to make any moves. Each attempt we throw out puts a dent in our defenses and they feast on every opportunity to exploit any weakness we expose.

The circle is closing, no matter how swift I am with my dagger, it's not enough to keep them away. If we could just find a gap maybe we could call the horses but our chances are slim.

A gap is not going to reveal itself.

I turn my head enough to see that just as Tatum's sword makes contact with a Howler's hip, a hand grips around her ankle, pulling her feet out from under her. A scream escapes my lips and my wrists are bound together by long gray fingers.

I know my brain is broken because I should have immediately started figuring a way to get out of this but the only thought bouncing off the walls of my mind is, you're going to die screaming like a little girl.

You're going to die screaming like a little girl.

All of the training, the confidence I thought I had, the moments I spent full of pride, reduced to nothing.

Just to die screaming.

I'm jerked forward into the cloak and blood pours over my face.

This is the end. A harmless sneak out to look at some fucking water.

I'm covered in blood.

Blinking the blood out of my eyes I look up to where the Howler's face should be. Blood is flowing from its neck. Its head is missing.

The long cloaked body crumbles to the sand.

Commander Garrith stands where the Howler had just been before it was beheaded. His green eyes are piercing and darker than I've ever seen them. His swords are out in both hands and one is dripping with blood.

Terrifying.

He is positively terrifying.

Instead of his normal hint of murder gleam, his eyes are beaming with death and destruction. He makes the color green look like murder and horror.

He moves like a dark shadow, not staying in one spot long enough to make out his entire figure. The dark fabric flows around him, his swords flashing as they find purchase with every swing. The smell of metal drifts up into my nose and my vision tilts. I wish I wasn't so affected. I wish I was stronger than the queasy apprehension settling in my stomach. Blood isn't supposed to smell, but the air around me is metallic and reeks of death.

Three Howlers are down before the other four even register their new attacker. Attention is torn from Tatum who looks shaken up but miraculously unharmed. The Howlers stand to their full height and tower over Garrith. It doesn't matter. No one and nothing is as swift and accurate as Garrith. His movements are fluid as he picks the creatures apart limb by limb.

He must be designed for this. Every step, every twitch of his muscle is intentional. He doesn't miss.

Danger.

This man is dangerous.

I'm useless. I know I can help. I have daggers and I'm capable. But right now, witnessing Garrith annihilate every Howler within feet of him, has rendered me speechless and unable to do anything but watch.

Blood flies, staining the sand around us. The once calm sand is now a field of gory evidence proving this massacre. Proving Garrith to be as menacing as we all thought he was.

Tatum is up, and like me, she can only attempt to gather her bearings. Shock is the only expression on her face. Her clothes are tattered and her tunic is split, now exposing her shoulder and top of her chest; blotches of pink skin creep from her shoulder to her neck. Her hand-to-hand combat skills allowed her skin to stay intact as there wasn't a single scratch on her. Both of us are unharmed, yet my pulse would have me believing I had lost a limb.

With only two Howlers still standing, one in front and one behind Garrith. He spins impossibly fast, with a flash of iron and blood, that the wounds don't register on the Howlers for three, four, five seconds.

They fall.

If Garrith has blood on him, it doesn't show up on his dark attire. Suddenly his black uniform makes sense. Killing is second nature, if not first, to him. How else is he to conceal his deadly talents without being dressed head to toe in black?

A part of me wants to run far away from him; a part of me wants to be him.

He sheaths his swords.

Garrith stands among the broken, cloaked bodies. His back is to us; his shoulders are set near his ears. I've never seen him so tense. He is a hulking image of darkness, terror, and destruction. Only the smell of blood and the sound of his heavy breathing inhabits the air around us. I open my mouth, only to close it. I'm too stunned to speak. I glance at Tatum and her expression mirrors mine. The moment is too heavy, and I inch closer to him.

He whirls around and his voice shakes me to my bones, "What the fuck is wrong with you!" Unbridled anger is surging out of him. I'm thankful for the coverings on his face for once. His eyes alone are holding enough fury to kill. It's a wonder how his glare hasn't killed me already. The distance between us closes in an instant and he's towering over me. The urge to strangle me where I stand is tormenting him as he clasps and unclasps his fists.

When he opens his mouth to speak, and I am not prepared for the volume of his anger. "How could you do this? Do you not care if Jo is alone?" He may as well have slapped me. He's at a loss and his anger vibrates the ground and every cell in my body. I don't want to turn away so I hold my ground and create a mask. I will hold my chin up. If I can run out into the Arid and nearly die from stupidity, I can take whatever berating remarks he can throw at me.

He seethes until he decides to yell again, "You could have died tonight. You would have died tonight." His eyes shift from anger to anguish. He's too intense. His pain is worse than his anger. I can't maintain the eye contact. I look down in shame and his hands are visibly shaking.

He walks to his horse and mounts. Tatum and I take that as our cue to do the same. It's clear that Garrith is trying to blow off steam when he takes off at a pace we won't be able to keep up with. We take off, closing the distance to Moria.

I see Garrith's point. The speeding hoof beats are doing something to my mind I didn't know I needed. Under the trauma of this evening are feelings I haven't been sure how to tap into. But with every hoof beat, I can see it.

Jo isn't here, as Garrith so merrily reminded me. I don't need to be strong for her right now.

She's not here.

She's not here.

She's not here.

I brought us here. And all that did was get us separated.

It's my fault.

It's my fault.

It's my fault.

How dare Garrith judge me for tonight? It would have been devastating had something happened to Tatum, but if my recklessness had gotten me killed, I would probably be doing Jo a favor. Maybe she would grow from it and be able to protect herself better than I seem to be doing. I walked her to her death, leaving us at the mercy of Megara, and then instead of looking out for her, I got caught up in feelings for a boy. Not to mention he's a boy that's been instructed to deceive me. And deceive me, he did.

I urge Winnie on. I can barely make out the dust that Garrith's horse is kicking up behind them. We aren't going fast enough.

I'm not sure if it's the sting of Reid's betrayal that's started a fire inside me or the inevitable sting that will ensue once my smug Commander hears about it. As if being reckless tonight wasn't enough of a reason for Garrith to talk down to me, he's going to enjoy every minute he gets to patronize me for being naive enough to fall for a traitor like Reid. And why did I have to receive all of his disdain? Tatum is just at fault for tonight as

I am. But he won't utter a word or look her direction. All of his hatred is saved for me.

I've opened the dam and all of my anger toward Reid and Garrith pours out.

At least that's what I tell myself.

Because deep down, I know I'm only angry with myself.

CHAPTER 27

Every step we take toward our rooms is like another log thrown into the fire that keeps me raging. Tatum seems to have already gotten over this evening when she pinches my arm and tells me she'll see me tomorrow. I think she wants to calm me but her retired state only makes me more irate.

Her room is one of the first ones in our wing so I have the length of our cave to listen to Garrith's condescending breathing.

Every breath that leaves his lungs patronizes me.

It isn't until we near the end of the cave and I can see mine, and Reid's door, that I remember I'll be sleeping back in my own room. Heartbreak hits me again for the millionth time today but right now I do not want to cry. I want to break something. Anything. Everything.

I take the first step up to my room when, surprisingly, Garrith breaks the silence, "I just have to know why."

I turn back to look at him but for once he isn't looking into my soul. His eyes are diverted to the wall. "I thought you were smart. I thought you had sense." His voice is even, but I can hear his resignation and I get the feeling that I didn't just let Jo and Tatum down tonight. For a second it feels like I let Garrith down too. Like he cares about my well-being, that is until he turns back to me and says, "Twice! Twice I arrived just in time. Do you like being saved? Do you plan on putting yourself in these situations? Do you *think* that someone is just going to be there when you fuck up? Use your head! I might not be there the next time you decide to be reckless."

"Then don't be there! No one called you to save me! If I put myself there, I can get myself out. And if I can't, maybe that's just how it was supposed to be."

Anger and heat radiate off of him. Rage forces him forward and he says, "So you'll abandon Jo? I know better than to believe you'd be so careless with your life. I know you'd be there for her! Is this just a cry for attention? Need to get back at your boyfriend? Put yourself and your friend at risk to get a reaction out of him?"

The fire is back and consuming all the reason and logic I have left. "You know nothing about me!"

"I think I do! I think you've spent your whole life in survival mode and now you're here and think you can kick your feet up and indulge in dramatics."

I've heard enough and so can everyone else in Moria. I refuse to allow him to keep the insults echoing down the cave for anyone to hear. I turn around and walk up to my door. My anger is overflowing and I can tell my actions are almost out of my hands. I slam the door behind me and rake my hands through my hair ready to pull it all out by the roots.

I know I threw the door back with some force but the crashing sound never comes. I turn back to find Garrith halfway in my door, his foot having caught it before it closed.

He takes another step inside and taunts me by leaning back

until I hear the quiet click of the latch falling into place. And all reservations are out the window. I launch myself and have my dagger pressed against his neck before he can utter another scornful slew of words.

The dagger is sharp and cuts through the fabric wrapped around his neck. There's surprise in his eyes and it gives me a surge of triumph. Nothing catches Garrith by surprise.

But then the scene folds out in my mind. Garrith just saved my ass in the Arid. And now I'm holding a dagger to his throat. I retreat, sure the shock on his face is now blanketing mine. I'm out of control. I want to box up all of my feelings and return them to whatever dark corner of my mind they came from. I'm supposed to be better than this. Or at least I thought I was.

"What's going on?" His voice is gentle and concerned.

"I'm sorry, I didn't mean to lash out." Close it up. Block it out.

Part of his neck is exposed from where I cut the fabric. More guilt. More shame.

"This is not you." He takes a step forward.

"Maybe it is." I take a step back.

"We both know you do not sneak out for joy rides and hold daggers to throats for no reason."

"I do not want to have this conversation."

"Well, you need to sort out your shit before you leave this room. There are other people here. And we can't all fall victim to your new habit of trying out different personalities."

"I know nothing about myself! I take care of Jo. I take care of Jo. I take care of Jo! I don't know what I want. I can't tell what I am or who I am when I'm not actively taking care of her. I only know that I live and breathe to protect Jo! And she's not even here, and I don't know when I'll see her again." My voice breaks on my last word and I'm suddenly exhausted and ashamed and whisper, "I'm sorry that for a second I wanted to do something for me. I wanted to see the water. I thought for a second that I could make a decision for me."

Silence stretches out between us.

I wish he would say something so that my selfishness wasn't the only thing at the front of our minds. "She's not a burden." My voice is low and resigned. Why am I still talking? "It's an honor to look after her. I love her. I think I was born to guard her. I'm only saying that if she isn't here, shouldn't I figure out what I am without her?"

His eyes are unreadable. And I'm about to reach out and rip the fabric off his face but he interrupts my impulsive thought, "You can protect the ones you love and live at the same time." The sense of relief he allows me to have is short-lived when he says, "But tonight, you were irresponsible. It's not selfish to want to live, but it is selfish to act without thought when people are relying on you. You were reckless and you should feel bad about it."

I feel the tears welling, threatening to free themselves from my eyes. I do not cry because he's being mean, I cry because he's right. I do not cry because the boy distracting me from these feelings turned out to be a fraud. I cry because I miss Jo and all I know is how to take care of her and she's not here and I have no way to make sure she's okay. What am I without her?

The tears are finally too much to hold at bay and they spill down my cheeks. I turn to shield my face from him. I lift the back of my hand to my face. Starting to wipe away the dampness from my skin, he catches my wrist. With his other hand he reaches out and cups my jaw. My momentary surprise almost sends the tear back up into my eyes. His fingers glide back to my neck while his thumb rubs across my cheek, erasing my tears. He lets go of my wrist and instead wraps his arm around my waist, reeling me in, while his other hand pulls my head to his chest. He's everywhere in my senses. A scented mixture of musk, earth, and him swirls around my head and it somehow centers me and plants my feet on solid ground.

The shock quickly wears away and it's like a dam has broken and my heart has split apart because the sobs that escape my lips sound like something animal. He's sturdy and holding all the pieces of me together so I can let go and break.

I let the tears flood my brain and wash away all the cobwebs. Wash away all of the boxes I've hidden away. I feel raw and weightless. My breakdown was embarrassing but necessary. I haven't felt this refreshed and light since my parents were alive.

I'm not sure how long we stay like that. My tears eventually come to a slow end. I can tell he won't move until I do. Maybe he hates me, but at the same time, he has compassion. And today I'm thankful for him.

I lift my head off his chest and tilt my chin to face him. His lids are heavy over his eyes and somehow it still doesn't dim the intensity of his viridescent eyes. I'm so tired of his face being covered. I need something to be wrong with him. I need him to be flawed.

I stiffen at the realization that my breakdown has ended but I've remained nestled in his arms.

Stepping back, I wipe away the remaining moisture under my eyes. A blush is inching up and my ears go uncomfortably warm.

I need to know if he's blushing too. Need to know if his body is reacting out of reason the same way mine is. I reach up to pull away his shemagh.

He's quick and back to business as he steps back to the door and grabs the handle. "You need to get some sleep before tomorrow," he takes a breath, "or I guess now it's today. Breakfast is in a few hours."

I'm at a loss for words and nod. It seems he's also unsure of what to say as well. Garrith nods and is out the door.

The roller coaster of emotions I've been on today catches up with me when I unlace my boots. Exhaustion creaks in my muscles and my mind. Though it will be brief, I know this nap is about to be one of the best I've had in a while, even if I am alone.

CHAPTER 28

Geneneral Pinnell starts strategies with a bang today. There's chaos and chatter throughout the room. He clears his throat and rattles the room when he says, "We are going to war in one week."

The havoc in the room goes still. Every conversation comes to an end.

"For the next week, we will plot the upcoming expedition within our squads. The soldiers you've been working with for the last few months will be your squad mates for this mission." That's a relief since the only people underground I'm certain don't want to kill me are the ones in squad ten.

"Each squad will have different missions. All missions are delicate in that this will be a domino effect. If one squad fails, we all fail."

Unease settles in my stomach. Garrith is our squad leader and I haven't seen him since the hug in my bedroom. That was two days ago.

I woke up yesterday morning expecting an awkward run-in, or uncomfortable icebreaker where we agreed to act like my moment of vulnerability never happened.

But he went missing. He wasn't in training yesterday, and he isn't in training now. My eyes scanned the room for him when I walked in and I hate myself for it. Hate myself for the disappointment in my chest when his looming presence was nowhere to be found.

My eyes do connect with Reid's. I also haven't spoken to him in two days. After I told him I needed space to think, he obliged, but still, his puppy eyes found me everywhere. It's a doppler effect where his blinks send waves of *I'm sorry, forgive me, I love you.*

I don't dwell on that betrayal. I can't.

"Over the next seven days," my attention is pulled by General Pinnell, "you will learn your place in this mission. The goal is to start a war. We need to lure the Howlers out of the North mountains, to the outskirts of Groth's base. Since we do not know the mountains, we must piss them off enough to bring them South where we will hide in the ruins of Audun and ambush them on their way to Moria." Pinnell takes a break to lock eyes with the squad leaders in the room. "Before any of that can happen, we need to piss them off. Later on, you will all get your personal squad missions. I'll address those individually. Now get to training quarters. We're about to bring home a war."

Cynrad doesn't miss a beat. I'm distracted while sparring and he uses it to his advantage. A kick to my torso sends me flying off the mat.

"Pick it up Jem. *We're about to bring home a war,*" Cynrad

imitates General Pinnell. I turn my head to the man who had me distracted in the first place.

King Cerastes is standing against the wall in training quarters. His eyes are on me, so he definitely just saw me get laid out. So much for his prized little project. I desire his disappointment.

Seeing his face makes Reid's deception wound feel fresh again. He grins and begins to walk directly toward me. Once he's close enough for me to hear, he says lightly, "I hoped you'd have a little more," he ponders his words, "power by now. My sweet Jemma, all of the potential and none of the follow through."

"Sorry I'm not measuring up to any of your expectations," I sneer.

He flashes his perfect teeth. His good looks should count as attractive but he only seems sick. "Oh, you're referring to your relationship with my son?" Before I can even respond he goes on, "Yes, I was displeased by your immature reaction. I was only helping you."

"Helping me? You sent Reid on a quest to charm me, to trick me. I think my reaction was fitting."

"That's where I see immaturity. You've had two nearly successful attempts on your life by individuals that also occupy Moria. And yet, now you want to cast out the prince of this kingdom. You want to abandon the additional protection that comes with a higher title."

"In case you've forgotten, I got out of the first encounter without Reid, and in the second he had us abandon a commander against the Howlers *and* wolves. I'm not eager to obtain the protection that comes with his friendship."

The king scoffs, "We'll see."

With that, he leaves. I don't want to think about the conversation with Amos. His words are always cryptic and seem to find purchase in the cracks in my mind. But today, I train. Something much easier to focus on while not being observed by the King of Megara.

Enon offered to help me and Tatum today with kicks. My speed and dagger skills have improved, but I have a long way to go before I can spar again with Garrith. On the occasion that I can safely land a kick, I need enough power for the attempt to be worth it.

Enon takes us into one of the side caverns in the corners of training quarters. In this room are large, cylinder sacks of what appears to be sand hanging from the ceiling. Enon has us stand at a bag while demonstrating proper form. Tatum, as always, is a natural. She looks like she could give anyone underground a run for their money against her shins.

Enon doesn't laugh at me, which is surprising given his usual reaction to my lack of grace. A new respect for Enon forms when he uses patience to refine my stance. What was supposed to be a power-building exercise, quickly became a lesson on the basics.

As discouraging as it is, not being at everyone else's skill level, there's comfort in knowing I can grow. I've come a long way since Jo and I were brought underground. The things I know now, the improvements, the achievements I never even knew to want, now grant me the ability to look forward. As much as I've grown, I have so much to learn. The idea excites me.

Once Enon considers my stance acceptable, we move on to building power.

"Your strength isn't just in your leg," he reminds me. Again.

As embarrassed as I am for not understanding his meaning, I get clarification, "But I'm kicking? How is my leg, not the driving force?"

Enon doesn't bat an eye, doesn't scoff at my idiocy. "Your

leg carries the power, but that power starts before your foot ever comes off the ground. It starts in your stance and grows from your core as you move. Yes, a jacked leg is definitely helpful to have in this situation, but you don't have to be 200 pounds of muscle to land deadly kicks." Enon swivels to face Tatum who has unleashed all her fury on the cushioned sandbag.

She's amazing.

"Can we do this again tomorrow?" I ask Enon, without pulling my eyes from the deadly assault Tatum is throwing at the sandbag. I want to be able to do that. I want these skills. I want to be able to flatten anything that separates me from Jo.

Everyone here is training for the war, but I train for Jo.

"Jemma Shayde!" I just walked into the mess hall for supper and I'm already being yelled at. I turn and it's General Pinnell. "You're needed at the East exit." I start to question him but he's already continuing past me.

Surely, this won't take long. Enon didn't go easy on us. I'm exhausted and hungry. I didn't realize how much I was looking forward to supper until someone postponed my meal.

The East exit is closest to the training quarters so I'm able to get there quickly. My pace increases when I realize there could be something wrong with Winnie. I'm taking the steps up to the exit two at a time. I turn into the stables and Garrith is standing with his back to me. My heart skips a beat and I'm not ready for this conversation with him. I haven't seen him since our embrace. Did he summon me here to talk about it?

He's facing his horse but his head and shoulders move slightly like he's speaking. He turns around and reveals Jo behind him.

CHAPTER 29

A shiver of joy rattles my spine. Jo is running toward me and I'm floating to her. This is weightlessness. This is relief.

This is happiness.

She's in my arms smiling and unharmed and all the tightness inside my chest disappears. This embrace mends all of my shattered pieces.

I hold her away from me so I can see her but she's blurring and I realize it's the tears in my eyes clouding my vision.

Jo giggles and gasps. "I have so much to tell you!" Her body is vibrating with excitement and I can't believe that she's here.

I must be mirroring her. "I've missed you," I breathe. My shoulders are shaking with laughter and it feels like the first time I've ever laughed. The dust on my normally still and lifeless shoulders is finally disturbed as I shake it off. Nothing and no one gives me life and purpose like Jo.

She takes a step back and beams at me. "Jemma, I'd like to introduce you to Niki." She holds out her hand and Garrith takes it.

My confusion is obvious. The corners of Garrith's eyes crinkle like he must be smiling and Jo giggles. Secrets are hiding behind her lips. Her smile widens, like secrets bursting at the seams.

Jo tells me about Commander Garrith in the orphanage. She tells me the same stories she told me months ago when we were on the brink of death in the Arid. Garrith, or apparently Nikolai, was Jo's protector. And it makes sense that someone would be inclined to look out for her. It makes sense that among the children she would make a great friend. She reminds me that Nikolai is exactly ten years older than her, and that's why they were destined to be an excellent team.

We sit in the mess hall and eat but I can't taste the food. The more Jo explains, the more confused I become.

How can the man that she describes from her childhood be Commander Garrith? In my mind, they're two different people. My suspicions become clear when I start questioning her, "You've seen Garrith at least a few times around Moria before you were sent away. How did you not recognize him?"

"He never spoke to me, and he's always so concealed. I thought he seemed familiar, and he reminded me a lot of my Niki. But his voice is deeper now and I wasn't sure it was him until he took off his shemagh."

An unexpected emotion punches me in the chest. I recognize the irritation and I try to swallow the feeling that I don't reserve the right to have. Jo has seen Garrith's face. This isn't a surprise because she's seen Nikolai's face when they were children in the orphanage. I throw a mask, toss a tarp, anything to cover the bite in my voice, anything to keep it steady. I'm ashamed of my irritation because at this moment I need to only be happy. Jo is here. And she's telling me all about Megara and her friends. She takes classes and has favorites and least favorites. She loves her instructors and she helps in the kitchen with the cooks. Her charm, no doubt, is leading her into all the wonderful parts of Megara.

Jo is thriving. I can hear it in the excitement around the stories she tells me. I can see it in the weight she's put on, finally hiding the skeleton she's been walking in for years. I feel it in the reassuring embraces she can't stop granting me.

And I'm so delighted.

I am.

I'm proud and relieved that she's happy. And I force myself to keep those emotions at the top. Please don't let any feelings but happiness and gratefulness surface. Bury any of my other feelings.

Because I know that my earlier, unpleasant reaction was ugly.

All this time I've been dying to see Jo. And it's here. And she's unharmed. Relief is all I should feel.

But something rose.

I've wondered about and wished to see Garrith's face more often than I'd like to admit. Jo got to see it.

And I am *jealous*.

Commander Garrith is my green-eyed monster. He brings out the worst in me and somehow the best of me. Everything about me is heightened if he has anything to do with it, whether that's good or bad, I have yet to figure out.

Garrith, Nikolai, leaves us to take Jo's bag back to our room.

"I have to go back tomorrow night," Jo whispers as we make our way to our room.

"So soon?" She just arrived. She can't leave. I have to talk to King Cerates.

"I knew it would be brief. No matter the travel, it was

worth it." Jo's grin breaks my heart. Knowing she'll be sent away plants a black hole in my abdomen. My gut swallows all the happiness and leaves me empty. And she isn't even gone yet. I wish things would stop. I wish time would stop.

Let me feel this for a little longer.

Holding out my arm, I let her rest her head against my shoulder, wrapping my arms around her. She is everything good in the world and I'm fortunate to hold her.

We walk to what was once our room, now only my room. Just because this time isn't permanent, doesn't make it any less beautiful.

She throws her pack on her bed, which hasn't been disturbed since the last time she was here. There's a cut across the belly of her pack.

I fetch my mending kit and reach for the pack once she's gathered her nightgown from it. She giggles at the hole in the fabric. "Yeah, that Howler didn't know what it got itself into."

My hands freeze on the thread and needle. "What!"

She waves away my distress. "Don't worry, I had Niki with me. It was one Howler. And honestly, Sto is fast enough that we probably didn't need to stop. But with how close it was to Moria, Niki said it was our duty. He killed it in a second. I could've killed it in half a second if Niki let me bring my bow."

"Who is Sto? The Howler was close to Moria? Your *bow*?" If they're coming close to us, are they closing in on Megara too? And Jo has a bow?

"Yeah, the instructors let me practice with a weapon sometimes. I really like archery, and I've caught on quickly. As for the Howlers, Niki says they've started coming up out of the dried river. And Stoic is Niki's horse." Jo shrugs.

"Are they teaching you about the howlers? In Megara?"

"Oh yeah," she goes on. "They tell us all about Groth and the wolves and beasts and the mindlessness of the Howlers."

"Beasts?"

"Jemma, there's just so much to tell you, I don't know where to begin."

The lack of knowledge I have about our enemy is nauseating and I wonder why I'm not being brought up to speed the way Jo has been. My face gives away my missing confidence and she quickly tries to stop my unraveling. "We have history class in Megara. All the soldiers you train with here have all taken the classes. But Moria is for combat training. I wonder if they even know that we weren't exposed to the wicked ways of Groth during our time at the oasis. I mean, until we had to leave."

A moment passes, and our minds fall to the oasis. The years we spent there, the peace, the bliss of not knowing what creatures were encroaching on the Arid.

"What did you mean by the mindlessness of the Howlers?" Curiosity pulls me from my nostalgia.

"They're brainless, an enchantment. A mixture of the wolves and humans forged together and brought to life with magic. They're created by the beasts of Groth, as their twisted soldiers." Her explanations sound familiar, like a story from a long time ago.

"Beasts?"

"There are many different words for them. I prefer Beast. They stay in the mountains. It's assumed that there must be a power source, in the mountains. But it's a maze. And even if a person wanted to map it, it's overrun with Howlers." I have so many questions for Reid.

Reid.

I can't ask Reid, after the events of today, his betrayal slid to the back burner of my mind.

Maybe I can ask Tatum.

Or Garrith.

No, not Garrith. Just thinking of him throws a hot coal into my stomach. I don't know what I'm doing, but steering clear of him might be my best option. I'm pulled from my thoughts when I catch Jo yawning.

"You should get some sleep," I tell her, as I start to stitch her pack.

She smiles and lays back, watching me work.

"And though we fall apart,

Though our efforts sometimes weary—" She falls asleep before she can finish her poem.

CHAPTER 30

When Sondra saw Jo, her reaction would lead anyone to believe she was being reunited with her long-lost daughter. Jo's always had that ability. To know her is to love her. Sondra keeps us in her living quarters while she goes to fetch the best snacks Moria has to offer.

No one says anything when I don't report to training quarters with my squad. Whatever the consequences of my absence, I'll handle them tomorrow once Jo is gone. Even though she's here, right in front of me, the dread of her departure is ruining our time.

I shake the thoughts and keep them on the good laid out before me: Jo feasting on knafeh, cheese stretching from her mouth to her chin, and certainty that I will never know a delight greater than in this moment.

"So update me on Reid," she teases. Her eyes gleam with mischievousness until she notices my torn expression. "What is it?"

I don't want to share the details with her, details I don't

exactly have yet myself. So I say, "Reid is Prince of Megara. His loyalty lies there before it lies with me. And it was silly to think differently."

"Want me to poison him? I mean it. He looks to be about 185. I know the right dose to keep him from dying but also ensure that he won't be able to leave the bathroom for twenty-four hours."

I fall back in my seat laughing and clutching my belly. I've missed her. Sweet on the outside, vicious on the inside.

"Come on, the squads should be finishing up their afternoon training. We can make sure you still know how to fight after all your *history classes*."

Jo rolls her eyes but follows me anyway.

My back smacks the mat and Jo swings her legs across my shoulders and chest. She's got me locked in place and threatens to snap my arm. I'm impressed with how much she's learned in the past couple of months.

"Who taught you that?" I'm breathless when she releases me.

"We spar in Megara too." She's smiling and I want to lock this moment in my mind forever. Jo smiles and turns to get ready for another attack; she glows. I want to keep this memory fresh and at the front of my mind, as a happy film to watch at the end of every rough day. "Maybe hand-to-hand isn't a top priority. But survival skills are pressed the hardest so we do have to spar occasionally. Mostly we learn how to live in the Arid, like if we ever find ourselves stranded. I know most of what they teach but you'd be surprised how much knowledge would have come in handy over the last eight years."

"I wish I could go back with you," I say. And it's true. I want to see what she sees. I want to meet her friends. I want to personally thank every person that has made our separation bearable for her.

"Me too." Suddenly she looks weary. "I'm not ready to go yet."

This sparring session is shifting into a goodbye that neither of us is ready for. I ignore the growing lump in my throat and choose strength for her. "We'll be back together before you know it. I know this visit was brief but it's helped me a lot to know that you're happy there." Her eyes are welling up but she shakes it off—my strong girl.

We pack up our stuff and head to my room to gather the rest of her things. We are supposed to meet Garrith in an hour at the East Exit.

Our time together is falling away, but I'm grateful for the day we got. As much as I despise the King, I'm tempted to thank him for giving me some grace. As we walk, I mention to Jo, "I'm surprised that Amos allowed you to visit. The last time I talked to him he was adamant about separating us."

Jo snorts. "Oh, the council didn't know Niki was coming to get me. And the king definitely did not okay my being here."

"That doesn't make any sense. Who made the order to bring you here?" Jo must be mistaken. Someone had to give the order to have Garrith bring Jo to Moria.

"He did it on his own. Niki showed up in the middle of lunch. He must have left super early in the morning and rode for seven hours straight because he was exhausted. I thought you were in trouble because the first thing out of his mouth was that you needed me." The realization hits me but before I can allow my mind to fall down that rabbit hole, Jo says, "I knew it was him. He sounded just like the last time I heard his voice." She continues to explain, "The elders convinced him to stay the night that day before the journey back to Moria. He needed rest and food. And once I realized you weren't in danger, I couldn't make him bring me to you before I was sure he was okay. He wouldn't take off his shemagh until we left Megara, but by then I was already pretty sure." Garrith took off after he saved me from the Howler attack, after my breakdown, and after our embrace. And he did it all without permission, to grant me time with Jo.

"What's he like?" My curiosity gets the best of me.

Jo smirks. "He's a lot like you." My expression makes Jo laugh. I'm sure my face is showing nothing short of disdain. "He comes off as rude. Nothing about his first impression, likely even his tenth, says welcoming. But he is fiercely loyal. There's nowhere in the world that I feel safer than when I'm with you or Niki."

"How did you separate?"

She hesitates before sharing and I can't help but feel like this is a story not meant for me. This is a story between Jo and Garrith, from a time before me. "He didn't leave me if that's what you are thinking." It isn't. Not that I know Garrith well enough, but he doesn't seem the type to abandon a person like Jo. "It's been so long, my memories are blurry. But I know he saved me, and then I was alone." Jo is so close to me but she's a thousand miles away. She thinks and tries to place herself there.

Concern and confusion settle in her expression. I know she's traveling back to unpleasant times.

"You don't have to tell me," I say.

"Niki might be a better person to ask about it. I've never understood how we split up. But I do know that he would not have chosen it." Like I would ever ask Commander Garrith about the details of his and Jo's separation. Like he would ever share the information.

I wrap an arm around Jo's slender shoulders. I think this is where I've found a middle ground with Garrith. We've both protected Jo and lost her. It sits heavy on my heart to know how deeply he understands my agony. He knew I needed her. But unlike me, he never received a surprise visit.

Outside, Jo breathes in the fresh, night air. Tears prickle from behind my eyes when I spot hers already glassy. Her breathing becomes ragged and remaining positive in this moment becomes nearly impossible.

I hold her to my chest. "Have I ever told you about when I first found you in the Arid?"

She sniffles and squeaks, "You said the birds were waiting on me to die so they could eat me."

"I mean after that." Garrith comes up out of the stables, guiding Stoic. I look up at his eyes and he stops, keeping his distance, allowing us this goodbye. "Well, when I first found you, your lips were cracked. You were starving and beyond dehydrated. I wasn't sure my efforts would keep you alive." She looks up at me and I cradle her cheek. "I started with water. And twenty minutes later you were smiling. You didn't have any parents. And you didn't have any teeth. And you looked up at me and said, "Hello, I'm Jo Thumont, what's your name?""

She starts shaking from giggles in my arms, and above her head, I can see Garrith's shoulders shaking too. "Thumont?" she laughs.

"It took a few months for your two front teeth to come in after I found you. You couldn't pronounce the D in Dumont." This keeps the laughter flowing. And I know it's okay to let her go; I'll see her again. "Jo, you are so strong. I knew it twenty minutes after finding you in the Arid that you would be okay. And as conditioned as I am to worry about you, deep down, I know it's in vain. Your warrior spirit has kept you alive as much as I have." Her white teeth shine. Her beautiful smile contradicts the tears that flow from her eyes.

She tucks her head under my chin and squeezes my ribs. "I love you, Jemma."

My voice doesn't quiver, and my breathing is steady when I grin down at her and say, "I love you too."

CHAPTER 31

L ast night I watched Garrith put Jo on his horse and ride back to Megara. It was painful but this time I will not fall apart. Jo is safe. And we both have our duties, hers are there and mine are here.

I can't dwell.

Despite every instinct to unleash my emotions and destroy anything in the way of my reunion with Jo, I will hold steady. I will do what I have to. As Garrith likes to remind me, "Play nice."

When Garrith met us outside I had so many questions for him, but it wasn't the time, nor did I have the words to express my curiosity. Garrith is only a mystery to me. I know so little about him but so much. I know what Jo has told me. But in my mind, Garrith and Nikolai are two different people. The more I find out about him, the more confused it leaves me. I'm also confused about the amount of time I spend thinking of him.

Don't.

I shake him from my thoughts.

Today we will receive the ins and outs of our mission. The

attack on the Howlers has to go smoothly. General Pinnell stands before the lot of us, his face holding a focus that keeps everyone quiet and attentive. The room is silent and full of anticipation. General Pinnell finally begins, "We have five days before we initiate our attack on the Howlers. Each squad will be receiving their specific mission. I am very proud of the progress I've seen in all of you over our time training. I am confident that every squad here is capable of working together and completing their objective without issue." He scans the room. "Maps and objectives have been distributed to each squad leader. Please follow your leader to a table, and they will walk you through it." Garrith is our squad leader and he won't be here until tomorrow night. "Squad ten! Stay put where you are, you'll be getting direction from me today since Commander Garrith isn't here."

General Pinnell lays out a map of Sahir. We are located South of Groth. On this map is a river that flows from the Howler territory to Megara. The map can't be accurate because the old river dried up before the Blight hit. General Pinnell starts grabbing pieces to add to the map. He marks our location and then places something that looks like a bridge near the top of the river. "This is a dam. The Howlers built this eight years ago, cutting off the water supply to Audun." That would explain the river drying up as quickly as it did. "We are going to bomb the dam. And you are the leading squad to do it."

There's silence until Enon says, "Fuck, yeah."

Pinnell doesn't acknowledge Enon's interruption. "The dam is heavily protected and without numerous distractions, we don't have a shot of getting close to it. The other squads will unleash a series of smaller attacks East of the dam. This will pull many of the Howlers from their posts. Commander Garrith will be there for half of the mission and you are to trust his judgment fully. This mission is the most dangerous as we have never gotten close enough to the dam to properly plan an attack. You will be acting on instinct and improvisation."

The anxiety swirling around our heads is palpable, and Enon's confidence is knocked down a peg. "So we are supposed to bomb a dam that we don't know the layout of or its level of fortification?"

"No, you follow Commander Garrith's orders. He knows the area better than anyone here. He's been sent on many mapping expeditions, but without distractions, weakening the dam's protection, and a full squad behind him, it's limited the depth of his research."

"So we're like the guinea pigs?" Tatum guesses.

"No. You are trained soldiers. And you are expected to handle this mission as such."

Uncertainty settles between us. I just have to survive. I have to survive to see Jo again.

"You have three days to come to terms with this. In three days, you start on the two and a half day journey to the dam. In the mornings we will go over Arid survival skills. In the afternoons we train and brush up on signs. If you are in an area where silence is a necessity, and given that we haven't gotten very close to the dam, it's a real possibility, signs will allow you to communicate with your squad mates."

Pinnell looks at Tatum, waves his finger in a circle next to his head, and looks at her expectantly.

Slowly she says, "Let's leave." It sounds more like a question.

"Rally point. There are fifteen motions we use on the battlefield. It's your job to know them. Use them often with your squad. If on the field you motion correctly, it won't matter if your squad mate doesn't know them."

A question floats around in my mind. I don't want to ask. I thought someone else would have asked the question for me by now. "You said Garr—Commander Garrith would be with us for *half* the mission? What does that mean?"

"Yes. We are planting two bombs on the dam. One of them will be closer to the East side and Commander Garrith is in charge of it. So when the dam falls and the water flows—"

I cut him off, "He'll be on the wrong side of the river."

"Yes." Pinnell eyes each one of us, "You'll be making the trip home without him. It will be up to you when and where you stop. The trip will likely be shorter on the way back with the Howlers on your heels."

Garrith will be trapped on the other side. And the word river is a wild understatement. Before the dam, Audun civilians said the river was wider than Audun itself, several parts too wide to see to the other side.

"How will he get back to Moria?" There's a rise in my voice. Irrational hysterics are clawing at my throat.

"Commander Garrith has his own orders in place. As long as it all goes as planned, Commander Garrith will join us back in Moria the day after your return."

He's not going to share the details. And I suppose he doesn't have to. I try to swallow but my mouth is dry. Panic holds me against my will and I have yet to know why.

"Squad ten, official first string in Moria!" Enon has been hooting and hollering since we opened Tatum's bottle of wine.

After dinner, Tatum suggested a trip behind the throne room. Cynrad stressed that it was a bad idea and I agreed with him. But Tatum and Enon make the most convincing arguments. *We could be dead in days, our mission is the most dangerous, we should celebrate it, this could be our very last bottle of wine together.*

They aren't wrong, I take pride in being part of the A team, though I'm sure the choice was made despite my involvement. And this time together makes Moria a million times more bearable.

I thought that the off and on again cycle between Cyn and Tatum would cause awkwardness in the squad. But Enon reminded me they've been doing this dance for a year and even if it's not genuine, they make it work somehow. The breakup still seems fresh but Enon assumes they're on the mend. Again.

Tatum asks me in a hushed tone, "Do you know what Reid's mission is?"

Guilt hits me in the face. Reid has a mission too. He could leave and never return. "I haven't spoken to him," I admit.

"Good. Fuck that asshole. And his dad," Tatum spits the words.

"Whoa ladies," Enon responds to Tatum's outburst. "Who's an asshole?"

"*Prince* Cerastes," Tatum mocks his title.

Enon and Cynrad look at me with sorrow and understanding. The moments are rare, but the fine line they both have their lips pressed into and the dimples carved deep into their cheeks, have them look every bit of the identical twins they are.

"Has he tried to talk to you?" Cynrad asks.

"Not since Garrith helped me kick him out of my room that night I learned of his *orders*."

"Garrith was there? How did that go?"

"Weird. He wasn't in his usual broody attitude. He looked at me with pity. Turns out, I like him better when he's pissed at me. I'm not sure where I stand with him. I also don't know where I stand with Reid. He wants to talk, I'm just not ready to deal with that." Once the words are out of my mouth I'm embarrassed for oversharing.

Tatum blows the hair out of her eyes and hands me the

bottle. Yes. This won't fix my problems, but it'll make them seem smaller. For a while.

I take a swig and learn that this is not wine at all. It burns and I sputter half of the contents back up. All three of them break out into unrestrained belly laughs. "What is that?" I can't get the foul taste out of my mouth.

"A waste, it would seem." Enon laughs, gesturing to the liquid I spewed across the floor.

The laughter ceases first with Cynrad. He sits up and I follow his gaze to the doorway where Reid stands. Everyone else sees him when I do. My suspicion that this is a place we are not supposed to be is proven when Enon and Cynrad quickly stand.

The only one not bothered by Reid's presence is Tatum, who has ingested more of the foul liquid than all of us combined. "Your Highness," she drawls, "come to toy with our darling squad mate some more?"

"Tatum," Cynrad warns.

Reid looks at me, hurt flashing in and out of his eyes. Finally, he speaks, "It's late, we leave for the dam in a few days. I recommend you all find your way to your dorms."

"Not going to turn us in?" Tatum stands, unsteadily. "Or are you trying to get back on her good side?"

Cynrad wraps a sturdy arm around Tatum's waist and starts to guide her out of the room. Reid steps out of the way.

Enon is the next to move toward the door. He looks at me, unsure if he needs to stay with me. I tilt my head, directing him to the door, and smile at him. I can handle Reid.

Once we're completely alone Reid says, "Stealing from my father's stash?" He gestures to the open bottles.

"I'd say he owes me. Compensation for being a piece in his project."

Reid flares his nostrils. "I've been trying to talk to you for days. You have to let me explain."

"I don't have to do anything." My syllables are coated in acid. The anger I thought I had overcome surges forward.

"You're right. I know you're right. But if you hear me out, I believe we can save this. Just, please, tell me you'll hear me out." He rushes forward and grabs one of my hands. He turns it over, looks at my palms, and looks back up to my face. "I'm so sorry. I know you must feel betrayed. But it's not what you think."

I pull my hand from his. "Fine, I'll hear you out." In an instant, he's glowing. "But not tonight," I say. "You were right, it's late. I don't want to hash this out now. I'll come get you when I'm ready to talk."

I move to the door before saying, "Don't walk me to my room. Goodnight, Reid." Facing betrayal, contemplating murder, and considering forgiveness is exhausting.

CHAPTER 32

Reid pulls me away from training. He's putting cracks in my focus and of all the feelings I've had toward him in my time here, irritation has become a regular sensation. I have to refrain from physically shaking his grip off of me. I can't find my center and he's making things harder than they should be.

The scale is tipping and I don't know which side to add weight to. My balance is gone. I need to be steady. I need to stabilize.

I need a list.

Things I want:

-Safety and happiness for Jo

-Outside air and dips in the ocean

-To laugh with Tatum, Enon, and Cyn

-To get through this training lesson *uninterrupted*

I don't know what else I want. But I do know that I'm tired. I'm tired of my conflicted feelings toward Reid. The usual guilt that keeps my aggravation at bay has expired. I'm tired of anything getting in the way of my list of wants.

He pulls me around the corner, out of sight. It's darker here but any light in a mile radius reflects off Reid; he acts as a human flashlight with his bright hair and pale skin.

I speak first, "When I told you we could talk later, I didn't mean in the middle of training." The bite in my voice surprises me. I'll be conscious to dial it back.

His hands rake into his hair before he thinks better of it and grabs both of my shoulders. "You have to know, Jemma. You have to know that my feelings are real."

I've been avoiding. For days I've averted my eyes and busied my hands. I knew this conversation was coming. I just wanted to wait.

I've been waiting for myself. I thought the solution to my dilemma would reveal itself. But now I stand before Reid, unsure what I want or what I should tell him.

I decide to share only what I know is the truth. "You hurt me."

A crease of pain grows deep between his eyebrows. "I know. And I am guilty. That day we met in the throne room, when I took you on a tour, and when I stole treats for you, I'm guilty. It was part of the plan. I was following orders."

Even though I knew this, it still hurts having it confirmed.

"You were a," he hesitates and says it slowly, "project." Reid holds his breath awaiting my outburst. I remain still so he goes on, "But then we were at the beach and you were all conscious of your scars and all I could do was aw at your strength." He slides his hands over mine. "After that, I was so thankful for the orders to be around you. I wanted to know more. I wanted to be there for you. I wanted you to lean on me, and let me in." His hands come up to cup my face. Lightly his fingers press against the back of my neck while his thumbs tilt my face up and I have nowhere to look but at his beautiful face. "I should have told you. And even though I have to regain your trust, I'm thankful for my orders. They allowed me to know you. They allowed me to love you—" and he kisses me.

And it feels amazing to melt. It feels amazing to stop shouldering the storm around me. For a moment I can live here in this bliss, in the swirl of colors warming all the coldest parts of myself. The tingling his lips pass on to mine spreads. It flows down my neck, and sweeps off my shoulders, sending heat down my torso.

I bring my hands to his tunic and grab the fabric against his ribs. He pulls away and I groan in irritation. My annoyance is met with a chuckle.

Reid pulls my body flush against his. "Come to my room tonight," his voice is low, sending goosebumps down my spine.

And I know it's wrong. I know it's *definitely* wrong. But I'm nodding anyway.

When I rejoin my squad I can't get my mind right. I accept that I'm in over my head. But I don't know what I can do about it.

Pinnell's shoulders fall at my piss-poor excuse for a sparring match. My reaction time is slower today. The girl I face lands more punches than what my recent progress should allow. I try shaking the fog from my head.

Pinnell says the match is over.

"I'm fine!" I shout back. I have to find focus. We head to the dam tomorrow and I can't find an ounce of fight left in these muscles.

"I said, get the fuck off the mat, Shayde!" He turns away to observe other sparring mats and I know the conversation is over. My ribs will be bruised tomorrow and my ego is bruised today. I've never heard General Pinnell curse before.

Maybe being back outside will help me clear my head. Right now I'm not in it. I want to be held. I want to feel whole.

Tatum notices me looking a handful of sparring mats down

from us. She catches me just in time to witness Reid send a wink my way.

The look on her face sobers me. I keep my face innocuous.

Tatum cocks her head to the side and raises an eyebrow.

"What?" I feign innocence.

"Just making sure."

"Making sure of what?" She has my attention and she knows it.

"Making sure you don't need reminding." I know exactly where this is going and immediately regret asking. "You don't need a reminder that Reid is the son of a deceptive and power-hungry king? Or a reminder that the king ordered Reid to befriend you? Bed you? Fatten you up like a pig for slaughter?"

"Reid did not *bed* me."

Tatum sighs. "Is that all you got from what I said?"

She's getting under my skin. "I know what I'm doing." My voice holds enough conviction to sound exactly like a girl who absolutely does *not* know what she is doing. Tatum shakes her head and turns back to the mat. She thinks I'm weak, that I don't have a handle on whatever is going on between me and Reid. Before I know what I'm doing I'm reaching out, yanking her to look at me. "What is it you're accusing me of?"

Surprise flashes in her eyes and I know it's from my unwarranted hostility. She recovers quickly and meets me with the same fire. "I think you know exactly what I'm referring to."

I take a step, impossibly closer to her. "If I were you, I'd sort out my own relationship bullshit before sticking my nose in another."

Tatum scoffs. "Relationship?" Her face splits into a menacing smile. "I know better than to be in a relationship, especially not one as fucked up as yours. Trust me, Jemma. You don't want people to hear you call *being a pet to the throne* a relationship."

I lunge. My hands are at her throat for half a second before she's got me pinned flat on my stomach with my hands caught behind me. She whispers in my ear, "I knew you were weak, I didn't know you were stupid too."

I writhe beneath her. Suddenly her weight disappears. I flip over to find General Pinnell holding Tatum by the arm. "If you two can't get your personal problems sorted out before tomorrow, your mission is doomed. Do you want to cause the death of any of your squad mates?"

"Only hers," Tatum bites.

I prop myself up on my elbows and stare her down.

General Pinnell orders Tatum to training quarters cleaning and I'm sent to the mess hall to help finish cooking dinner and clean the kitchen. I roll off the floor and find disdain coating the eyes of every observer I set my gaze on.

I go to the mess hall, eager to be done with this day, eager to go to the only place underground where I'm not a disappointment. Only 300 trays to clean away from Reid.

CHAPTER 33

My moves are sluggish. I can't run, can't move my arms. I try and try but I'm suspended. The water is slowing me down.

I reach but it takes days for my body to react as it's supposed to. The back of Jo's head is bobbing as she runs away. She is quick. Something is wrong. I don't want to waste time looking back to see what she is running from. I need to follow her.

But in the time I take one step, she has taken twenty. She's not stuck underwater the way I am. I will my arms to pump, my lungs to expand, my legs to extend. But I can count handfuls of seconds before any of my appendages respond.

I'm losing her.

I have to be faster but my body isn't on the same page as my mind.

There's a glimpse of light and relief when I realize she will make it. Jo will survive, but she will have to do it without me. She looks back to find me.

"Jemma," she says, or maybe she screams, but I'm too far gone.

All my emotions contradict one another. I find solace in knowing I've done everything I could for her. But she's not ready. She's not ready to tackle this life without protection.

My pleas get stuck in my throat, blocked by the water.

I'm choking.

I cough and heave and gasp my way back into consciousness.

Reid's hands rest on my shoulders. "Jemma!"

I blink away the water trapped in my eyes until his face comes into focus. His eyebrows pinch together while keeping his eyes wide open. I release a ragged breath; the pain in my throat tells me I must have been screaming.

He sits back on the bed, keeping one hand on my hip, allowing me the space to control my breathing. The feeling that I need to apologize bubbles up, but before I can start he says, "What was happening?"

"It was Jo."

He tilts his head up, resting the back of it against the headboard. He grabs my hand, and runs his fingers over the lines in my palms, "I'll go start a bath."

There's comfort in not having to explain the nightmare any further. When he enters the bathroom, completely out of sight, I let the tears fall. It's brief, but the passing of tears and minutes allow me to create distance from the dream. Thankfully, it starts to fade.

Reid's head pokes out from the bathroom door. "Ready?"

I nod and get out of bed. When I enter the bathroom, full of steam from the hot water, I expect him to leave.

He stands in the doorway. I give him a quizzical look, and he takes a step forward, shutting the door behind him. For a split second, I feel caged. My heart speeds up when he takes another step closer and says, "I have to leave soon. My squad's departure time is an hour from now."

The bathtub is nearly full so he reaches around me and shuts off the water. The silence is suddenly consuming. The only sound besides our breathing is the drip, drip of the faucet.

Reid studies my face as he comes impossibly closer, his chest only an inch from my own. His hands trail down my arms until grabbing handfuls of my blue nightgown. He bunches the fabric at my hips and whispers, "Arms up."

Alarms sound, and somehow, I want him everywhere and nowhere. I can't decipher my feelings from my head, heart, or hormones. I don't know what we are or what is true. I stand on a tightrope and use the faith that he loves me as my balancing pole.

He's leaving in an hour. He'll be a part of a mission, and so will I. He could die. I could die. And a switch flips when I think of the potential tragedy this expedition could entail.

My arms rise.

In a swift motion, my gown is pulled up, away, and thrown to the sink. I'm almost completely bare, except for my underwear. I attempt to move my arms, to shield my breasts, but Reid's hands gently hold my wrists. "Beautiful," he breathes.

Warning bells commence and I force my mind to quiet them. He pulls my wrists up until they rest on his shoulders. My hands come together on the back of his neck. When he's sure I won't pull away, he runs his hands back down the length of my arms across my shoulders. His fingertips glide down my back and rest at the waistband of my underwear.

Goosebumps erupt on my skin. Reid's forehead falls to the nook between my neck and shoulder. His breath is hot and tickles the skin of my breast. Muscles tighten, and he turns his face into my neck, runs his lips over the delicate skin, and whispers, "God, I want you."

He backs me up until my bottom collides with the vanity. The cool countertop sobers me. And mixed with the steam in the air, I feel suddenly light-headed. "I know you want me, too." Uncertainty runs in my veins. He brings his lips to mine but when his tongue tries to open my mouth I swipe my face to the side. My stomach twists itself into knots and though it's empty, I can feel a session of heaving coming on. My breathing is ragged and irregular and when I turn to find shock and confusion on his face, dread and embarrassment spread across my skin.

Reid steps away. His eyes close, lips are pursed, and his hands reach up to latch behind his head. He will say something. But when he finally opens his eyes, he finds me with my arms folded. I can tell my body is unconsciously caving on itself but there's nothing I can do to stop it.

He averts his gaze. With a sigh, he leaves the bathroom, closing the door on his way out.

I don't know what's wrong with me. I wipe the fog from the mirror. My eyes are crazed and my skin is a splotchy mess. When I get into the bath I'm thankful the water has cooled. I need cool water and air; I need space to breathe and think. I feel for Reid, but every time he is close to me, he's too close to me. If he had it his way, I would ignore my unease, the warning in my gut, he would have me ignore my instincts. But it's my instincts that have allowed me to survive this long. I have to trust my gut if I want to continue working to find ways to protect Jo.

I get out of the bath and get dressed in my normal tunic, belt, and pants. Reid is supposed to leave soon so I don't waste time getting dressed. I want to tell him goodbye.

I find him sitting on the edge of the bed, his elbows resting on his knees, his chin on his fists.

"I just thought," the fists under his chin shift into fingers rubbing his temples, "I just thought the worst was behind us. I thought you liked me." He stops fidgeting and drops his hands in his lap. For once, he seems completely resigned. Guilt pulls me to him. Guilt pulls my hands to his face. I hold his face and wish for him to have patience with me.

I wait for him to open his eyes before I say, "Today we go to war. I can't bear the thought of you going into today thinking I don't have feelings for you. Because I do. And I'm sorry for my retreat." I close my eyes, and press my forehead to his. "There's so many ways to split myself. I have to be good for Jo. I should be good for Moria. I want to be good for you. You are my most conflicted indulgence. How can I allow myself to feel the things you make me feel while keeping a handle on what I have to do?" I press my lips to his. It's a feather of a kiss; light, but reassuring. "Wait for me. And after this mission, come back to me."

Reid looks up at me from under heavy lids. He smiles, pushing my guilt to the back burner. But it could never really be gone, as I'm still not certain I mean the things I've said.

Reid left a while ago. I started getting my travel pack ready. My nerves are already shot and the need to get out of this room and clear my head outweighs the need to pack. I close the door behind me, my to-do list will still be here after a walk.

I see Tatum further down the hall. I lift my hand. It's a white flag, an apology, a call for peace. She looks at me, doesn't lift her hand, doesn't bat an eye, and turns away.

I know I deserve it. I know that the things I said were unfair.

When I walk up to Enon, eager to learn how to make amends, he seems jumpy and uncomfortable. "I don't know,

Jemma. The whole thing was fucked up." His eyes flash up to something above my head.

"I just don't think she has the right to accuse me when she doesn't have all the facts." I cross my arms.

"Yeah, well," he tosses his shower bag over his shoulder, "I'm not getting in the middle of it. I hope whatever is going on you sort out before the dam. We can't afford any petty business out there." He doesn't wait for my response and walks back to his room.

And suddenly it's my first day here all over again. I'm the outcast. I might have made friends with Tatum, Enon, and Cynrad. But they've been together for years. Seeking support from people who have never owed me loyalty was foolish. Embarrassment burns my cheeks. I want to run back to the embrace of Reid, someone who wants me and listens to me. I know it would be wrong to show up as he is taking on his mission. He has his duties to report to, and I can't interrupt those because I'm being shunned by my squad members.

It's going to be a long day.

We leave in two hours for day one of our mission travel. And perhaps, during our journey, I can figure out how to make amends.

I go to the mess hall to eat breakfast. Sustenance is vital today. I clean my plate despite my lack of appetite. None of the food has taste, and I'm not sure I'm in control of my body. Numbness seeps in and I don't have the willpower to fight it anymore.

Just as I allow my mind to retreat, to check out for the day, the hair stands on the back of my neck.

In a second I'm alert.

I can feel Garrith's presence. My body feels it before my eyes see him or my nose smells him.

I turn to find that he's just entered the mess hall. He's moving toward me. I hold my breath.

But, no.

He's only passing me on his way to his room. He's back from his journey and it makes me anxious and adds a lightness in my stomach and I don't know how to navigate these feelings. I feel pulled a handful of different ways but every direction that doesn't lead to him pinches and plucks at the strings around my heart.

He brought Jo back to me, though it was for a day, it was needed. And he did it against council order.

I have to say something. I have time before we set out. My feet are moving before my mind can catch up with me.

It's rare that I get to look at him like this, his back to me, unaware of my presence. His bag hangs over his shoulder. He's twenty feet ahead of me, his feet moving with a purpose. I'm sure he eagerly awaits his shower. The idea unlocks curiosity and I wish I could be there, to witness him remove his shemagh, to see his face. I wonder what his skin looks like. My steps falter and my face heats.

I stop and look down at my feet, suddenly aware that I was on a mission to talk to Garrith and have no idea what I would say. Moisture collects in my palms so I wipe them on my tunic.

When I look up, Garrith is no longer walking to his room. He stands facing me, his green eyes like beams looking into my thoughts.

My head falls empty, he hasn't said anything but I know he's expecting me to speak. I try, "I, um, how was your trip?"

His eyebrows become impossibly heavier as he sees through my question. He says nothing and allows me to squirm for several more seconds before saying, "It was fine. Jo's friends were happy to have her back." He moves his head to the side, attempting to gauge my purpose for following him.

"That's good." I clasp my hands, unclasp my hands, pinch the skin between my thumb and pointer finger.

He nods and waits. I say nothing. When I look into his eyes, confusion swirls in the storm green. He nods again and turns to keep walking to his room.

"Thank you!" Words keep falling as he looks at me again, "for bringing Jo. I didn't know. I wasn't sure how to picture her. Sometimes I would think of her crying to sleep every night because I wasn't there. And I just—" I know I'm telling him more than I intended and I need to pull it back. "I guess I just wanted to thank you. You didn't have to get her, but you did."

Everything comes out staggered. This encounterer is completely unfamiliar with grace.

He cocks his head to the side and says, "Is your bag packed yet for the next couple of days?"

What the fuck?

My eyebrows shoot into my hairline. "Yes, well almost. I still have to—"

"Pack. Your. Bag." With that, he walks away, leaving me to wonder what kind of strange wind derailed that conversation.

I don't know what I expected, or why I had to thank him today, or ever. I can't read Garrith and I don't think I ever will. He brought Jo to me, an act of kindness, but blows me off every chance he gets.

I'm spiraling and have no one here to throw me a rope.

Winnie has unofficially become my horse. Since our close call at the beach, I've been sneaking to the stables to check on her. No one says anything when I lead her out of the stables. As great a horse as Gideon is, he's several years older than our company and if we find trouble, his lower threshold for speed creates unnecessary risk.

I attach my pack and get on the saddle. The usual banter among my squad mates has gone quiet today. It's unlikely but it would be ideal if today's travels don't require much communication.

For hours we head North, following the old ridge of the empty river. In an attempt to remain out of the way, I stay at the back of the pack. I know we are getting close to Audun. If we stay near the old river, we shouldn't have to see it. I haven't allowed myself to think about my parents in months. I don't want to break that streak today, but I continue to find my gaze falling to the left of us, in case there's a recess in the dunes.

After my tenth stolen glance, I turn back to find Commander Garrith stopped out ahead of us. His eyes are on mine when he says, "You have five minutes. Get a drink, and tend to your horse. We're four hours from tonight's camp and we won't stop until we get there."

He means it.

We don't stop again.

We also don't speak when we set up camp. Not a word is passed while Cynrad builds a fire.

That is until Enon pulls a bottle of amber-colored alcohol. He passes out wooden cups to everyone.

After that, conversation buds among the squad. The only interaction I receive is from Enon when he offers me a cup. The taste is offensive but the burn starts to warm me up, loosen my chest, and calm my nerves. So I drink the rest.

CHAPTER 34

"I shouldn't have said those things to you." I catch Tatum by surprise, interrupting her gaze into the fire. I motion with my head to the available spot next to her. She nods so I sit down. "I don't know why I attacked you like that. I think you were just saying the things I knew, the things I was trying to ignore. I guess I didn't want to hear it and the anger I had at myself, I threw it all at you."

She looks at me and for once her intimidating demeanor seems vulnerable. She ponders my words before responding, "I shouldn't have pushed you. I knew what was happening and I let pride get the best of me. And you were right too. All the talk about relationships, I'm in one. I've been in one. And pride has kept me from enjoying it."

She looks across the fire and I follow her line of sight. Cynrad sits by himself, his eyes already on Tatum.

She sighs, smiles, and looks at me. "Jemma. If you find it," rolls her eyes and says, "Love or whatever. Do what you have to. Make it work. Even if you have a bitch in your face telling you you're ridiculous. Trust your gut. Even more important, trust your heart." Across the fire, I watch Cynrad stand and Tatum follows suit. "And if you ever tell anyone I said that, I'll kill you." Her expression is stern until it breaks into the biggest smile I've ever seen. She pats me on the head. "See you tomorrow, Shayde."

With that, she leaves me. She reaches out and grabs Cynrad's hand on their way to their tent. I don't look around to see who witnessed her display of affection. They never mattered anyway.

Dawn is upon us. The sun has yet to break over the sand, but the sky has hues of lavender, ensuring that day is on its way.

I'm breaking down my tent when Enon rolls out of his. His groans and stretches are as expected, exaggerated. When he reaches for the tie on the opposite side of the tent, his tunic catches on the stick, ripping the material. He stops, stares at his shirt, and puts his hand through a hole in the fabric that starts at his armpit and ends under his ribs. He gives me a tight-lipped smile of disappointment. It shows off his dimples and for a second he's an adorable, ten year old child.

I don't have to say a word. I hold out my hand as he sheds the tunic and tosses it my way. I fetch the mending kit from my pack and get to work.

"Thanks." He has a seat next to me. "So where did you learn how to sew?"

"My mom. I've stitched together a lot of shemaghs, tunics, tarps—" I trail off. Jo always seemed to bring me something torn during our days in the Arid. Jo was mesmerized by it. She even had a sewing poem. Whether or not it had anything to do with the craft was beyond me. But she always said it.

I look at Enon and smile. As I stitch the fabric I recite:

"What is broken,
Sure will mend.
If not, sometimes,
We must pretend.
For if our hope,
do ever perish.
There's not a thing for us to cherish."

A booming voice knocks me from my work. "Do you think that words will save us from tragedy?" Garrith stands on the other side of the dying fire. "Do you think, because you run extra laps in the morning, you'll make it out of this alive?" His voice cuts through the air between us. And he's moving.

He steps over the fire and continues his verbal assault, "You land yourself here, you walked out into the Arid with Jo and crumbled nearly to nothing, you come into Moria like it's a vacation, like King Cerastes is your savior." Enon stands while I stay seated. I don't trust my legs.

Garrith is right in front of me but his words sound like they're echoing down a tunnel. Like I'm screaming them at myself from a million miles away.

Enon presses a hand to Garrith's chest. "What's your problem?" All the usual lightness in his voice is gone.

Garrith brushes away his hand and brings his face near mine while he sneers, "You think some pretty verses are going to protect us? You're doomed. And so is Jo. And that's on you."

Every word out of his mouth is a nail in my coffin. Garrith walks away. And keeps walking. He walks until we can't see him, until the dunes swallow his silhouette.

He hates me.

He *hates* me.

The months of training, the pride I imagined he took in me, the hints of smiles, the solace I thought I had found with the

Commander, all reduced to delusion. My imagination allowed me to construct a person I believed to have warmed up to me.

I'm a fool. I'm a fool. I'm a fool.

My hands shake. My progress is slower now. My stability is unreliable. Stitch. Mend. Piecing fabric back together is therapeutic. This makes sense. The fabric is torn but we can put it back together. I cling to the certainty. This makes sense. Keep going.

Keep going until the tunic is mended or until my hands cease to shake. Whichever comes first.

I won't think about Garrith and how everything he's done to me, done for me, doesn't make any sense at all. I won't think about the times he's saved me. I won't think about how he went against orders to grant me time with Jo. It doesn't make sense for a person with such detest for another to make such gestures. It doesn't make sense but I think about it anyway. My hands still. Is it all a game? Is it a grand series of events designed to disorient me? He convinces me he hates me, to convince me he cares, to convince me I'm nothing. I'm spiraling and get the feeling this is what he wants. Whatever game he's orchestrated, I know I'm on the losing end.

I wasn't going to think about it. I look at my still hands. I look at my unfinished running stitch.

Keep going.

Busy hands, quiet mind.

Busy hands, quiet mind.

Busy hands, quiet mind.

"Jemma," a whisper.

Busy hands, quiet mind.

"Jemma." A statement.

Busy hands, quiet mind.

Busy hands, quiet mind.

Busy hands, quiet mind.

A sigh comes from close behind me.

Busy hands, quiet mind.

It's finished. This makes sense. The fabric was torn so I mended it and now it's as good as new. Peace settles. It starts at my skin and seeps into my bloodstream sending relief to all corners of my being. I turn around, ready for whatever new wrench he wants to throw into my plans, but Garrith is walking away.

CHAPTER 35

At first, I thought we had made it. The top of the dam was peeking out over the nearest dune, and I knew we were here. But no matter how much we trotted along, the dam didn't get any closer.

I look to Tatum, still trying to avoid contact with Garrith. She gives me an understanding nod and says, "It's bigger than anything you've ever seen. The river is nearly as wide as Audun. I'm still not sure how the five of us are going to take it down." That doesn't help the nausea.

The closer we get, while still being at least a couple miles away, the taller the structure grows. Garrith uses one of his hands to signal to the rest of us to stop. He gets out a telescope that looks old enough to go back a few generations. He signals for us to dismount. We gather in a circle and Garrith says, "The Howlers are crawling all around the dam. There are at least fifty. Bombs should sound in a couple of hours." In a couple of hours, the sun will have gone down. For some reason, I have been picturing us doing this during the daytime. "We hunker down here until the Howlers are pulled away." Garrith moves a rotted tree trunk behind him revealing four crates of what I presume to be explosives. Garrith hands one crate's contents to Enon and another to Cynrad and instructs them to pack it behind their saddles. Garrith takes the remaining explosives from the other two crates and attaches them to Stoic.

He then unrolls a roughly sketched map. It looks like one of Ray's pieces of toddler artwork. An unexpected pang shoots through my chest.

Garrith starts sketching over the sad piece and Enon interrupts, "Is this all we have to go off of?"

Garrith ignores him and continues to sketch. "This is the closest I've ever gotten myself, the first time being two weeks ago when I brought the explosives. Pass around the telescope and look for yourself, but this is how I'm going to explain the game plan, regardless of you pissing your pants." I watch over his shoulder as the picture grows clearer. When he's content he spins it around. "We are here," and points to the bottom left side of the page. At the top center, he's drawn the length of the dam. In the empty river, he's drawn a scribbled rectangle at the base of the structure. "At the bottom of the dam, there's a massive pool. On either side of the pool are two cave-like structures. You four are in charge of getting those bombs inside the West cave. I'll take the East cave. The caves are in the empty riverbed. You have two minutes from lighting the fuse to get out of the river. Once it blows and the dam falls, the water will wash anything in the river away."

Enon fidgets. Cynrad, noticing his anxiety, rubs a hand on Enon's shoulder.

"How far into the cave do we light it?" Tatum is all business.

"Use your gut, you're as familiar with the structure as I am." Garrith suddenly seems aware of the lack of confidence spreading throughout the group and he says, "You were chosen for this. Moria chose you because there is not a better squad to complete this mission. Plus you have me." Cynrad snorts.

Garrith shows us how to light the bombs. We are supposed to stay on our horses no matter what so that if we find trouble, our getaway will be swift. Tatum is supposed to assist Cyn and Enon in the cave to ensure they get their bombs lit. I'm supposed to wait at the entrance, keep a lookout, and signal to Garrith once we've lit the fuse so he can follow suit. "Supposed to," lacks the confidence in this mission that my nerves would appreciate right about now.

When I try to push that I can handle a duty of higher importance, Garrith dismisses me without a second thought.

We get acquainted with the bombs and secure our packs.

I think I hear something in the distance but no one else turns to look. Except Garrith, who eyes me and nods.

Just then, loud booms echo in the distance. It's too far away to see any explosions, but I can feel them rattle up my spine. Unease gathers in my shoulders. When the bombs go off at the dam, I'm almost certain it will bust my eardrums.

Enon goes around the circle and bumps knuckles with everyone before getting on his horse. Cynrad pats me on the shoulder. Tatum punches me in the arm. "Don't get silly out there, Shayde."

Everyone is on their horse. Garrith looks through the telescope, watching, waiting for the dam to be clear enough.

We wait. I count.

I've swallowed nine times before he gives the signal.

We're off.

Winnie is faster than any of the horses in Moria but I stay at the back of the back. A mile out, Garrith splits off. He rides down the steep slope of the river and starts to cross.

I haven't spotted a Howler. Surely a few explosions wouldn't justify the entire protection of the dam taking off to investigate. The hair on the back of my neck stands as we come to the river's edge. I've lost sight of Garrith.

This can't be right. This can't be empty.

Sweat rolls down my neck and under my clothes. I start to itch. I want to turn around and go back.

I'm ashamed of my thoughts. We've come this far. For all this time I've trained. I can't turn back now and I shouldn't want to.

Our horses gently handle the slope. The top of the dam looms above us. Once in the belly of the river, the dam's height appears taller than the tallest mountains. The pool stretches out before us, black water reflecting the stars shining in the sky. It's eerie, the perfect reflection in the pool. Not a single ripple. If I look long enough, I can convince myself it really is the sky.

Get in, light the bomb, get out. I look out across the pool for Garrith. I still can't find him. Panic is surging in my blood.

What if he doesn't show? Do we still light the fuse? If we still bomb the dam, what if the river washes him away?

Tatum reaches the entrance of the cave. She stops, listens, then motions for us to move forward.

I shake my head and mouth *Garrith*.

Their heads turn to look at the other cave. From this distance, it's difficult to see if he's even over there. The night blankets everything in darkness. Stoic and Garrith both are dressed in black and I feel like this could have been a more thought-out part of the mission. I guess that's why he has the telescope, and we're just supposed to trust that he sees my signal.

Tatum shrugs and motions the boys onward.

This is where I stay.

I watch them from the entrance. Watch for signs of Garrith across the pool.

I'm a sitting duck and I can't do anything about it.

The cave is dark while the boys undo their ties on the explosives. They're lowered to the ground and Tatum takes the fuse, lighter in hand, and nods at me. I strike a match and light the miniature torch Garrith gave me to use as the signal. I wave the lit torch and pray to God he sees it.

I turn back to Tatum as she lights the fuse. Sparks fly and she drops the length, ready to run. But the sparks emit a light on the cave, lighting up the walls around them.

A gasp gets lodged in my throat as rows of Howlers come into view. Shadows are cast across their gray faces.

As if on command, all yellow eyes snap open. Every muscle in my body freezes. Tatum, Cynrad, and Enon are barreling back out of the cave. Enon's horse knocks into Winnie and she rears back. My grip on the reins is weak and I can't clutch back onto them before I'm falling off her back.

I land with a thud on my shoulder. And it takes a moment to catch my breath and roll out of position.

Scrambling to my feet, I notice the Howlers have started moving toward the opening in the cave. Their moves are slow at first as if they've only just woken from a long sleep. Winnie is already nearing the crest of the river, following close behind Tatum and the boys. I need to get up there. I start to run.

My squad has panic-stricken eyes.

And I see it. If I run up the side of the river, I expose my squad's location to the swarm of Howlers closing in behind me.

If I make it out of the river, I'll bring fifty Howlers with me, ready to slaughter my squad. I slow down before I reach the incline.

Cynrad's eyes widen from under his floppy bangs.

His horse begins to step back down in the embankment. The other two understand and move with him.

And I'm not sure if it's the strength in my voice making an appearance for once or the resignation in my eyes, but they listen when I scream, "No!"

An explosion blasts to my right knocking me face down in the cracked ground.

Sound doesn't exist.

Only this ringing.

My head splits in half, from one ear to the other. My jaw locks and I'm sure I'm chipping my top teeth on my bottom teeth.

I seal my eyelids shut, anticipating the water. And at least I didn't endanger my friends. Tatum, Cynrad, and Enon are all accounted for. My only loose end is Garrith.

Garrith.

My eyes fly wide open. Where I thought I would find a compromised dam, there's only a large crack spanning over halfway across the concrete. Smaller cracks break away from the aperture. And eerie quiet falls upon this borrowed time.

We need the second bomb to go off. I need to know where Garrith is.

Without Winnie, I'm not sure I can outrun the Howlers. But I'm out of options.

I run toward the East cave.

One step in front of the other.

Don't look back. I don't need to. I know they follow me.

Another step.

Another.

Another.

Faster.

Faster.

The closer I get, the better I can see.

I start hearing my labored breaths, it's sobering, and I realize my hearing has returned.

I fail and look back.

My stomach sinks when I see more Howlers pouring out of the entrance.

Every second that passes is another five Howlers on my trail, and in a few more seconds I'll be guiding a hundred Howlers, to where, I'm not sure.

Understanding of this predicament settles in my bones. I'm suddenly tired from the sprints.

I'm not going to make it. Perhaps I've done my job. I've drawn the Howlers away from the group. Please let the dam blow. Let it wash us away. Let it take us out.

There's a crashing sound. But it's not the dam.

Garrith is at the river's edge. He bangs his sword against a small building. "Come on!"

What the fuck?

"Shayde!" Garrith's eyes are wide, in warning.

I turn my head and in my peripheral, I can make out a spindly hand reaching for the back of my tunic. I unsheathe my dagger and before its sharp nail can graze me, I slice across its wrist.

It's momentarily thrown. Its long, gray fingers from its other hand come up to hold its wrist as it bows over me, giving me the perfect angle to swipe my dagger across its throat. It tumbles over, nearly taking me with it.

Behind its billowing fabric is movement, not dark like the Howlers, and definitely faster. He comes into view.

Cynrad.

Has to be a hero.

He soars down the west side of the river. He's behind the Howlers; they haven't seen him yet. I scream to go back. God let him hear me. He can still turn around. He can make it.

But I lose sight of him as the group of Howlers from the cave are all moving in on me, swallowing the rest of my limited vision.

I reach the east side of the river but the incline forces me to dig with my hands into the ground. I climb on all fours. Some of the ground is hardened and I jam my fingers, trying to claw into the surface. My fingertips split and blood gathers in the lines of my palms.

Up. Up. Up.

Faster.

My eye level comes over the river's edge. Garrith and Stoic are seconds away, Garrith's eyes trained on mine. His expressions are always so hidden that he's never revealed more than a handful of emotions. Maybe that's why I feel a new weight. True fear creeps into my senses because shock and pain are painted across Garrith's eyes.

He's thrown from Stoic's back.

An unnerving howl slices through the air.

A scream is lodged in my throat when a Howler steps out from a cluster of dead trees. Its eyes shine a brighter yellow than the others. *Mindless Howler*. Mindless being how Jo described them. This Howler wields a sword.

Its movements are swift and accurate.

It is certainly not mindless.

And it is not alone.

Another Howler comes into view. It carries daggers.

I can't get there quick enough. Like I'm stuck in the mud. I'm stuck underwater again, my movements are too slow. I have at least twenty feet left to go.

Garrith is up, swords drawn. And I don't have time to

breathe a sigh of relief because another explosion bounces off my eardrums.

This time cracks surge up and across the dam from the east cave. There's a rattling moan from the structure and water starts to spew from the center of the dam. It's going to come down.

The triumph never reaches me. Victory is replaced with dread.

Cynrad.

Cynrad is smack in the middle of the empty river.

My brain stalls and I look to Garrith for guidance but focus just in time to see a sword become buried in his side.

This time the scream escapes my lips and the dagger Howler whips its head in my direction.

The Howler's fingers are too swift and I'm a second late to register the flick of his hand.

The dagger goes flying. His aim is perfect as it sails to my chest.

I wish I weren't a coward.

I close my eyes.

CHAPTER 36

Death. It's here. This is how I will go. And I will bring with me the only person in the world capable of protecting Jo. Garrith has saved me more in the past few months than anyone else has in my whole life. He's saved Jo. But meeting me will be his death sentence. I've ruined him.

This can't be it.

Can't be it.

Can't be it.

Make it stop.

Let me think. Let me *think*.

Garrith. Garrith sticking his neck out for me. Garrith taking the time to work with me, instruct me, and prepare me. He would have been fine if I had made different decisions. All he's done for me, reduced to nothing because in the end, looking out for me will be what kills him. Garrith. Nikolai Garrith. Think of Jo. Think of the news reaching her.

My heart breaks at the same time desperation drowns me.

You are more powerful than you know. Trust your mind. Trust your voice. Take care of her. Take care of you.

I'm as cowardly now as the day my mother told me those final words.

Always with my eyes closed.

I never looked.

I never look.

I never look.

I couldn't look at her dying. And this is my final moment.

And I can't look.

I feel a ripple. It starts in my chest and makes its way to my toes, makes its way to my fingertips. Goosebumps coat my skin. What an odd sensation. Every particle and every molecule around me surges and then finds a center in my chest. I'm tripping forward and backward, my blood runs cold and confused and in the wrong direction. Arteries turn to veins and veins to arteries until everything settles in my heart that still manages to ring beats in my ears. The ringing in my ears is only broken up by the sound of my pulse which gives its best efforts to jostle my eardrums. It should frighten me but it steadies me. I've never experienced death but at least it isn't unpleasant. Ironically enough, death feels powerful. Anticipation floods my veins and I open my eyes.

Somehow, I can still open my eyes.

I gasp. Everything was happening quickly but for some reason, it's all coming in slow. My brain must be full of static because the scene unfolding before me starts to slow down. It keeps slowing down until I'm sure it's stopped. Unless I focus on one specific spot, I would almost believe my vision has frozen. But everything is moving.

Everything is moving.

Everything moves but in slow motion, in tiny ticks. But the

ticks in a clock have gained extra minutes, wedged between every second rests additional time.

This is the opposite of a dream. In my dreams, everything happens fast, yet all of my attempts are slowed. But this isn't a dream. I wave my hand in front of me and it's normal and moves at a usual pace. Everything and everyone is trapped. But I turn my head to the left, to the right. I'm not stuck in the mud.

I'm not the one underwater this time.

My eyes find the water rushing out of the broken dam. But the water isn't rushing. And I'm grateful. Because Cynrad is right in the path of the soon-to-be river. I yell. Tell him to move. But he is trapped in slow motion. I move forward but run into something sharp. A piercing object starts pressing into my chest. I move back, out of the way. I watch it continue on its path. Inch by inch, a perfectly aimed dagger intended for my heart sails by.

I look to Garrith. He's fighting off a dozen Howlers with more on the way. One has a hand around his neck. It won't be long until he's overwhelmed and outnumbered. Or it will be long. I can't tell.

And then I see it.

The gift. The opportunity. The opportunity to be the nightmare.

Time has slowed for everyone but me.

I realize everyone here is trapped in this sliver of time with me.

I will not fail.

I go. I will not waste seconds or minutes or whatever version of time I'm using. I send my dagger through carotids, into hearts, I slash everything. Every threat to me. Every threat to Garrith. Every threat to my friends is completely at my mercy.

The devastation at the tip of my dagger multiplies. And I can't stop. If I wait, if I watch, I'll get to see realization, pain, and death on the faces of the Howlers I slaughter. But I don't wait. I keep going. Dozens and dozens of Howlers. Even their blood spews in slow motion. An interesting feeling. Power. To kill someone before they even get to know they've been killed. Before they send a final prayer. To manipulate the situation and make it whatever I need it to be. The power should make me feel guilty but I only feel light. I only enjoy it.

I'm no longer in my nightmares. Everyone here is in mine.

The Howlers crumble. Slowly, one by one it becomes clear that their wounds are fatal. I take the sword from Garrith's hand and behead every Howler within ten feet of him. Remove the hand from his neck and let the pieces fall down around him. Garrith is safe.

Garrith is safe.

Heaviness punches through my chest. Tiredness spills into my blood. I turn to the river. In all the time I've spent slaughtering Howlers, Cynrad's horse has only managed to move a few feet. The water is coming.

There's a whooshing in my ears.

I have to get to him. Get him out of the way.

The whooshing grows louder. The water speeds up. I'm almost to the empty river's edge. I can make it to him. I can move him out of the way. I can get him out of the water's path before it falls over him. But my vision is narrowing. My ears are ringing and maybe they were this whole time and I can only hear it now. I'm stagnant. I'm spent. And suddenly the ability to move my legs becomes strenuous. I've lost all peripheral vision.

My eyesight becomes a dark tunnel leading only to Cynrad. Relief washes over me when I see that his horse's legs are moving faster. They're speeding up. Maybe he'll make it. The horse's frozen stance is breaking and turning back into a run.

But the water.

I was so focused on Cynrad, I didn't notice the water gaining speed.

I go to launch myself into the river's path but my muscles are slow. A hand firmly grasps my bicep.

I scream for Cynrad but my mouth moves as if I'm sedated. My screams for Cynrad come out longer in a deeper tone than I've known my voice to be capable of. I'm still able to see in slow motion but unable to move against it.

All the sounds within a five-mile radius come rushing. It's a shock wave in reverse. I am the originator and the resolution. I am the source and the recipient. The humming starts far away and gets closer and closer. Louder. Unbearable buzzing grows and rattles every particle of my existence.

Until it becomes my reality. The buzzing turns to the sound of crashing waves in real-time. And I am being pulled backward, away from the water, away from Cynrad.

"No!" And finally, my screams comes out normal. I'm pulled back against a solid chest. Garrith.

But I get to watch.

The water, swift and unforgiving, swallows Cynrad in an instant. He was here and then he was gone. My throat vibrates as inhuman sounds erupt from my mouth. Tears cloud my vision and I blink them away.

I don't believe it. I can't believe it.

Tatum is across the river. I can't hear her screams but I can feel them. I want to run across the water. I want to take her pain away. But I know better.

She has to feel this. She has to feel it so she can be reminded every day that it is real. Cynrad will never return from this mission. He won't go back to Moria. He'll never see Megara again.

Cynrad will never have children with Tatum, never grow old with her.

So many dreams. Every tomorrow, reduced, swept away in an instant.

All their plans, all their whispers of the future. All their kisses, all their looks, all their love, diminished to could have beens.

Enon is without a brother. Enon without a twin is not an image that seems possible.

I'm shocked by my own sobs.

"We have to go!" Garrith is pulling me back, farther away from the river, away from my friends. But I can't leave them. I can't move. Grief is leeching into me, straining my circulation.

"We can't stay here." Garrith blocks my vision. His face is inches from mine and his eyes reach for mine, demanding my attention. "We are in Howler territory with a river between us and our allies. You have to get up. You have to move." And he makes sense. His argument makes sense. But that sense won't reach my legs, my arms. I'm stuck in the sand and my nervous system is shrieking, malfunction, malfunction, malfunction.

"For fuck's sake..." and I'm moving. Nothing is gentle. I'm jostled and shifted so Garrith can put his fingers in his mouth. He whistles for Stoic. I'm in his arms and my head bangs against his shoulder until I'm thrown over the saddle. And we're off.

CHAPTER 37

G~~arrith Nikolai~~ Garrith's breathing is labored. His chest rises and falls in sporadic and rushed intervals against my back. He's gathered the reins in front of me. He's a blanket of safety around my shoulders and I mold into his large frame. He must have been running on shock and adrenaline and it's wearing off with every mile we put behind us.

Any hint of dusk has expired. Now we ride in the dark.

We destroyed the dam. We massacred fifty Howlers. But at what cost?

Cynrad won't feel the sun on his face again. Won't breathe in the scent of the ocean when we get over the last dune.

Won't see Tatum.

Won't see Enon.

I don't even know what's come of my other friends. Did the river hold off the Howlers? Did the rest of our squad make it out?

Nausea creeps up my neck. The back of my mouth fills with saliva. I choke it down. I will not throw up now.

After a few hours, Garrith's breathing levels out.

"We're almost to the outpost," he says. The outpost. That was part of the entire mission, but it didn't include my squad's assignment. The outpost is part of the plans laid for Commander Garrith.

We ride another mile. Stoic slows and Garrith slides from his back and takes the reins to guide us down the sand. There's a rusty, metal roof poking out from a recession between the dunes. When he said outpost, I was picturing something bigger. However, we are still in Howler territory and a sanctuary large enough to be spotted wouldn't provide the safety we need right now.

Garrith ties Stoic to the post and then reaches for me. His hands grip my waist and I put my hands on his shoulders. He lowers me to the ground but I look at his eyes and he's wincing and breathing like he's the one who sprinted here instead of the horse. He's wincing like bearing my weight was too much strain to keep his face neutral. He's supposed to be a master of the neutral expression.

"I am not fat," I quip.

He looks at me, blinks, and rolls his eyes. "Of course you're not fat."

"Then why is my weight offending you so severely today?"

He turns away from me and starts toward a small, wooden door. It creaks open with a shove and grunt from Garrith. "I'm not offended. I'm fucking stabbed." He stumbles into the small area inside the "outpost."

"WHAT!!!"

He sits on the sandy floor and waves me off. "I put two full water skins in that cabinet a week ago." He points to a cabinet sitting just next to the door. The moon shines in from the open door providing enough light to see. The outpost is no more than an eight-by-eight-foot room with a low ceiling. I'm five foot eight and have to tilt my head to keep from hitting the ceiling. Garrith is a hulking six foot six; he takes up half the room by himself. There are three small cabinets on the floor and a stack of boxes. I rush to the cabinets to fetch him water. I whip around to find him unwrapping the shemagh from his face.

And I think remnants of my new-found abilities flow. It seems to happen in slow motion. But I know better. It's not me but my stubborn heart.

His piercing eyes alone have left me light-headed. But his face as a whole is a new kind of beauty. He's so painfully beautiful, looking at him is nearly unbearable. But as difficult as it is to look at him, it would be harder to look away. His bronze skin is flawless. His nose has a small bump at the bridge, like God said, let's give him a flaw to disguise him as a human when in reality he belongs in the heavens. He belongs in robes of white instead of black. A tortured angel with dark, angry eyebrows and a gaze designed to plant jealousy in the hearts of everyone around him; everyone who will never measure up. He has a shadow of facial hair dusting the underside of his face, surrounding a set of full lips.

I'm suddenly thankful for the fabric over my face. My cheeks are simmering with heat, nearly setting my shemagh ablaze. He pulls the rest of the turban from his head revealing dark curls that fall over his forehead and down his neck. Air isn't entering my lungs as smoothly as it should be. And he's pulling the bottom of his tunic and his undershirt up, up, up. He's removing his shirt and my blood has set on fire. I look away, only now realizing the trance I had fallen into.

I can't breathe. I can't swallow. He's too much to look at, too much to share such a small space with.

"Jemma," he breathes. I look up. "The water."

"Oh! Yes. Sorry!" I hand him the waterskin. "Here." He

snatches it from my hand and lifts it to his mouth. Water runs from the corners of his mouth to his neck, down his chest, and into the blood that is smeared across his torso.

There's a wound on his left side. A perfect slit about two inches long runs parallel to this body. That cut couldn't have been the cause of so much blood. There is so much blood. He sets the water down and takes a deep breath. "Grab the cloth in the cabinet. I'll clean this up."

I do as I'm told with my wits intact this time, for the most part. He pours water on the cloth and starts cleaning the blood. He looks like he got all of it, the only imperfection left is the cut on his side that I swore was bigger a second ago. "Will you get my back?"

"Why? What's wrong with your back?" He just holds out the cloth until I take it. He gets to his knees and turns around. Just as much blood, if not more, is spread over his lower back. "Garrith!" There's another slit on his back, on the left side too, identical to the one on his front. He was stabbed completely through. This is the exit.

"It's not bad now. I was dehydrated and things won't heal as quickly when I'm weak."

"What do you mean heal?"

"You should know better than anyone. How is it that one second a sword entered my side, and the next second, the Howler responsible was falling dead in front of me? Along with the rest of the Howlers surrounding us. How was I holding my sword, and a split second later, you're far away from me with it tight in your fist?" I'm not ready to unpack what happened when the dam broke. I'm not ready to figure out that part of myself. I start wiping the blood from his back. "You're gifted, Jemma."

Keep cleaning his back. Stay numb, stay tepid. Clean his back.

His back is an expanse of muscle, unlike anything I've ever seen. Everything about his appearance is hearty and full and beautiful. I inspect the thin gash on his side. And it does the impossible. It comes together and shrinks into a small pink line. Soon the pink line fades as well. Garrith turns on his knees to show me that the wound that was a few inches above his hipbone has now vanished as well.

Incredible.

In the last five minutes, I've learned more about Garrith than I have in all my time at Moria. Garrith's face, Garrith's ability, Garrith is more than I could have imagined. He stands as well as he can. He bends at the waist but his head and shoulders still brush the ceiling while he makes his way to the cabinet. He gathers new shirts and struggles to put them on in such tight quarters.

He catches me watching. "I was up here a few days ago putting away anything I might need after the dam bombing." He pulls out a bucket and bag of oats for Stoic then manages to get his giant frame back out the door.

I slide back against the wall and watch through the small doorway as he feeds Stoic and pours water into the bucket for him to drink. He's had a hard day. Stoic is the fastest horse we have and Garrith pushed him beyond what we knew him to be capable of today.

"We'll rest here for a few hours," Garrith says as he ducks through the door again. "Sto needs a break and we could use some sleep."

"I don't feel tired." Especially now that I've managed to earn the right to view his face. I don't want to sleep. I want to revel in these moments looking at his uncovered face. Every time I look away, not a second goes by and I'm already back, soaking it in, memorizing all the lines of his face. Studying the way his lips move around certain words. He's mesmerizing.

"That's the adrenaline talking. Lie down. Even if you don't feel the exhaustion, you look dead on your feet." How sweet. He hands me a blanket and a waterskin. I take them and curl up in the corner. I place the waterskin on the floor next to me and something catches my eye.

There is a hint of faded purple. I reach out my hand. Tied to the water skin is a piece of violet fabric—the fabric from my mother's curtain. I ripped this ribbon from the curtain months ago in my parents' home.

"This is my water skin," I say. Garrith looks at me, I think he might have been watching me the whole time. I rub the cloth between my fingers. For a second I feel like she's here with me. "Why do you have it?"

"It's a waterskin. We aren't going to throw those away." He shrugs.

"And this ribbon?" He stills at my question. His eyes fall back to the purple in my hand.

Ten breaths pass between us before he speaks. "When I found you, you had one arm wrapped around Jo, and the other hand was tightly wrapped around this." He starts to grasp the ribbon in my hands but stops an inch shy. "I knew it must have been of value. Not material value, but value to you. I couldn't discard it. So I left it." He sighs and stretches, "You can have the ribbon back. But that waterskin is mine now."

I wait a moment. Rub my thumb into the tattered fabric. He doesn't move so I say, "It's from a curtain in my parent's house. My mother loved purple." My throat is closing from the memory creeping up. He nods in understanding and retreats to his small corner in the outpost.

Garrith is without a blanket but he keeps the single pillow for himself. He puts the pillow behind his head and lays back. His long legs almost reach across the whole room. Cold air blows in from under the door. He crosses his arms over his chest, I'm sure he's chilly without a blanket. And he's right. I am tired. I lie on my side curled into a ball and my eyelids suddenly weigh a thousand pounds.

All the cells in my body are turning into feathers. They fall and land so lightly, soundless. It's calm and relaxing, and I've never enjoyed falling asleep as much as I do right now. If only the feathers would stop tickling me, I could fall all the way asleep and turn off my mind. But the feathers tickle. They shoot goosebumps down my arms and span my skin. They send chills all over me, and I can't help but shiver.

Something stills the feathers. Something warm. I jolt awake.

Garrith is crouched in front of me, his hand resting on my side.

"Turn around." It turns out Garrith is bossy all hours of the day.

"Why," I whisper.

"Neither of us will get any rest with your teeth chattering like that. And I'm cold too." He lays the pillow down where my head just was and instructs me to place my head back on it, but this time I face the wall. The cool air doesn't hit me anymore and Garrith is to blame.

He slides under my blanket behind me. His arm folds under the limp pillow, better cushioning my head. His body is inches from my back but the heat radiating off his chest causes the frost on my bones to evaporate. The warmth swirling under this thin blanket is intoxicating. I wish I could bottle this feeling, save it, and drink it later. Reid's luxurious mattress always seemed so plush and inviting. Yet, here under a shabby blanket with Garrith, I've never known such comfort.

CHAPTER 38

I don't want to get up. I don't want to leave the outpost. Here, Garrith and I are allies. Here, I can pretend that Cynrad is alive, just at the camp across the river waiting to head back to Moria. Here, I can pretend that Jo is waiting for me, and I'll see her tomorrow when we get back. Hope manages to swell as I inhale but I tap it down. Exhale.

Garrith's breaths are even and deep. I woke a few minutes ago but I'm trying to stay as still as possible. I try in vain. His breath whispers past my ear. The tickle causes an involuntary shudder to rack through me.

While we slept we melted into one another. He's so close. He's so close and I can feel every angle of him lightly hugging every angle of myself but he's touching me nowhere. All I would have to do is scoot just a little. What am I thinking? A blush creeps up my neck and cheeks and I'm grateful that I'm facing away from him.

I can't help my breathing. It's sporadic but I'm as in control of my lungs as I am my thoughts. An even breath in, an even breath out. But in our bubble of quiet, I hear the difference. His breath is as uneven as mine.

Garrith is awake, and for once, he breaks the silence. "I didn't mean it yesterday. About the poem, I didn't mean it."

"I didn't realize the depth of the poem. I wouldn't have said it had I known. It was just something Jo used to say a lot. Especially the first year we were together."

"I know that." Pause. "I felt exposed. My parents used to say—" It seems like his thought isn't complete but he decides not to continue.

"You don't have to explain if it makes you uncomfortable," I tell him. He's never been keen on sharing and I know I'm the last person on his list of individuals he'd ever want to share with anyway.

"I don't remember anything bad about my parents. Every moment I had with them was a gift. To be in their presence was to feel infinite happiness. And almost every moment after watching them die has been..." He trails off, unable to express his grief.

"I understand."

"Until I found purpose in protecting Jo, things just didn't make sense. And she centered me. She brought so much balance and perspective to my life and I still failed her."

Silence falls between us. His breathing is heavier than it was a minute ago.

"How did you separate?" I whisper. Like I have any right to ask him questions. But he's too guarded, too reserved. I want to shrink down to the size of an ant, find my way into his ear, and hike to his brain. I want to turn a light on every dark corner of his mind and uncover all the things about himself he keeps hidden. I want to see his worst and show him mine because deep down I believe they wouldn't be all that different.

"They were going to burn all of us in the orphanage. Amos Cerastes believed the bronze of skin was to blame for the sickness since we weren't catching the Blight. He had a small following of civilians who believed him. And it was enough." He sighs then inhales forever. "They barricaded the doors. The smoke was thick but Jo and I had a tunnel that we'd used to find trouble and pastries at night. It wasn't very wide and it was difficult for me to get through. She slipped through quickly. I took too long and the flames had already swallowed my legs. By the time I was completely out of the tunnel, I hadn't made it a foot from the exit before I passed out. At first, they thought I was dead. I wished that I was. The pain was excruciating. But I wanted to find her. Needed to find her. And looking back, I think that's what saved me. I can only heal while I possess enough strength to do even the most basic things, like walking, standing, breathing... you get the idea." He's a thousand miles away, stuck in a memory that haunts him. "A lot of the civilians that tried to dispose of us that day are part of the Megara population."

"Is that why you keep your face covered? If so many people in Megara and Moria prefer you dead, why do you stay?" I can't keep the questions from bubbling over.

"Amos knows I've been looking for Jo. Since the day they found me. They left me dying on the ground outside of the orphanage. A week later a wagon came through Audun. I was nearly healed, some of the skin still appeared scarred, but I was up and scavaging for food. I wasn't strong enough yet to fight them off so they brought me to Moria. The King had suspicions that I might be *gifted*. So they threw me to the wolf."

He didn't need to finish his story. I knew what time on the wrong end of the wolf cave could mean. And I had daggers.

I had a hunch that Garrith was the other survivor, but I

only pictured him dominating. The idea of him being wounded never crossed my mind.

"I was nearly torn to pieces, and when I healed at an unbelievable pace, the king offered me a deal. He would allow me to organize regular searches for Jo. It wasn't the sole purpose for going above ground. Mostly, he let me tag along with the above-ground parties and called it a favor."

"What was the other end of the bargain?" I knew the king well enough now to know that his grace comes with a debt.

"My blood. I have to donate every week. Not only can I heal myself, but my blood can heal the wounded. They actually used it on you the night you faced the wolf."

I ponder his revelation. An injection of his blood mixing with mine. The idea feels intimate, though I'm sure it's been used on many Megara inhabitants. But it's comforting, and somehow I think his blood could heal more than just my physical wounds.

"For eight years, I looked for Jo, only to find her dying a few months ago in your arms. I failed her. I should have been there." Guilt smacks me in the face. Garrith is tormented with thoughts of losing Jo, and my brain is swirling with the feeling of his blood mingling with mine.

"It doesn't sound like you failed her, Nikolai. You saved her. She made it out. And that's thanks to you." I want to turn around but I don't think my heart could handle his face right now.

His voice is low and filled with rage. "I wasn't there. She ran from the orphanage and straight into the Arid to die. If I had acted faster, realized what was going on before the smoke hit, I could have gotten through that tunnel and been there to take care of her. I hate myself for not putting it together sooner." And I get it. His resentment toward me mirrors his resentment toward himself.

"Like you hate me. For bringing her here."

"You love her," he whispers. "Even on the brink of death, even starving, dehydrated, and blind, Jo was the center of every desperate plea on your lips. You did everything that I couldn't. You stayed with her and protected her. I led her to death, but you found her. And a few months ago, she nearly met that same fate again, but she wasn't alone. You would've died holding her before leaving to save yourself."

He blows out a breath that rustles the hair resting on my shoulder. "I could never hate you."

I turn around to face him. The depth of his emotion is shining across his face and it's too much. All this time I've wished to see his exposed face and here it is and it's painful to see so much of him. He's too intense, too terrifying, too beautiful. All of my thoughts contradict one another as I fight the urge to look away and the urge to study his face forever.

I want to reach out and touch his cheek. Kiss away every ill thought he's directed at himself. My thoughts terrify me. I don't have to say anything because he can see it. His gaze shifts and his eyelids are heavy as he takes in my face, no doubt reading every thought I have written across it.

I turn back away from him, embarrassed. Heat has spread across my chest and neck and it's too warm in this little nook. I'm certain steam is visibly rising from my skin like traitor particles exposing my thoughts. I feel like I've done nothing and everything wrong. I don't know how to even begin to explain to Reid what happens to me when I'm near ~~Nikolai Garrith Nikolai Garrith~~ Nikolai.

Reid would not approve of this. Not that he approves of anything I have to do or say lately.

I shut out the thoughts of Reid and focus on calming the fire spreading in my body, down my legs, and up my neck. I close my eyes but I can hear my heartbeat in my ears. Squeeze my eyes shut until it subsides.

Nikolai's warm hand reaches to cup my hip and he pulls me to him. He envelopes all of me in a matter of seconds. My back pressed to his chest, my bottom tucked against his pelvis, my knees bent against his. Every inch of his body is hugging every inch of mine. His hand is splayed over the curve of my hip and he starts rubbing his thumb over the small bit of exposed skin at my waist.

A dangerous game.

It's a dangerous game and terrible things have happened, are happening. But I can do nothing about any of it. All I can do right now is be here. And there is nowhere I'd rather be in this moment than here.

I arch my back, bringing us impossibly closer. His hand moves up and he drags his fingertips over my side and slowly up and down my arm. His touch is light. It's a whisper of contact that tickles and feels heavenly at the same time. Goosebumps erupt all over. His hand slides up my neck, taking my hair up with it, to massage circles across my scalp. I melt into him.

I think it needs to stop. He is ecstasy. I think it must be wrong to feel this good. Nothing has ever felt so good, it must be bad. Very, very bad. My reservations evaporate as he brings his lips to my neck.

I gasp. His nose traces the base of my scalp while his tongue tends to my neck. His hand comes around to my stomach and pulls me to him, pressing me against him. I can feel him and the contact ignites a fire inside me.

Nikolai's mouth is full and his tongue is skilled and he's leaving me a panting mess. He tugs at my tunic and slides his thumb past the hem of my undershirt. He rubs over my belly button as he kisses down my neck, following my spine. My thoughts trip over one another, not making any sense, all I can decipher is *yes* and *this*, this is everything.

I've never.

I've never.

~~I've never felt something as good as this moment.~~

His palm goes flat on my stomach and his pinky slips under the button of my pants. "Jemma," it's a sigh, it's a statement, it's a question, it's asking permission for something I hadn't considered until now. His voice is strained. His breath is hot against my neck and I need to tell him.

I need to tell him but I can't find words. I'm breathless but manage to rub back against him. He wastes no time. He pulls his hand from my shirt and starts on my button; unzips the zipper. He pushes my pants and underwear down a few inches. My hip is exposed along with the soft skin between my hip bones. I feel his enthusiasm hard against my bottom. I hear his excitement in his breath at my ear. He's strained, coiled tightly and I wish he'd let go. I wish he would let go and take me with him.

His hand slides below my underwear and he's there. He's right there, teetering between knowing and not knowing. Slowly, he presses his fingers further down. His intake of breath through his mouth, through his teeth, almost startles me. "God," he moans and presses into me. "Jemma," he hisses. And before I can register the sensations, he rolls over me, putting me on my back. His thigh lands between mine. His other hand lands next to my head, his arm stretched out, holding him above me while he starts working his fingers below my pants.

All of it. It's too much, deliciously suffocating, and I can't imagine a better way to go. His eyes are locked on mine and his fingers are unraveling all my composure. I'm breathing like I just sprinted a mile and sweat is prickling around my hairline.

I see the sheen of moisture in his brow and, against reason, against all logical thought, it encourages me. I tap down the instinct to sit up and lick the sweat from his forehead but I can't help but rock my hips against his hand. He groans and brings his lips to mine.

These lips. I wondered, wished, and fantasized about these lips. What would they feel like? What would they taste like? And here it is. And they're mine.

There's a tightness building below my stomach. Nikolai grazes, strokes, and teases until the feeling grows. It's unbearable and exhilarating.

His tongue sweeps through my mouth, his breath mingles with mine and I tangle my hands into his hair. What would be a moan translates into vibrations in our connected mouths. He removes his hand from my pants and starts kissing his way down my neck. He's pushing the fabrics of my tunic and undershirt up. He grips the waist of my pants and I'm anticipating the moment they're pulled down. And something is missing. Something is off.

"Jemma," he whispers against my neck. I love the sound of my name on his lips.

And I want to stay here but something isn't happening that I know should be happening.

The alarms. There are no alarms. A man is trying to remove my clothes and there are no warning bells, no flashing lights; all I can find is the desire to get myself naked, get him naked.

It's never like this with Reid.

Reid.

Reid is probably at Moria losing his mind, unsure if I'm safe, unsure if I'm dead or alive.

Nikolai feels me still against him. He lifts his head, concern in his eyes, "Are you okay?" His breathing is still ragged.

I'm going to be sick. "Yes. No. I just—" I just what? "I just think—" The pitch of my voice is higher than normal and breathless. He sits back and places his hands on his knees.

"You just what?" His words aren't aggressive like I expect them to be, his face only shows me that he's worried.

"I just think that maybe this isn't the best thing for me to be doing." That's not what I want to say. "Since, you know, I still have a boyfriend." A boyfriend? Is Reid even my boyfriend?

Nikolai doesn't say anything. Shock is etched into every one of his beautiful features. His mouth parts like he can't believe the words he's hearing. And in all honesty, neither can I.

I try to save it. "Well Reid's probably not my boyfriend but there's definitely still something there." Words are tumbling, mindlessly spiraling from my mouth and it's my fault.

"Still something there?" He's slipping his neutral facade back into place, or at least trying to.

I try to backtrack. "Yeah, I mean, he betrayed me but he's been working on making it up to me." Not that any of his attempts would ever work. But I also don't want to be a girl that hops around from person to person.

"So what was this? Were you just bored? Needed a pick-me-up since Reid's bedroom is too far away tonight?"

"You know I wouldn't do that. You just... You're here and you took off your shemagh and I was distracted and it was a lapse in judgment."

"I'm a lapse in judgment for you?"

Neutrality is damned. Nikolai is enraged. "What the fuck, Jemma! You know damn well you aren't committed to Reid. You know what you want!"

I'm shrinking against the wall as Nikolai shifts from sitting on his heels to being upright on his knees. "I haven't thought about it. I've been busy. I never thought for one moment in the past week that I was going to end up on the wrong side of that river. I never thought I'd end up here with you. Plus, none of this makes sense. You don't want me. Why are you even bothering touching me?"

There's so much tension in his face; his eyebrows are set low enough to cast a shadow over his eyes. "You know why!"

"I don't!"

"I'm not going to feed into your need for assurance. If you're fishing for compliments, you'll just have to wait until you get back to Reid. Don't worry, it'll be like this never happened." It stings like he had slapped me, tears are forming behind my eyes. Nikolai's face softens slightly. "You know who you are and what you're capable of. And it's weakening you to lean on him for constant reminders."

"I do not lean on him." I want to scream it but my voice doesn't have the strength I wish it did.

"You do." His voice is softer but the urgency and anger are still projecting. "You've gotten comfortable. Your mind grows weaker by the day. You think you need reassurance but the coddling isn't going to help you." He won't stop. "And it's embarrassing; he is nothing compared to you. He's holding you back. I know it's nice, and I know you're on some sweet vacation, but we are in a war and the Howlers aren't going to care how many compliments your boyfriend gave you."

"Enough!" I'm done listening. "Reid loved me and I won't let you make me feel like I was his charity case. He's not coddling, he's caring, and he tells me how he feels." I can't tell if I'm convincing Nikolai or myself, but I keep going. "He shows me kindness, which is more than I can say about you."

"Don't compare me to him." His voice is steel, his glare sharp as razors. It's hard to think. Minutes ago he was a swirling storm of fire and desire. Now he's ice.

"This was a mistake," I whisper. An incredible mistake, I don't say.

I wanted him to touch me. I wanted him to kiss me. I wanted him to kiss every piece of me. And he knew it. And I'm ashamed. I won't look at him. Train my eyes on the ground. I won't look up, I can't.

"Don't." Finally, his voice is soft. I watch his hand come up, stopping short of my arm. He pauses before deciding to touch me, only barely. He runs his fingertips across my skin and makes everything feel okay. But it's not. I'm wrong. I'm guilty. I've done too much, said too much. So I pull away.

He gets it. He doesn't try to coerce me back to common ground. That beautiful common ground where we shared a moment of excitement. I risk a glance in his direction and break my own heart. Shock has taken hold of his face as if my retreat burned him. The shock is quickly covered up. His attributes are reacquainted with their walls, and he is a perfect soldier. Nothing gets to him. All his thoughts and feelings are held out of reach from me.

It's for the best.

Allowing anything to come between us would be selfish. Nikolai is too selfless for my poor offerings. I convince myself that he is better off. This hurt is nothing compared to the storm I would cause him. I am a coward.

Nikolai does his best to storm out in such tight quarters, but he forgets to turn sideways to go through the door, and his shoulder clips the frame, breaking the wooden frame right off the wall.

Almost a perfect soldier.

CHAPTER 39

I'm not eager to break the silence. Nikolai isn't either. The only words exchanged this morning were of absolute necessity. Syllables were limited and nods were suitable answers.

We take off on Nikolai's horse at dawn. Our positions are the same as yesterday but the spaces between us seem to stretch on forever. Nikolai's movements are careful. Every brush of his chin against the back of my head is met with immediate withdrawal. Every time I'm jostled back into a tighter embrace, I shrink and Nikolai bends his arms to keep a barrier of space between us.

Our awareness of one another, once warm, has turned cold. Hours ago I would have melted into the inevitable clash of our bodies. Now we are rigid, frozen, statues never meant to collide.

I want to fix things but the possibility of resolution falls away the closer we get to Moria. Every urge I get to tell him I didn't mean anything I said, I can't think of the sentences, of the words to piece together to explain myself.

We've been riding most of the morning, following close to the reborn river, until the river grows wider, slowly opening up into the ocean. Stoic comes to a stop when we spot an old, raggedy dock. It's clearly from a time before the river dried up, and now that the water runs, it looks like it's holding on by a thread. Nikolai swings his leg over Stoic and lands with a graceful thud. He extends his hand to help me down. It's different. It's robotic. Nothing he does comes with eye contact. It's been half a night and a morning since our dispute and I already miss his eyes. I'm unnecessarily startled when he speaks, "A small ship from Megara is supposed to pick us up here thirty-six hours after the river runs. It should be here around noon."

I nod. I'm ready to be home. I feel so lost. I am lost enough to consider Moria my home. I need space from Nikolai. I need to talk to Reid. I need to see Tatum.

Tatum.

I don't want to think of her grief.

It isn't fair that Cynrad is gone. And I realize how lucky I've been, how selfish I am. It's been years since I experienced such a loss. I lost my parents and my sister. And enough time has passed that I've taken that time for granted. Cynrad is dead and I've been taking the people around me for granted, taking our time together for granted.

Nikolai leans against the trunk of a dead tree with his arms crossed. His shemagh rests high on his face, back to only exposing his eyes. He looks out over the water waiting on a ship that might never come. Already, I feel like I've lost him. He looked at me last night, openly and exposed. So vulnerable and I still threw it all back in his face. I can't take it.

Maybe it doesn't have to be pretty. Maybe my words don't need grace. Perhaps they just need to be said.

As if he feels my gaze on him, Nikolai turns, his eyes connecting with mine. I move toward him and pull my shemagh down to speak. He pushes off the tree and steps away from me.

"Nikolai," it comes out as a plea, and in a way, it is.

He doesn't turn around. "Sit down, Shayde."

I don't force him to shut me down further. Maybe the common ground is something we can find later on. I wish we were back in Moria already. Nikolai's silent presence always makes me think, ideas bouncing off the walls of my brain. I've never been in control of myself when he's around.

He slides down the trunk of the tree, crosses his arms, and gets comfortable. I drink from the waterskin and try to clear my mind. Lying back on the sand, I pull the fabric over my eyes.

Minutes pass.

And pass.

And pass.

And my anger grows. Cynrad is gone. Tonight, I will find Tatum in pieces. And it's killing me that I can't protect her from it. I can't take it. Sitting up, I notice Nikolai is still propped against the tree, his eyes closed now.

I often blame God. I beg God. But when I think about it, I always decide I don't believe in God.

I've unlocked a part of my head, a part of my heart, and despite the crumbling bridge between me and Nikolai, words are spilling out of me. "Do you believe in heaven?"

I've taken him off guard as he whips his head my way and opens his eyes to ensure he's heard me correctly. I keep my expression neutral and he takes his time considering my question. "Do you?"

"I think so." I don't want to think about it but the dam broke and washed Cynrad away and it broke a dam in my soul at the same time and one thought tumbles into the next. "I thought I didn't. I thought when you die, that would be the end. The end of your thoughts, your feelings. You cease to exist." He remains quiet. My words continue to spill, gaining speed as they go. "But when bad things happen, anger surfaces, and I always have a bone to pick with God. And if my default reaction is to blame our creator, that would mean we have one."

His eyes crinkle slightly in their corners. He uncrosses his arms and rests them on his knees. His head tilts back against the tree's dead trunk, recognizing my mental turmoil. I wish I could do more than notice my spiral. I wish I could fix it, stop it, but I don't have the tools. What good is awareness of my problems if I can do nothing about them? He sighs. "My parents were murdered. They were killed right in front of me. I knew my mom was dead first. The sound of her head falling into the bucket before the guillotine plays on an endless loop in my dreams." The ground falls beneath me. His mother was beheaded and any sense of balance fades. His mother was beheaded. And he saw it.

I don't want him to continue but he does. "I never thought my father would die. He is where my healing powers come from, so I thought we would be more difficult to kill. But a dagger to the heart will do it." His voice is low. As much as I don't want to know these things, whether or not he tells me about them, they happen. "I was raised Christian. I had deep faith. But in my anger, I didn't blame God. I questioned him, questioned his existence. I didn't think the all-powerful God could allow such a thing to happen. So I lost my faith."

I can taste salt on my lips. A few rogue tears have slipped down my cheeks. I want to comfort him but I'm too late, too wrong.

He continues, "Well, I thought I lost my faith. And maybe I

did. Because my beliefs now are different. Tragedy happens all the time. No power in the world can prevent the unimaginable from happening. But when I think of my parents, I don't see them reduced to nothingness. I see them waiting for me. I mourn their death but I'm only mourning the time I have to be without them. I will see them again. Someday. A different faith was born when I realized that. The grief, the loss, the pain, it's for us. We hurt; we cry for ourselves and those left behind. It's not for them; I believe that they are okay. When I picture them, I can only see them happy and together. And I can't help but believe that souls have to go somewhere. And anywhere is better than here."

I can see it. It's only for a time. It's wrong that, in this life, Cynrad will not grow old with Tatum. He won't be able to act annoyed with Enon. He won't bless us with his sarcasm. But only for a time, because we will see him again. A sturdy foundation rests in the back of my mind. And when I step on it, I know my parents are not gone. They are just somewhere else.

Just then, a faint horn blows. I blink the tears from my eyes. Nikolai is on his feet in an instant. Just below where the water meets the sky I see a small ship.

We gather our things and approach the rickety dock. Nikolai brings his horse. While we await the ship's arrival I tell him, "Thank you." He only turns his head to look at me. "For sharing that. I had no idea." I move my hand across the distance between us, but when I graze his knuckles he pulls away. I can't hide the hurt on my face, and the pain in my throat echoes in my voice. "It doesn't have to be like this." It was only a day ago that the air between us was very different than it is now. He moves away from me. "Nikolai," I plead.

"Don't be fickle, Jemma. You're toying. And it isn't right." He dismisses me and watches the ship, adding more than physical distance between us.

I won't have it, and follow. "I'm not toying."

His whole frame turns to face me. "Then what is Reid to you? Tell me, so I can figure out where I fit here."

I don't know what Reid is to me but he's not nothing. He means something to me and until I talk to him, I won't have an answer for Nikolai. So I say, "I'm not sure yet. I haven't talked to him."

Nikolai rolls his eyes.

"But it shouldn't matter. You and I are friends."

He flinches, slightly. "Do you normally do with your friends what we did?"

I knew he'd throw it in my face. All day I've thought about it and cursed myself for thinking about it. I want to wipe it from my memory and at the same time I want to hide it for safe-keeping.

"That was a mistake. You have to admit, it had been a pretty intense twenty-four hours. *Pardon me* for slipping up. My decision-making skills were spent and sometimes when I'm close to you it's like my blood operates differently, and when I look at you, I can hear my heart beating. You'd think it would be a bad thing, but at the same time, your presence is like a blanket of calm and you *always* leave me lightheaded and I'm sorry. I'm sorry. You're a lot. And I got mixed up." Almost to further prove my point, my breath comes out in erratic spurts and my cheeks, neck, and ears have all been set ablaze.

He just stands there, looking at me while I'm eaten up with a fire fueled by regret and embarrassment. He finally crosses his arms and says, "Alright."

"Alright, what?" I'm still breathless and every syllable across my tongue seems soaked in desperation.

The boat is almost here and he readies for our departure. "Alright. We can be friends." He walks away and doesn't speak or look at me for the remainder of the trip.

We were fortunate with the wind today. The ship went West for an hour before we could finally see land again, bringing us to the docks nearest Moria. I spent the entire trip positioned at the stern, and out of the way. I can't deny that it was fascinating to witness the muddy, river water bleed into the ocean. Garrith's horse was anxious on board, and I'm sure that's where Nikolai stayed. I did not see him and did not turn around to look.

I didn't recognize any of the hands on the ship when we first boarded except one. The man that took Jo to Megara—Tiago, I think. Nikolai immediately dove into reports with the gentleman I believed to be the captain. So I made my way to the back of the ship. I've never been on such a device. Floating through waves, and watching the crew run around adjusting sails to control our course, it's captivating.

We approach the dock and I sneak a peek to find Nikolai soothing Stoic. His eyes immediately connect with mine and he looks away. Triumph blooms in my chest for having caught him watching me.

Nikolai, Stoic, and I are the only ones going ashore. Wordlessly, Nikolai helps me back onto his horse and we begin the final stretch of our travels.

No one is in the East stables, but in the stall, nearest the entrance, stands Winnie. I worried she wouldn't make it without a rider. I pat her nose and brush my hand down her neck. She calms under the pressure of my palm like she was as anxious over me as I was her. "My fierce gal," I whisper.

The sun was going down beyond the dunes when we

arrived. I leave Nikolai and Winnie and start down the tunnel, taking me deeper into Moria. Shock and smiles are the common expressions worn by those on patrol when I pass them. At this point in the day, the mess hall should be cleared out.

I follow the flickering torches down the cave until the light of the mess hall falls on me. My eyes lock with Reid's. Dread and surprise are washed from his face when his mouth splits into the largest smile I've ever seen.

His happiness is contagious and I feel my lips crack as I return his excitement. His hair is sticking out in a million different directions like he's been raking it with his fingers for days straight. He moves toward me, arms extended, and the closer he gets I can make out the dark circles under his eyes. Something like relief tugs at my heart. Relief that my absence caused a man, who can sleep under any circumstances, sleepless nights.

Relief is quickly replaced with guilt. Guilt that while Reid was here, stressing about my well-being, I was exploring all the delicious slopes of Nikolai.

Reid sees my face falter as his hands reach my cheeks. He's gentle, cradling my chin. "What happened?"

Nothing! Everything! His eyes search mine as I come up empty of explanations.

Over Reid's shoulder, I see two others. More blond hair.

Tatum and Enon stand rigid, hope and fear palpable in the air around them.

Vomit threatens.

I step out of Reid's embrace. And close the distance between me and Tatum, taking her hand.

Her voice is strong, stronger than her appearance would have you expect. "He isn't with you, is he?"

Before I can even shake my head, she pulls her hand from mine and barrels out of the mess hall.

Enon is still. Silent tears stream down his face. I extend my arms and he accepts my embrace. Full-body shudders explode from him as he allows himself to sob. His voice is hoarse when he says, "We assumed he didn't make it, but hoped he was just washed to the other side of the river. We swept the whole shoreline from the dam to the ocean. He was nowhere." Another round of sobs erupts from the deepest canyons of Enon's heart.

He cries until I'm sure his body is devoid of tears. He sniffs and releases me. When he steps back, the red rim of his eyes and pink splotches over his skin almost bring me to my knees. "I'm happy you're okay, Jemma. We were really worried about you." I rub his arm until he gives me a weak smile and turns to go to his dorm, a room he no longer shares with his brother.

I wrap my arm around my ribs and pinch the bridge of my nose. My nose is too full of snot to breathe so I have to continue forcing strained breaths from my mouth. I close my eyes. Arms snake around my waist and I lean back into Reid's chest

"Let's go to bed," he says.

Yes. Bed. Please.

He takes my hand from my face and I open my eyes as he starts to guide me. My gaze connects with the bright green from across the room. Under heavy, dark eyebrows, even with his face covered, his glare sends daggers.

Reid takes me down the hall to our dorm, his dorm. And for the first time since childhood, I pray. Or I think it's praying. I'm not sure anymore.

I ask for forgiveness.

I ask for forgiveness for the things I've done wrong that felt right and the right things that felt wrong. And forgiveness for my error in differentiating which is which.

Maybe Nikolai's words were just pretty ideas to help me stand on solid feet, on solid faith. But I lean into it anyway. I picture Cynrad. He's sad but calm. His calm flows into me. And I recognize that his sadness is only from knowing that it will be a while before we see him again.

CHAPTER 40

Sondra is almost finished with my appearance. My hair falls in waves, reaching my waist. Abundant gold and jewels are sitting on the counter in her room. All the embellishments are meant for me. I'm supposed to wear these fine jewels to celebrate the start of a war. Celebrate King Cerastes.

Celebrate his son.

Celebrate the death to come under his command.

I'm an imposter.

On the bed is the most stunning gown. Hues of blue decorate the silk and sheer material. Sondra completes my hair and moves on to my earrings.

"How much time do I have before they need me?" Suddenly the decoration wished for me grows heavy. I wish for a moment alone before I cuff myself into this role.

"About an hour." She eyes me like I'm made of glass. And in this moment I am.

I need to think.

I need to think without the weight of the kingdom's jewels sitting on my head.

I need to summon my ability. Slow down time. Grant me extra time.

Narrowing in on the wall, I urge the buzzing to reappear. I know using the power right now is uncalled for, but who would know?

Focus. Breathe. Summon the surge.

Sondra's hand moves normally, reaching out to rub her thumb into the formed crease between my eyebrows.

"I need a moment; I won't be long." I stand and walk out of her room, ignoring the dress meant for me. I want to stay in this ivory tunic dress forever. I don't want to let the King dress me up for his enjoyment.

My steps are speeding up. And before I know it, I'm running as if I can outrun expectations. As if I can outrun my feelings. As if I can take the thoughts out of my head and leave them far behind me.

But I can't do any of those things.

I run through the tunnel and to my own safe little corner of this luxury prison. At the entrance, I grab the torch and continue down the steps toward the gates of the wolf den, passing rows of seats. It's quiet here, and my thoughts have enough space to bounce off the auditorium walls and grow into something I can organize in my mind. I can build compartments here and file away all the things I can not control. In this dark corner, I know how to center myself.

I reach the lowest level, and I can barely make out the cage. I reach through the gate and toss the torch to the fire pit. The fire pit erupts with flames. What dim illumination the torch gave off is now amplified and casts a warm light across the walls. The crackling of the fire is soothing, and I can finally take a breath deep enough to completely inflate my lungs. My thoughts are out of control, and I know my newfound confusion is to blame.

Nikolai is filling my brain with too many ideas. I don't trust Reid, but I do.

There aren't enough minutes before tonight's event to unpack my confusion.

"Before you call on Satan or get naked, you should know that I'm in here too." I spin around and Nikolai is sitting in the first row of seats near the wall. Of course, he is.

"I'd appreciate some space right now."

"I was here first. You're who intruded on me." He looks up through heavy lashes, his eyebrows casting a faint shadow over his eyes. His shemagh, swords, and tunic are all sitting in the seat beside him. He has set up camp to decompress here. And I stormed in on him. He remains seated, the light from the fire illuminating his beautiful face. I don't think I'll ever get used to seeing his whole face. His eyes alone were enough to intrigue me, and that was before he removed his shemagh. He's wearing only a snug, black, long-sleeved shirt and black pants tucked into his boots. I meet his eyes, and there is no kindness within them. He is not in the mood to argue today, but neither am I.

He's the brightest of flames, and today, I sprouted wings and became a moth. This encounter has no chance of ending happily, but I can't stop my feet from bringing me closer to him. Instinctively, he stands. Always on alert. I stop in my tracks. He's over six feet of pure intimidation.

"Are you almost finished here? I could use a second." I try to stay as cool and calm as Nikolai.

"No." Prick. One word, and I'm ready to hurtle chairs.

Stay neutral. "Why are you even down here?"

"For conversation. You?" He's a closed-off prick with tons of snide remark ammunition.

"I told you. I need a minute. I've got some things going on and I need to sort them out." I pause. "I don't know where I stand with Reid." I gamble that a moment of vulnerability will get him off my back. Maybe he will leave.

"Then maybe instead of hiding down here, invading my sanctuary, you should go sort it out with your non-boyfriend, boyfriend. Have you told him about your power yet? Or are you afraid that information would scare him off? Afraid he won't baby you if he knows what you're capable of?" His breathing grows heavy, and I watch seconds tick away on his face. As taut as his stance and expression have become, I can still see the regret wedge between his eyebrows. He got it off his chest, but defeat coats his features.

Nikolai rakes both hands into his hair until deciding to turn away. He walks back to the end of the aisle and lands heavily in his seat. His hair is sticking out in a million different directions, and he's never looked more vulnerable or human.

I can't help myself when I walk up to him. "I don't need your advice or judgment." He grips the arms of his seat, but I continue, "You want to think less of me because I chose to find a sliver of joy in this world. That's fine. But you can't stop me from indulging in things that help me find a way to hope. I've earned it. The world could end in a moment, and I'm through wasting moments doing anything outside of protecting what's important to me and finding happiness in that."

For a moment, I let my words hang between us. They swirl in the air until I realize our time is finally up.

I step away, but he reaches out to grab a handful of my tunic just below my chest. I'm not ready for whatever slaps of reality I'm sure he's got planned for me, so I beat him to speak. "Let me go. You were right. I don't need to be down here. I have better things to do than wallow in misery like you do." His fist is holding tight to the fabric. I can see the strain in his white knuckles, the veins rising from his wrist and winding up his forearm. The familiar warmth I felt at the outpost spreads across my chest and creeps down my arms and up my neck.

His face shifts and the hand loosens on my tunic. His hold on my top becomes a whisper of a touch, his gaze set on mine. His restraint is written all over his face. I can feel the war in his head like it's in mine. His eyes slip down to my lips and return so quickly I'm sure I imagined it. I want him to look at my mouth. The feeling causes my lips to part. He lets this tunic rest only between his thumb and fingers, and gently rubs the fabric together. I take the tiniest step forward, putting my left foot between his boots. Even when he's seated, he's nearly my height. I tilt my head down and watch the rise and fall of his chest. His breaths are inconsistent. The heat radiating off of him is intoxicating, and I want to drown in it.

We stay here. I never imagined this bubble, this silence, this moment before, could ever be so comfortable. I know he's letting me decide. He's waiting for me, and I know he'd stay in this place for years waiting for me if that's how long it takes me to make up my mind. I can take my time. Nikolai would never rush me.

Nikolai. What tears me apart is that I'm not torn at all. This time I will say something.

"Nikolai," I breathe. And his large but gentle hand presses forward and flattens against my stomach.

Slowly.

So slowly, he rises. He towers above me. He takes another step forward, slides his hand from my stomach, and circles it around my waist, leaving a trail of fire. His other hand finds my cheek. I can only remain still; I'm petrified and curious and at a loss for what I need to do next. Every move he makes is hesitant, like he's waiting for me to shut it down. He tilts my head back, and his fingers slide back behind my neck. He rubs circles with his thumb softly over my cheek. His thumb grazes over my lips.

His eyelids are heavy as he studies my face, the normal lightness of his iris gone. Every syllable is faint and hoarse when he whispers my name, and it's taking everything in him to talk to me like this. To touch me like this.

"You." His voice is gravel but still manages to flow like water into all the cracks of my mind. I can't breathe. I can't think with him this close. I shouldn't want but all I can do is want.

I want. I want.

I want.

"You hold me here. Where you are is where I have to be, Jemma. My allegiance is not to Megara. It's to you. To those living life the way it should be. Please."

His voice breaks. He swallows. Tries again.

"*Please*," he murmurs. "Put me out of my misery."

I lift on my tiptoes, and he brings his head down. Our lips brush and there's a balloon in my chest and my body is on fire and chilled with goosebumps all at the same time. It's light and delicious and I want more. I press closer against him and he groans and crashes his mouth to mine. All restraint is gone and the hand he had on my waist slides to my back pulling me up, pulling me closer. I place one hand on his chest while the other tangles the hair curled at the back of his neck. His mouth opens mine and I can't get close enough, can't taste enough, and all the hair on my head is standing while I try to bring him impossibly closer.

It feels like my stomach has disappeared, like I might start floating any second if I keep allowing this moment to take full control of me. But I don't want control. I want this. He breaks the kiss, and I gasp as he braces his arm around my arched back and hauls me up. My legs wrap around his waist, and he turns to press me against the cave wall. I lean forward, eager to find his mouth, and he quickly obliges. His tongue massages mine and sends my head swirling. He grasps the back of my knee, pulling me higher.

I feel heavy and weightless and his hand wraps around my thigh while the other comes up to the back of my neck. With every inch his hand travels up my thigh, I feel more and more like my heart will burst from my chest. He pulls his face away from me and a whimper slips from my throat.

"Fuck, Jemma."

Fuck, Jemma.

Fuck, Jemma.

And his mouth is at my throat. He kisses his way down and pulls the neckline of the tunic so he can kiss along my collarbone. My fingers intertwine in his hair and I let my eyes shut.

I'm bombarded with sensations and he adjusts his position between my legs and I can feel him against me. Heat soars down my spine. A trail of fuel ignites, starting in my joints, and ends south of my stomach. He's taut, pressed in my thighs. I roll my hips, eager for the friction. My silent plea is enough, he knows what to do, and how to do it.

His lips find their way back to mine and continue their intoxicating assault. Every rake and roll of our hips is another shovel of sand digging my grave and I'm happy to go. This grave doesn't spark my claustrophobia as sand is tossed on top of me. The grains aren't coarse or heavy; they're light and languid and where I expect my skin to itch, it glows. The sand buries me, and suffocates me, but I don't need oxygen— only him.

I tilt my head back and a moan escapes my lips. I rake my nails across his scalp and am rewarded with another groan from deep in his chest. I anticipate my panic anytime now but it never comes. I'm tripping through need and desperation. More. More. More.

"Tell me to stop," he begs.

"No." And I mean it from the bottom of my heart. He kisses me again and I can't believe how much heat I'm carrying for how cold I normally am in these caves. I glide my fingertips across the sweat on the back of his neck and have to refrain from licking my fingers to taste it. I want him in every way a person can be had.

"Tell me to stop," his voice is strong but holds hints of hysteria.

"No." His hand slips under my tunic and my undershirt. He's skirting my side and his fingers grazed the bottom of my bra. Again, no panic; all I find is content to stay here in his arms forever. I want to tell him. I want to yell at him that I am his and I will be or do anything he needs from me.

"Jemma." He pants and his eyes are wide and it's like he can feel it. Feel me realize that I belong to him.

A growl erupts down the cave and someone may as well have thrown a bucket of cold water over us. Our surroundings completely disappear when Nikolai has his hands on me. After the wolf's growl ceases the only sound in this cave is our heavy breathing. Nikolai steps back and lets me down slowly. I fix my tunic and he turns toward the seat with his belongings and pulls his tunic on over his undershirt. He doesn't say anything while he puts his belt on. Already.

Already, I'm losing him.

I open my mouth to object to his withdrawal. He slides his swords back into place. Say something, anything to stop this moment from turning into the next.

Insecurity creeps into my mind. What if he's feeling regret? The unease must be spelled out on my face because when he looks at me he says, "I'm sorry."

It feels like he's just punched a hole through my chest. "Me too. Another error in judgment. We have to stop this," it leaves my lips in a breathless rush, like my mouth is on autopilot, thinking with a consciousness I'm unfamiliar with. The silence stretches, and I mourn the loss of the moment. When he looks at me, I shrug but I can tell I need to get out of here as soon as possible. The lump in my throat is growing by the second. "I don't know where my mind is lately." I try to joke but my laugh is stale and dies in the air between us. The words tumbling out of my mouth don't make sense. I'm still catching my breath from the sensation of his hands on me and apologizing for it. I'm not sorry. Not even a little.

His chest rises and falls while the corners of his eyes crinkle. I'm under the scrutiny of his quizzical brow, but I don't know how to tell him I am eager to know what he's analyzing. I'm a puzzle he can't figure out, but I can't figure me out either. Slowly the neutral mask slides over his features. "Right," he says slowly and begins to wrap his face in the black shemagh. I won't be able to keep my hurt disguised for much longer so I slap a smile on my face and turn to run up the stairs, and out of the auditorium.

CHAPTER 41

It's a whisper of a touch over my eyelids. Sondra runs a brush over and over. She lines my eyes with a black pencil. I've never worn makeup, I was too young to wear it myself when I would watch my mother outline her eyes. She had a pale pink lip color that she would wear on special occasions. She was beautiful.

I keep my eyes shut and wish I could shut my heart as well. I have an open valve of pain and desire pouring out of my chest, making everything harder. Harder to breathe, harder to eat, harder to sleep.

I don't realize Sondra has finished my eye makeup until the pad of her thumb wipes away the tear that trickles down my cheek. I open my eyes. She knows nothing of the cracks in my heart but understanding sparkles in her blue eyes.

Sondra holds a gold piece in her hands. It looks like the most intricate necklace. A hundred gold coins hang on tassels. I hold up my hair so she can clasp it behind my neck.

She shakes her head. "This is not a necklace. This is a special piece, worn only by the highest-ranking women of

Megara. This part rests on your head while this drapes over your face." The women, the wives, at the first dinner I had in Moria; they all wore these.

Sondra points me to the full-length mirror. The headpiece settles into place. I can only see my eyes which resemble that of a cat. The bold eyeliner comes to point at every corner of my eye. It's stunning. But I don't look like myself. Sondra appears behind me with the blue gown. Months ago I would be blown away by its beauty. Now it screams royalty and ruin. Charm and chains. Superiority and suppression.

And I don't want it. I don't want it. I don't want it.

Moria started as our salvation but we've only been met with layer upon layer of expectation.

Sondra slides the dress up over my slip. I hear all the locks clicking into place. My breathtaking prison. Every clasp yells fraud.

The sleeves glide up my arms revealing that they are unnecessarily long. The front of the sleeves stop at my wrist but the end of the bell somehow sweeps the floor. My mother used to read me a book, and I can see the wizard donned in drapes on the cover. Despite this monstrosity, the memory makes the dress feel lighter. The only part of the illustration I'm missing is the enormous hood.

In the mirror, I inspect the dress further. The neckline is wide, barely resting on my shoulders. I'm decorated in the same gold hues as what reflects off my face. A golden sheer material splits to reveal the base is a solid blue. The train extends several feet behind me, and the sheer, glimmering cape that starts behind my shoulders falls over it.

"You're ready." Sondra sounds sure of herself.

I wish Jo were here. I'd give anything to hear her tease me. Just thinking of her allows me to smooth out the pinched expression I hadn't realized I was wearing. Perhaps this mask will prove to be more helpful than I thought.

Sondra opens the door behind me. "Time to go."

I follow her out into the hall where King Cerastes waits. My eyes instinctively widen. His smile gives away that he is pleased to have caught me by surprise. "You look beautiful, Miss Shayde." He holds out his arm to escort me.

Being this close to him is less than comfortable. My blood runs colder, rejecting his presence. His smell is familiar like he intentionally chose a scent made to relax me. Initially, it does.

But the smell is wrong on him. It's too clean, too fresh, too saturated in citrus.

Citrus.

He smells too much like Reid. My head whirls as I turn to look up at him. It's hard to imagine that if I close my eyes, and block out his sickly smile, I wouldn't be able to tell if I was holding the arm of Reid or his father.

I focus my attention straight ahead. I don't have the time or resources to allow cloudiness into my brain. And seeing Amos but smelling Reid is a kind of confusion I'll have to sort through on another day.

Amos steers me to the throne hall. We're almost there. In a moment I can leave his arm. "I hope you know how proud you've made this kingdom." Amos has no interest in keeping this final stretch silent. "Such courage. Such bravery. Such power. Your actions at the dam did not go unnoticed." My power. Does he know? How could he know? Thank goodness for his coat or he would be feeling the slimy reaction in my palms to his apparent accusation. "I am very pleased that you've pledged your alliance, your skill, to protecting Megara. Tell me, what do you want your future here to look like?"

His question catches me off guard and I, again, find sanctuary behind the gold coins shielding my expression. "I, uh."

He skips over my lack of answer quickly. "Because I'd like to paint you a picture." I try to speed up our pace. I will the throne room to appear. "A strong woman always has choices. My son, if given the choice, would commit to you today." I see where this is going. I haven't worked through things with Reid, and after the past week, I'm not sure I have the right to. "I believe in taking care of those who take care of mine. You would be an incredible match for Reid and an incredible queen for Megara." His voice is low but the sounds seem to echo down the cave. Queen. Queen. Queen.

"I'm sorry." My mouth is dry and the syllables feel like cotton balls lodged in my throat, "Reid and I haven't talked about our relationship. I don't feel it appropriate to discuss a future with your son without talking to him myself."

He chuckles. "Do you not feel I would be a suitable father-in-law?" He laughs as if this isn't the most absurd conversation ever had. "Jemma, I want you to remember that I take care of mine. If you were a part of my family, I would extend my protection to not only you but your whole family as well."

"My family is dead." This conversation has gone stale. The light of the throne room is coming into view.

"What about your sister?" He presses. Just a few more steps and I will be rid of him.

"Jo is not my sister. But she is my family in every sense besides biologically." I start to pull my hand from his arm as we enter the lit hall. Amos places his hand over mine, securing me to him.

"Forgive me," he says. I look up at his grinning face. "I was referring to Darian."

The air is knocked from my lungs. The room tips sideways. His grip on my hand tightens to provide support. My Darian, my Ray. Ray at one year old. Ray at two years old. Ray at three years old being put on a wagon. Ray crying. Ray reaching for me. Ray being wheeled out of Audun with a dozen other toddlers to safety. Ray would be 11 now. Where is she? How is she? My mouth is parted with questions that refuse to tumble out. Shock is an iron fist wrapped around my throat. Shock is a dagger lodged in my chest, deep enough to penetrate my heart but not deep enough to kill me.

"She is okay," he answers my unasked question. "She is in Megara with the other children her age. I wouldn't be surprised if she's met Jo by now." Amos pats my hand. I want so much to be comforted. I wish his motives were something I could trust, but I know better.

Take a moment. Take a breath. Mourn the years Ray was out there and I wasn't there to take care of her. The pain is a knife and I'm bleeding out. It's gutting. I hear my pulse thump erratically in my ears. In my mind, I double over. Sob until my throat is raw and my vocal cords snap. In my mind, I rip the skin from my bones. Tear myself apart. The selfish girl who chose not to keep her sister. In my mind, I dig a hole deep enough to keep me from ever getting out.

But in this throne room, I am still. My turmoil will be unknown, buried miles into the depths of my brain. I am calm and collected and breath will enter and leave my lungs. Robotic.

I look ahead. The columns lining the hall, once bare, are now decorated. A large expanse of gold fabric draped between them. To the left and right of the line of columns sit long tables dressed as royally as their company. I only recognize some attendants from Moria. The rest of the company is older, all wearing the most ornate clothing of which navy and gold are most common. Most of the people in this room must have traveled here from Megara. The light has not yet fallen upon us. The people still have a moment before noticing their king.

Amos slows my stride. "As I said, choices are to be made. As king, I possess the power to make life-altering choices every day. I can reunite you with your sister. And I would be happy to do it. But she isn't yet the age to be here in Moria and you are not permitted to go to Megara. I think I will allow you the honor of making this choice yourself."

"What do you mean?" He's being cryptic, and at this point, I know it only to be for his pleasure.

"Jemma"—he smiles down at me—"Rules would need to be bent to bring you to your sister. And I'm afraid I only bend for *family*." He releases my hand and I pull mine from his arm. "Why don't you take your seat? Reid is waiting."

On both sides of the throne are pairs of seats similar to the king's, only smaller. Reid is seated on the right, closest to the throne, I'm sure mine is beside him. Finally, I step from the shadow and make my way down the long aisle. I accidentally make eye contact with some of the men I remember from my first meal with the councilmen. Today their wives sit with them at the tables.

Two men, appearing to be near the age of the king, sit to the left of the throne. I wonder about their title. They must be higher than a councilman, as the council is spread out among the tables.

I look to Reid who stands when he sees me. He is dazzling, a smile plastered to his face. And I think I don't deserve his kindness anymore. Will he still smile at me when he knows of my moments alone with Nikolai? I want to tell him so many things and this isn't the place.

He walks down the steps and extends his hand. I take it as he leads me to my seat. We don't sit. Everyone joins us in standing as King Amos is announced. All eyes are on Amos as he makes his grand entrance. I am the perfect guest, steady and silent. But inside, a storm brews. Dust flies in my mind. Ray is alive. I don't know what I'm doing but I'm about to do it.

My gaze is set on the king. My vision begins to blur and fray at the edges.

The storm grows.

I'm not in control.

A hand slips against my palm and grabs my fingers. At first, I don't feel it. I'm here in this hall but it seems miles away. I've remained still for so long that when I finally turn my head to see who has taken hold of my hand, every movement creaks and quakes.

I tilt my head down and find large, brown eyes looking up at me. Her grip on my hand tightens and wrinkles appear at the corners of her eyes. She smiles. The storm subsides and I realize I am smiling too. She's here. Thank God.

Jo is here.

CHAPTER 42

"How?" I whisper to Jo. I can't wipe the smile from my face and neither can she.

"Niki is pledging his allegiance officially tonight. My presence was one of his conditions." Jo is dressed in a long, black tunic dress with her hair pulled back. Her curls spring out in every direction from behind her head. She is the most heartwarming sight. She opens her mouth to speak but when she turns toward me, something glitters on her nose that I hadn't noticed before.

I cut her off, "Josephine Dumont. Is that a ring in your nose?" She brings her hand up to the gold hoop and grins.

"Do you like it?"

"I do," I wrap an arm around her shoulder, "my bad-ass girl."

For a moment my smiles are genuine. Amos takes his place in front of the throne. "Thank you all for traveling and attending today," he continues with formalities. I'm split a million different directions. I'm so happy to have Jo here with me again, thinking of Ray growing up without me there sends waves of nausea through my body, and I can't help but constantly scan the room for the face—or eyes—that occupy the remaining space in my brain.

There's not enough space for my thoughts but Jo is the perfect antidote to quiet my whirlwind of a head space. She is my ground, and I know that right now, there's nothing I can do.

I focus on the king. "Before we can move forward this evening, some things must be addressed." He glances at Reid. "This week, the cold war between Megara and Groth was warmed. We successfully bombed the dam that the Howlers built all those years ago, and the river runs again." At the expense of Cynrad, he doesn't say. "I take immense pride in our soldiers and their training. Harder days are coming, but I am confident in our brave men and women of Moria." The king steps forward, away from his seat. As he raises his palm, gesturing down the hall, he says, "That brings us to another part of the evening." I follow his gaze to where Nikolai is stepping into the light at the end of the hall. He is back in his usual, head-to-toe black, covering everything but his eyes. He walks the long distance to the throne and as he grows nearer I realize that today his attire is more formal. He's traded his tattered tunic for crisp threads, the darkest black found in fabric—gold stitching glimmers, around his collar. Even a cape flows behind him, stopping at the backs of his knees. The darkness of his clothes offsets the lightness of his eyes. He is a sharp blade capable of cutting anyone in half with only a look.

Once at the steps to the throne, Nikolai halts.

Amos says, "Commander Garrith, please remove your shemagh."

Oh, no. This can't be a good sign. I must be squirming because Jo gives me a reassuring squeeze of her hand.

Nikolai unwraps the fabric from around his head, exposing one beautiful inch of his face at a time.

A hushed gasp fills the air of the hall as some of our Megara company recognizes Garrith from the orphanage in Audun.

King Amos turns away from Nikolai to grab something at the arm of his throne. He then faces his people holding a book. Upon closer inspection, I recognize it to be the Book of Moor. Before Groth invaded the northern mountains, citizens of Audun—now Megara— occupied the land and called it Moor. It seems that as the generations pass, our civilization continues to move South. I've only seen the Book of Moor in the chapel of Audun. During service, I always chalked the stories up to, just that, stories. But after the things I've seen, curiosity gets the better of me and I wonder what other "stories" the book holds.

"Commander Garrith," the king pulls my attention from Megara's history. "Place your left hand on the Book of Moor, raise your right, and repeat after me:

"I, Nikolai Garrith,"

"I, Nikolai Garrith," his voice is like velvet without the muffling of his shemagh.

"Do solemnly declare,"

"Do solemnly declare,"

"To be for Megara, a beacon of honor, power, and wisdom,"

"To be for Megara, a beacon of honor, power, and wisdom,"

"To all those who stand with her, I pledge myself,"

"To all those who stand with her, I pledge myself," Nikolai's eyes are fast. So fast, that I'm sure I imagined the look, the connection, for a split second that he looked at me.

"And swear to protect her and all of her dust, until to dust I too return,"

"And swear to protect her and all of her dust, until to dust I too return,"

Nikolai removes his hand, takes a knee, and bows his head. The king unsheathes the sword at his hip and rests the blade across Nikolai's shoulder. "Nikolai, you have proven your loyalty to Megara and all of her people." The king puts away the sword and lifts his hands. "Rise, General Garrith."

The room erupts in applause as Nikolai stands. He bows to the king and turns to face the room, but not before leveling me with another undecipherable look. He leaves the steps to the throne and joins a table straight ahead of me and takes a seat next to a grief-stricken Tatum. Her expression is hollow, and I'm not sure she's aware of Nikolai sitting beside her. Next to Tatum, Enon gives a polite nod to Nikolai and then exchanges words. I want to be at that table. I want to know what they're saying. I want to check on my friends.

Enon appears to be holding up well enough, but even his light demeanor doesn't disguise the circles under his blood-shot eyes. Perhaps once the night gets started, Jo and I can sneak away to see my friends.

Reid stands and clinks his glass. A toast. I grab my glass in unison with everyone else in the hall.

"Thank you all for coming to celebrate the start of many victories. We are on the horizon of a war. War is ugly. I won't stand here and pretend that with this time won't come heartache. We are about to embark on many days, weeks, and months full of loss. At a time like this, celebration may seem foolish. We only mean to keep spirits up since the hardships that will soon be faced," he looks at Tatum, "if not already faced, will surely prove to be tragic. To every soldier and every person who loves a soldier, I am with you. I will train with you, face Groth with you, be afraid with you, cry with you, laugh with you, and someday be victorious with you." The rows of tables erupt with applause. Reid is a natural. He will make an exceptional king one day.

I glance at King Amos. He beams with pride, a pride not doused in his usual cruel intentions, but a pride born from love. And I realize just how much the king does love his family.

As the excitement dies down Reid continues, "I do have a favor to ask of you all, while the opportunity is here. It is rare that so many amazing people are gathered like we are today. I have something important I need to say, something I need to do. And I can't imagine a better setting. Despite the grueling months ahead, I've decided to make the most of any time I have left in this world. And I don't want to spend a second doing less than holding tightly to the one I love most."

Reid turns and looks at me, a grin glued to his perfect face.

He holds out his hand for me so I take it and get to my feet.

It happens in slow motion even though I am not using my power. Reid places his glass on the tray, and glides down on one knee, paralyzing me as he goes. I want to stop it. I want to have never left my room this evening. He's opening a small box. He's opening his heart, expectation gleaming in his eyes.

The ring is exquisite. An oval sapphire on a twisted golden band. The final lock clicks into place.

I look above Reid's head where Amos stands. He moves, barely, giving me the slightest nod.

I have no wish to be married, but Ray is out there. I must control what I can. I must find Ray.

I look into Reid's eyes. There's only hopefulness. I could swim in the swirling blue. He is everything positive and safe. And I think there are worse things to be forced into.

I respond but I can't feel the nerves in my lips. I can't feel my mouth form the word. Reid's hopeful face cracks into the most earth-shattering smile as he slides the ring onto my finger, as he rises and reaches for me.

I focus on his happiness, on his arms wrapping around me, and I push the ugly truth deep into the archives and choose not to dwell. I try not to notice. Try not to notice. Try not to notice.

But I do notice. Nikolai is not here.

And I realize, no matter how much I play pretend and celebrate my new alliance with Reid, to Megara, the truth tugs and creeps, reminding me.

My future is not mine.

JEMMA'S STORY CONTINUES
IN 2025.

ACKNOWLEDGMENTS

Vulnerable is not something I like to be. Putting your words into a world where anyone can read them forces all vulnerability concerns aside. I owe an abundance of thanks to those who supported me fiercely through my self-doubt.

Writing the story was easy. Sharing it was hard.

To my husband, thank you for your patience when you sit beside me but I'm a million miles away in a fictional land, filled with fictional people. Thank you for believing in me when you have watched me start (and never finish) project after project. Thank you for setting an example for our girls that a husband should encourage the pursuit of dreams. You are my perfect person.

I owe an enormous thanks to the rest of my family. It takes a village, and mine is spectacular. My mom, for teaching me that you *truly* can do anything, and never being surprised when I create something grand. Also, my meemaw, my papaw, my dad, my mother-in-law, and my father-in-law, the most amazing lineup of people that I can call for anything at any time and you would always be there for me. I hope you feel all my love for you the way I feel yours for me.

Shayna, my good pal, my wild reading lady. Your opinion of my writing meant more to me than you will ever know. Thank you for your honesty and for being a safe place to share my ideas.

To my friends who have grown with me from childhood.

Thank you, Meghan, Rylee, and Kaylin, for cheering me on every step of the way. Special shout to Meghan, who's been reading my stories since student base in the sixth grade.

To my Mary, for being the confidence that I could do it when I had none. You've inspired me in more ways than I can count. And when the odds are stacked against us, we move forward with it anyway. Thank you for believing, without question, from the very beginning.

My phenomenal editor, Kay, thank you. Thank you. Thank you. You touched this story more than anyone else and left me feeling better after every round of edits. Thank you for being gentle and treating this story like it was your baby as much as it is mine.

To Jess, my genius map-maker. Thank you for taking on a project outside of your norm and creating a better image of Sahir than I could have ever dreamed of.

Thank you to every person who has touched and inspired this story. To my readers, thank you for taking a chance on a debut novel, let alone a self-published novel. At this point, all my anxieties of vulnerability have dissolved, and I am only grateful for the amazing and accepting company I keep. If I missed you in these acknowledgments, this is a series, and I'll catch you next time.

ABOUT THE AUTHOR

Keela Jones is a wife and mother. When she isn't chasing around her three young daughters, she spends her time reading, enjoying live music, and tearing into DIY projects around her home. She works in the school corporation and finds peace in numbers and correct answers.

Keela appreciates the quirky corners of art and loves collecting funky pieces equipped with eccentric stories. Her discovered passion for writing is inspired by the love she has for her family and satisfaction when creating something that will make them proud.